NETTIE

 ## AT THE

WELL

To Kristi,
Best wishes!
gaolson
10/1/18

A novel by

J. A. OLSON

Published by St. Jehanne Press
Vancouver, Washington

Nettie at the Well/ J. A. Olson -- 1st ed.
ISBN: 978-0-9855275-2-5

Copyright © J. A. Olson, 2018

Book Layout by Guido Henkel

Publisher's Note: This is a work of fiction. Names, characters, places, and incidents are a product of the author's imagination. Locales and public names are sometimes used for atmospheric purposes. Any resemblance to actual people, living or dead, or to businesses, companies, events, institutions, or locales is completely coincidental.

Consider it pure joy, my brothers, whenever you face trials of many kinds, because you know that the testing of your faith develops perseverance.

James of Jerusalem

For Sandra and Heather,
mes amies dans la vie.

"Youth, new beginnings, and a secret that won't die... Ms. Olson masterfully weaves a story of deception with the truthful struggle for meaning. Engaging and witty, the past and present knit together as the reader journeys with the characters to unravel the mystery—one beloved page at a time." ~ Seraphina Book Club

"A deeply evocative story of hope and despair, *Nettie at the Well* captures the desperation of loneliness and the triumph of God's love." ~ Booktown Review

Chapter One

NETTIE STEPPED OUT OF THE DIM COOLNESS OF her house and into the low morning sun. Silence hung in the trees like a shroud, interrupted only by an occasional bird here or there summoning its mate or announcing a worm. Carrying an overstuffed backpack on her shoulders, she closed the door behind her and fumbled with the key, not quite sure why she was locking it anyway since she would never be back. But it had been her beloved home for eighty years and held everything dear to her: her clothes, her belongings, her keepsakes, and the bed where she had given birth to her daughter—the same bed she had shared with Thomas every night of their marriage until his death nineteen years earlier.

She trudged around to the shed at the back of the house, pulled open its creaky door and entered the dusty, still interior. Going to the back corner, she pushed a rusty lawnmower out of her way and kneeled down on the rough wood floor. Prying up a loose floorboard, she found a dirty wool satchel hidden in the space underneath. She opened it up, and a quick inspection assured her that the money was all still there. She replaced the floorboard and returned the mower to its spot. Picking up the satchel with its precious cargo, she walked out of the shed, the door slamming on its spring behind her.

With the reality of the satchel in her hand came the reality of her leaving, pummeling her with dread. It was time to go, nothing else to linger over, all loose ends tidily wrapped up in a bow.

The old woman put one foot in front of the other, each labored step sounding the death knell of her life here, dragging her into her unknown future. She stopped and looked at the house one last time before entering the woods, hungrily absorbing the sight of the porch swing, empty and swaying lazily in the breeze, the same swing where she had rocked and sang to her sweet baby and later to the babies of her baby.

A burgeoning community slowly continued its encroachment upon the once secluded farmhouse where Nettie had been brought as a young bride those many years ago, sowing its seeds of new construction where Thomas once sowed his crops. The peach orchard where little Emily had run and played now sported a sea of brand new houses that all looked the same, dwarfing her old house with its graceful lines and wrap-around porch. With the selling of that last orchard five years ago she had received enough money to prepare for reestablishing herself when she would be compelled to move on someday, and today was that someday.

Life is one big loss, she lamented as she hurried on her way, the strengthening summer sun warm on her cheeks but failing to penetrate her inner chill. Her daughter's funeral yesterday had been hard, as they always are when losing someone you love, especially when that someone should have been burying you. Sad hymns from the service echoed through her head—her darling Emily whom she took care of as she grew old, whom she had resisted loving in the beginning but then grew to love so much that she now felt in her soul she could not live without. But Nettie didn't have a choice, as does no one when their special person dies.

Following the path along the river which led to town, Nettie stopped and stared over the shining waters, bidding farewell to the sparkling lights dancing atop rippling waves, soaking in memories of picnics with her family, of menfolk fishing, of lively children growing up and having lively children of their own. The squawk of an egret pierced the silence, stabbing through the quivering flesh of her heart and jerking her back to the reality of her aloneness. She kicked off her shoes and threw them into the water as a final ode to her former life.

Arriving at the train station, she shuffled into the ladies' room and tucked herself in a toilet stall. She pulled off her hot, gray wig and ran her hands through her shortly cropped, chestnut hair, raking it into some semblance of order. Shimmying out of her baggy dress, she removed her bra with its stuffed, pendulous cups and the huge granny-panties with the towel wrapped under its waistband. She was a girl again. She slipped on a pair of jeans over her slim hips and put on a teeshirt, wadding up her old clothes and cramming them deep into her backpack—didn't want anyone finding them.

Nettie started to emerge from the stall. Oops, one more thing. She dug into the bag and found a packet of cleansing cloths and wiped the makeup from her face, erasing the artfully applied lines and wrinkles that added seventy-five years to her appearance. Walking out of the ladies' room she worried that people would stop and stare, but no one did. No one looked at her despite the monumental change quaking inside her.

How old am I? Nettie pondered as she settled herself into a seat on the train. She added up the years in her head. I was born in 1773, so that makes me 235 years old, not the ninety-nine that everyone thinks I am. I invented that identity long ago and now I must invent another one.

Nettie determined that she must have stopped aging in her twenties. Every night when she washed her face she scanned for wrinkles and gray hair, but never were there any. She searched for the subtle sagging at the jawline that she saw on other women's faces as they approached their forties, but her skin remained firm and tight. Being married to Thomas and having a child had necessitated the aura of aging, and the youthful old woman had become quite the artist of radiating a grandmotherly illusion as the years rolled on.

Thoughts of her gentle, loving parents warmed her as the train carried her through the unfamiliar countryside to yet another new life. Papa had been a furniture maker in the St. Antoine district of Paris during the reigns of Kings Louis XV and XVI, and, of course, during the dreadful Revolution. He worked long days in his shop, designing chairs and cabinets for the rich folk in the St. Honoré neighborhood. Nettie liked to chat with him and listen to his stories while he sanded and shaped his objects, taking pleasure in the beautiful artistry which served the functional needs of everyday living.

"There is a solution to every problem," her father liked to tell her when he was stumped on a project. "You just have to sit silent sometimes and listen for the answer to come to you, and it always will."

Nettie sighed, wishing she could bask in the presence of her father's wisdom these nearly 250 years later. So Papa, what should I do? Everybody gets old and dies but me. She watched forlornly as the scenery passed by her window. She wanted to fling herself in the river and feel the water enter her lungs and snuff the life out of her. She had tried that once when she had first learned of her curse, but a fisherman came by at just that crucial moment and pulled her from the water. Another time, she had entered the woods with a knife to cut her wrists, but at that moment a little boy who was climbing a tree with his brother fell, and she was obliged to race him to the doctor's house.

Yes, she brooded, everyone is sure they want to live forever, but the reality is that it is a nightmare with no chance of escape. Maybe if all your people lived forever too, then it would be all right, but to suffer one loss after another, to be lied to and betrayed by people you trusted, to have your dearest soul-mates die and leave you alone and empty, to be in a world of perpetual strangers ....

Nettie tried to drag herself off the path that only led to despair. She had a plan. She was going to go to college. Girls nowadays went to college and had careers. She would invent a new identity as she always had when it was time to move on. While the days when one could start anew with no questions asked were long gone, she was armed with the birth certificate of her great-granddaughter who had drowned at the age of two.

What a sad, lost day that was, Nettie recalled, easily careening down this vortex of melancholy. Her mind reeled from too many images from times past, too many losses. Antoinette was an angel, but it only took one time of her mother forgetting to close the gate to the pool for an adventurous little girl to get loose and decide to go for a swim on her own. My namesake, with curly blonde hair and ocean blue eyes, the great-grandmother mourned.

Focus on the future, she scolded, trying again to pull herself out of her grief. Yes, the birth certificate. With that I can get a driver's license, and as a college student I can get a credit card. Three necessary items in today's world. Little Antoinette would have been twenty-one now, so then I am twenty-one and I get to keep my name, but maybe a modern nickname would be more suitable and attract less attention.

"I am Tonie Stevens. I am twenty-one years old, and I am a student," the woman previously known as Nettie rehearsed to herself as she finally fell asleep to the gentle rocking motion of the train.

Chapter Two

L AYING THE HAMMER DOWN ON A STEP STOOL, Tonie stood back to admire her diploma hanging on the barren wall of her apartment. A college degree—quite an accomplishment for an old lady, she applauded herself. The new graduate thought about the four years of hard work that it represented and the unanticipated goal it provided for her.

Glancing over at her roommate sitting amid the pile of moving boxes in the furniture-less room, she asked, "How does it look?"

"Great spot," Kassie approved. "We have one thing on the wall, that's progress."

"Hang yours, too," prompted Tonie, eager to transform their bare living quarters into a home.

"My stomach says I'll wait. If we find pots and pans we could make spaghetti."

Tonie eyed the formidable heap of boxes in the middle of the floor. "Or, we could go out for pizza," she countered, shaking her head at the improbability of finding a needle in this haystack. The two girls jumped up, grabbed their purses and raced out the door.

Friends during their college days in Portland, both students had been accepted into graduate programs at the University of Oregon—Tonie in botany and Kassie in psychology—and had decided to room together for their next adventure. Kassie's father and brothers had driven the girls and their belongings here this afternoon, then hurried back to Portland for a baseball game, leaving the students to explore the new town on their own.

That night, Tonie lay in her unfamiliar bed, once again uneasy in a strange place, reflecting back on the past four years since making the propitious decision to go to college. During her first year as a freshman, taking a required biology course, the professor had explained that in the current view of aging and death, scientists believe there are tiny "death genes" inside of cells that over time release an enzyme that cause its death. The professor went on to describe how as the effects of cell death accumulate they lead to the progression of aging and the eventual death of the individual. Scientists also postulate that certain plant enzymes may be able to slow, or even stop, the progression, perhaps leading to greatly extended ages—even immortality.

Fascinated, the young student had digested this information carefully, wonderingly, as to its application to her. Had the opposite of "cell-senescence" happened to her? It explained every symptom she had experienced of never aging or dying. Could there really be a simple physical reason for her immortality? Had she lived by a plant or eaten something that could have shut off the natural mechanism of cell death? A memory came back to her of eating berries as a child and becoming violently ill.

She had been playing in the woods near her home and came across some opaque red berries growing near the ground. Believing, with her inexperienced eight year old mind, that they were raspberries, she ate three, but, finding them tart and bitter and not sweet at all like raspberries, she had not eaten any more. That night she started retching horribly and couldn't stop. Diarrhea came fast and furious, and she fell so ill that she could only lay motionless on her bed, eyes glazed over. For three days, Mama told her later, she hovered close to death, and Mama and Papa had prayed and prayed for her. The priest finally came to perform the rite of extreme unction, but at the last moment she made a turn for the better and slowly recovered. Mama and Papa called her their miracle.

Upon hearing this lecture and remembering the berries, Tonie had abruptly changed her major to biology and became driven to learn as much as she possibly could about these killer genes and find an antidote to whatever had gone wrong in her body. She deduced that the berry incident made sense with what had been happening to her for the past couple hundred years. The berries must have turned off her aging mechanism. After eating the berries, she surmised, she continued to grow until she was about twenty years old, but there she stayed, never aging past that.

Even now, only four years later, people were telling her how young she looked for twenty-five—the made up age she claimed using Antoinette's birthday. That made sense, Tonie concluded, because no one begins their aging decline until their mid-twenties, so even if the mechanism turned off when she was eight, the effects would not be noticed until a person normally would start to deteriorate.

Deteriorate, the immortal sighed. Oh, how she longed to deteriorate. She lived in a nightmare with no escape—a hell on earth. Other people got old and died, it was the natural progression of life, but not for her. Everyone she loved eventually left her. Her mama and papa died, and she still missed them. Her brothers and sisters all died, and she had no one. And before that, before she knew her curse, her darling baby Henri died. Not exactly her baby, but her baby brother.

Mama gave birth to little Henri when Nettie was sixteen. Mama thought she was past having children, being that her youngest, Jacques, was seven. Nettie fell in love with Henri from the first, and he became like hers because Mama was so busy with six other children to care for. She fed him, rocked him, changed him, and he slept in her bed at night. But, when he was seven months old, diphtheria ravaged their small village. It had been a harsh winter, food was scarce and the house cold, but Nettie kept him warm and ate only after Henri was fed.

Henri's death devastated his sister-mama and she reeled in God's betrayal. Where was God when she needed Him? Where was Henri's miracle? Why would God send an innocent baby, an unexpected gift, only to take him away so soon? Sweet, smiling Henri, with rose petal cheeks and fragrant baby neck that she loved to kiss. She loved Henri more than life and had begged God to let her die instead. But as her prayers were not answered and she held her tiny brother's lifeless body in her arms, she cursed God, wretched in her powerlessness to save him, trying to hurt God like He hurt her. But nothing she could scream at Him was bad enough. The words rang empty, not changing God's mind nor easing her pain. She hurled every profanity she ever heard from the men working over the forges next door, but none were strong enough to mitigate her raging pain. She wanted to die, and God would not even do that for her.

After Henri's funeral she quit cursing God, because she knew then that there was no God. God would not have taken her baby in the first place and, if God existed, He would have destroyed her for cursing Him. In the Bible, Job was encouraged to curse God and die, but he refused. Nettie cursed God but did not die. Baby Henri was innocent but did die. People are fools to think there is a God, she bitterly spat out. I could pray to that rock over there, or curse it, and get the same result. I will never waste my time praying again.

Tonie choked up and blinked back tears at the memory, finally falling asleep buoyed on by her belief that she would find the cure for her undying state in her advanced plant studies.

With the advent of the school year and the breakneck pace of her classes, the grad student adjusted to her new life on campus. She enjoyed living with Kassie, saying quick hellos while rushing past each other with their busy schedules. Kassie often went home on weekends since her family lived so close, leaving her roommate with the apartment to herself.

On one such Saturday morning, Tonie was preparing to take a shower when the telephone rang, and she saw that it was Kassie who had left thirty minutes earlier. Worried that she may be having car trouble to be calling so soon after leaving, Tonie grabbed the phone quickly, but without a good hold of it, and fumbled it into the toilet just as it was flushing. Down it went, and up rose the water, higher and higher until it reached the lip of the rim and started to spill over. Horrified, Tonie ran out of the apartment into the hallway to search for help, bumping into a young man walking by her door.

"My toilet is overflowing and I don't know what to do!" the frenzied girl blurted out as if World War Three had just erupted.

"Oh," the startled passerby replied, "I can help you." He ran after Tonie into her bathroom and took the lid off the back of the offending commode, nestling the plug back over the hole.

"My cell phone fell in," she explained, flustered and embarrassed by the easy fix. "But I'm sure I can get it out now that you've stopped the water from overflowing."

Rolling up his sleeve chivalrously, the man dipped his arm right into the bowl, retrieved the phone and washed it off in the sink for her.

"It may not work anymore," he mused. "I've heard some people say they've had success putting them in rice for a day or two to dry out, but I've never tried it myself, because, well, I've never dropped mine in the toilet." He handed the soaked phone back to her with a grin.

Tonie threw a towel onto the floor to soak up the water. "Thank you very much. I can handle it from here since you've got the water under control," she stammered, wishing he would leave sooner than later. She nervously tugged on a strand of hair, keenly aware of her disadvantage in her ratty bathrobe and him in a sports jacket.

"No worries. Glad I could help. Also, you need to tell the landlord that your toilet float is not working properly. Do you ever have to jiggle the handle to get it to stop running?"

"Oh, yes, almost every time." Tonie's face turned red to be discussing her toilet with a stranger.

"By the way, my name is Paul Delaney and I live just down the hall in apartment 203. Paul's my name and plumbing's my game. Feel free to give a call anytime the phone goes for a dip," he teased.

The damsel in distress grinned. "Well, I'm hoping my shower works, obviously."

Her rescuer took his leave. Mortified, Tonie shook her head. How awful to be caught in such a state. The guy was good looking and chances were high that she would run in to him again since he lived in the same apartment building. She vowed to always check the peep hole before going out the door in the future.

The humiliating toilet affair was retold to Kassie as soon as she returned—acted out in full drama—becoming a joke between the roommates as how to meet a man and scare him away at the same time. The event was soon forgotten. However, it didn't remain in obscurity for long.

Shortly into the following term, a guest lecturer in Tonie's plant evolution class was scheduled to speak on plant fossils of the Paleolithic Era. She was looking forward to this lecture, hoping that it might shed light on the life spans of the early peoples of the Bible. Adam and Noah both lived over nine hundred years, Methuselah nearly one thousand. Did they have different diets that led to their longevity? Had plant life evolved over the years since then, losing the nutrients that led to these long lives?

While Tonie did not believe in God anymore, she willingly acknowledged the Bible as a well-written history book—an accurate depiction of life thousands of years ago. The progression of shorter and shorter lives could be describing the loss of certain foods from the diet, maybe the very berries that she had eaten. Maybe these berries had grown bitter and people stopped eating them, leading to the loss of the grand ages attained by these ancestors. The inquisitive scholar hoped to gain some enlightenment into the changing diets of humans over the millennia.

Nestled in her chair-desk early on the appointed day, armed with a myriad of questions, Tonie's anticipation turned to alarm when in walked her plumber with his notebook, stepped up to the podium and introduced himself—Dr. Paul Delaney, Paleoanthropologist.

"Oh terrific," Tonie moaned. "My plumber is an expert on the origins of humankind." The disconcerted scholar slunk down in her chair, hoping not to be recognized. But the good professor did not miss much. Pausing as he began his lecture, he gave her a smile and nod then launched into a brilliant insight into plant origins. The man was smart, a world expert, and his hand had been down her toilet.

Mustering up her courage after class, Tonie asked her questions, pretending she had never seen him before. Their discussion outlasted the confines of the time for the class, and they continued talking as they walked down the hallway. As they turned to go their separate directions, Professor Delaney asked if the rice had worked or whether she had had to buy a new phone.

"Yes, I did have to buy a new one, but mine was old anyway so it wasn't that much of a setback," she admitted, pulling it out of her purse to show him.

"Oh, wow, that is the newest one." He pulled out his phone and showed her his clunky last year's model. "It's starting to lose battery pretty fast. Maybe I should throw it in the toilet." He handed his phone to Tonie and took hers. He dialed his own number, and his phone rang in her hands. "Yep, it works, too. There, you've got my number in case you ever need a plumber again."

"Thank you," Tonie laughed, handing his phone back to him. "It's very considerate of you to care about a lowly student's toilet."

"We plumbers aim to please." Surprised at himself, Dr. Delaney laughed out loud. "I can't believe I said that. I think I've missed my calling!"

Three days later Tonie received a phone call from her favorite plumber, asking her out to dinner and a movie. She happily accepted, figuring that she didn't have to worry about making a good first impression because that option was already off the table.

Chapter Three

A S THE BLUSTERY WINTER SLOWLY LOST ITS RAGE
and mellowed into spring, Tonie and Paul moved as
one—whether huddling together under an umbrella
as they dashed through the rain to the coffee shop, or
eating lunch together on a sunny spring day on the grass
outside the commons—their love blossomed along with
the pink flowers on the trees. What started as a fun,
intellectually stimulating friendship caught fire and grew
into an attachment which surprised Tonie, who had
convinced herself that it was nothing more than an
amusement that she could leave at any time.

Her interest in the longevity of Paleolithic man
paralleled Paul's passion for the origins of humankind,
although for diverging reasons. While she was seeking
any clues she could find to shed light on her curse, Paul,
in addition to being a man of science, was a man of God
who did not subscribe to the accepted scholarly concept
of human evolution.

Based on his vast research into the origins of man,
and his habit of not accepting the face value of any

opinion, Paul theorized that humans did not evolve from the apes but were created as fully modern humans. He told his girlfriend that the more he studied human anthropology, the more he saw evidence for this. While this was Biblical teaching from the beginning of time, in scientific circles it was unheard of that any educated person could actually believe in such a fairytale. Paul didn't disagree that mutation occurred at some level—he disagreed that it occurred at the sweeping dimension necessary to account for human life. Tonie was shocked, chin down to the chest shocked, when Paul told her this. This was the opposite of what every scholar in biology accepted as truth, and Paul was at the top of his field. He said that he did not yet have enough evidence to start writing papers on it, but the evidence he did have did not fit into the box called "evolution by mutation."

"So why do all the researchers say that it is only a matter of finding the missing link to prove the theory?" Tonie asked, surprised that he was comfortable divulging his radical ideas to her. This kind of thinking could turn him into a mockery among his colleagues.

"Each time there is some discovery it is twisted to make it fit because it pleases scientists who have all propounded the theory. Then they all assume they are brilliant and pat themselves on the back for not believing what the 'common man' believes. These studies don't add up, and I don't think they always realize that they subtly change facts to make them fit the mold, but each time they do, it seemingly adds to the mountain of evidence that doesn't really exist."

"What about the ages of the fossils that are found? Doesn't that prove that man was around long before Adam?"

"No, they are very inconsistent at best. There are different methods, and every few years they prove to be off by thousands of years here and there. They are too unreliable for me to accept. And, I'm not sure yet how long ago Adam was created. The stories of him were passed on for centuries, or more, before they were written down. In those days people lived a very long time, as you pointed out about the ages of the patriarchs of the Bible. Adam and his descendants lived in the nine hundred year range. It wasn't until a thousand years after the flood that life spans began declining, and there was a big climate change at that time. These ages are also found in literature of the Greeks and Romans and Chinese. Why would we discount these writings when they all corroborate each other, and they were written independently?" Paul was passionate about his subject and loved that Tonie shared his enthusiasm.

"So, do you think that the decline in life span could indicate a change in diet? That their food supply changed, and their former staple foods died off?" Tonie quizzed, enthusiasm growing in her as the focus shifted towards her favorite topic.

"Yes, that and, I know this will be an odd concept to you, but I believe mostly that the further man traveled from God, the shorter his lifetime became because of sin. And while I do believe that is the overriding cause, I also think God caused it by physical changes. God created the world, and He works within that framework. The world was meant to turn on people's relationship with their creator. When Adam was created he was meant to live forever in a beautiful garden."

Tonie squirmed as the conversation turned to Paul's belief in God. She had shared with him that she wasn't a believer, but she had not shared why, or that it hardened her heart just to hear God's name. Trying not to openly disagree with him, she instead veered the conversation back to science.

"If people once lived that long, and it was a dietary condition, don't you think people could find that again? That there must be some 'elixir of youth' somewhere that would support one thousand year life spans?"

"Men and women have searched for the fountain of youth throughout the ages. I've never contemplated the reality of finding it. To me, it is a spiritual issue and not a matter of finding a specific substance. Would you like to find it and live for a thousand years?" Paul asked playfully.

"Well, I suppose if everyone lived that long it would have its merits, but if it were only me, then I would have to say no. I would not want to outlive my loved ones," the old young woman asserted, having first hand experience of this phenomenon. She hoped this was generic enough of an answer to not raise any suspicion. Although, she told herself, it was stupid to imagine someone might suspect she was centuries old, because even if she claimed her real age no one would believe her. But for some reason, she still worried that her secret could be found out at any moment.

"Yes, I agree," her boyfriend echoed the sentiment. "Life would lose its meaning without your special someone."

As the school year wound to a close, Paul grudgingly began his preparations to leave for a summer job in Israel. He had been appointed as the temporary Director of Paleoanthropology for three months at the ancient site of Bethsaida. Having applied for the position the previous fall before meeting Tonie and falling in love, he now wanted to go about as much as a hairless cat wants to hunt mice in a snowstorm.

Tonie dreaded the separation also, while trying to assure herself it was really okay—that she had projects of her own and would use this time to focus on her research without any distractions. But her heart sank when the day finally arrived for her boyfriend to leave. After driving Paul to the airport and watching his plane disappear into the big blue sky, she returned home with emptiness howling in her brain.

That first night as she lay in bed trying to go to sleep, a little voice kept whispering in her ear, "Danger, danger, don't get attached. It'll hurt too much when he's gone for good."

"No," she shouted the voice down. "I'm not attached. We're just friends, and I need to have friends to be sane."

"You love him, and he's going to die and leave you. What will you do then?"

"I have a clue to my immortality," she argued against the voice. "For the first time I have a clue. I will figure it out before he dies and, who knows? Maybe I'll be the first to go."

"You cannot die. Your life is a black hole that will last for eternity, and Paul will be gone."

Tonie leapt out of bed and began pacing back and forth in the little space between her bed and the wall, not wanting to wake up Kassie in the next room. She squeezed her head between her hands, trying to shut out the voice.

"No, no, no! I am going to figure this out. I have a clue." She continued pacing until the hysteria died down and she could return to bed. She rallied her mind to focus on her research. It was promising, very promising, and it made perfect sense. Eventually, she fell asleep, clinging to the hope of the berries.

Kassie was leaving also, quitting school and moving back to Portland to get married. On her weekends home during the year she had met and fallen in love with her older brother's best friend, and he had proposed.

"I'm sad you're going," cheerless Tonie told her peppy roommate, helping her pack up a year's accumulation of stuffed ducks, green and yellow flags and Walmart apartment décor. "What am I going to do without you?"

"You've got Paul now, and maybe he'll be popping the question soon, just like Justin did." Kassie lifted her left hand to admire her ring.

"We haven't been dating that long, but I do like him a lot," Tonie confessed. "He'll be back in the fall, and he writes every day. I'm going to keep busy with school this summer and try to graduate by next year."

"If he is back by September third, bring him to my wedding with you. That will give him ideas!" Kassie happily twirled around her empty bedroom, unable to imagine any joy more awesome than marrying the man she loved.

"I suspect he might already have ideas. He was sure singing the blues about having to go to Israel without me, but he committed himself to it before we met. And, it's important for him to study these archeological digs because he has such a passion for understanding the past, and he needs to do them for his career." The left-behind girlfriend sighed.

Before long, the car was loaded and Kassie cheerfully hugged her friend. "Come and visit me whenever you have a chance. I'm only two hours away. I don't want you pining away for the plumber all summer!"

Tonie laughed and waved goodbye. "Don't worry about me! If I get lonely I might come camp on your doorstep!"

Tonie pumped up the tires on her bicycle and checked the pressure on the gauge. Satisfied, she strapped on her backpack and helmet, joining six other riders for a three-day bike trip to the coast. Sparkling sunshine accompanied them as they silently glided on their way in the coolness of early morning.

With two weeks to go until Paul returned, Tonie had finished her summer classes and was looking forward to this outing to enjoy new vistas, free from all school responsibilities. An easy sixty miles to Florence, the cyclists anticipated that it would take them about five hours, plus lunch and water stops. They would spend a couple nights there in a hotel, explore the town and beach life, then make the return trip. After a year of biking around campus, Tonie felt confident in her ability to keep up with these speedy riders.

Rolling along in a single file on the shoulder of the highway, the morning traffic was light and singing birds could be heard serenading the bikers as they pedaled their way westward. Tonie mused about her new life and the difference between it and all the years that had preceded this era.

A midwife for most of her years, that profession had disappeared in the fifties when women began putting their faith in hospital births away from the comfort of their own homes. Living on the ranch with Thomas, she had no longer needed the income and willingly retired, having done it for nearly two hundred years at that point. She turned her attention to farm duties, raising Emily, making jam, sewing curtains and clothes. It was a borrowed life, as were all her lives, but for the most part she was able to quash the nagging of her impostor status always lurking in the back of her mind. Until the death of Thomas. He was the link to her old life in England and France, and with him he took away her sense of continuity with her former self.

Thomas's death was the harbinger of her soon required exit. He was a marker of time. With a grownup daughter and a granddaughter, the thread of life continued weaving its tapestry, drawing Nettie into the fabric, in and out, her life intertwined now, important, established, but one that she would be forced to abandon.

The old dread returned, a constant shadow gnawing and tearing at her.

By noon the traffic picked up. The shoulder had narrowed a few miles back, not giving much of a buffer between cyclists and cars, but the team confidently pedaled along, drafting behind each other to reduce the wind resistance. Hearing a loud diesel truck roaring up from behind, Tonie glanced back to check on the girl behind her, causing her front wheel to slide on the gravel as she took her eyes off the path for that instant. Rocking off-balance, she plummeted over the embankment. Pain shot through her right leg as she tumbled to a stop at the bottom of the ditch. Her left forearm and wrist hurt too. She heard the shouting of her ride partners as they descended the sharp incline to help her.

Ride leader Kirk ascertained that she had a broken arm and leg, and was unsure if any internal damage had been done since Tonie couldn't move. He climbed back up to the road to retrieve his cell phone and call for an ambulance. Paramedics soon arrived and drove the injured biker to the hospital in Eugene, where x-rays showed fractures to her right leg and left arm and wrist. The doctor scheduled surgery to set her leg for the next morning.

With her brain fogged by pain killers, Tonie emailed Paul that night and told him her plight. He wanted to come home immediately, but she argued that there was no reason to because Kassie said she would come and stay with her for a week until she could travel, and then take her back to Portland while she mended. A worried Paul acquiesced to this plan after talking to the doctor, secretly holding the reservation that he would decide after the surgery the next day.

The next morning, Tonie woke up chipper and bright, her leg and arm not hurting at all, even after the pain medication wore off. A nurse came and wheeled her down for the pre-operative x-rays, but, to the confusion of the doctors, no breaks were detected in any of the patient's limbs.

"I've heard of this before," paranoid Tonie assured the nurse who was clucking around her back in the room. "I know a woman who was told she had a broken arm, but then she didn't. Also, I wonder if the x-rays were mixed up and weren't mine. I think I was just bruised and sore coming in." She swung her feet over the side of the bed and made a big show of walking stiffly. "Yes, I am fine. And my arm is good, too."

"Oh my goodness!" the nurse exclaimed. "You lay right back down, missy! Maybe it is the second set of x-rays that is wrong. We'll get to the bottom of this, and I don't want you hurting yourself any more." She tried to usher the patient back to bed, but Tonie was determined to break free of her jail.

"Let me just put my clothes on." She made a lunge for the closet. The nurse tried to grab her shoulders to steer her back to the bed and sent the water pitcher crashing to the floor in the process.

"Oh dad gum it! Don't slip on that water, stand right there!" She ran out of the room to get a janitor, and Tonie swiftly dressed and left.

That night, she emailed Paul about the mix up of x-rays and reported that she was perfectly fine, just sore and bruised. Relieved, he agreed that broken bones could be hard to properly diagnose. Tonie danced around her apartment. Two more weeks until he came home! Life was good again. She had Paul, and she loved her new career path. If she must live forever, she concluded, it was better to have someone to go through it with than not, and this time, she knew an answer lurked on the horizon.

Chapter Four

T ONIE ARRANGED THE ONIONS ON A LONG TABLE AT the front of the laboratory classroom, then set out knives and cutting boards. Unlocking the closet, she brought out microscopes and distributed one to each student station. This was her first day as a teaching assistant for the lab portion of a Biology 101 class. About to graduate with her Master's Degree in Botany in May, being awarded a teaching assistantship was not only an honor but also helped pay the bills. The budding professor surveyed the room and nodded with satisfaction that everything was in order for the first session—studying cell structure.

Tonie watched in happy anticipation as students began arriving in class. She smiled at the first young man who entered and gestured for him to come in. "Take any seat," she told him, trying to be casual and friendly, but always aware that she was a pretender that could be exposed at any moment.

The classroom was filling up when an older student, a woman who looked to be in her forties, came in and took a seat on one of the tall lab stools.

"Amanda!" Tonie whispered, shocked to recognize her granddaughter, and immediately on guard against being discovered. Amanda, not sure if she had heard her name or not, glanced at the teacher expectantly.

Amanda was the mother of Antoinette whose identity she had assumed. The girlish grandmother froze, pasting a bland, disinterested smile on her face while she rapidly assessed the situation. Amanda looked away, figuring she must not have heard her name after all. Trying to relax, Tonie realized Amanda would never imagine her dead grandma was alive and now a young college student, whatever the resemblance. However, Tonie's heart ached at seeing this familiar face that she loved so much. It was a double torment—being desperate for even a glance of her loved ones, but then the pain of knowing you may never cross the threshold into relationship again. She was as invisible as if she really were dead.

As the quarter progressed, Tonie tried to resist taking a personal interest in Amanda, but her efforts were in vain. One Friday afternoon when her granddaughter was the last one cleaning up after class, Tonie suggested going out for coffee together. Walking to the student union café, the two kinswomen chatted about upcoming finals, the weather, and tidbits of gossip about who would be teaching what for the summer courses.

"What are your plans for your education?" Tonie asked, sipping her coffee on the veranda as the sweet spring air danced around them.

"Oh," Amanda sighed. "My husband ran off with another woman last year, and rather than sit home and stew, I decided this was my chance to start my life over, too. I always wanted to be a nurse, so here I am at forty-six going back to college. I feel so old around all these teenage girls. I look like their mother!"

Tonie gasped inside herself. That rotten Duncan! He ditched his wife for another woman? She had never liked that man, he was so self-centered and such a shmoozer. She struggled to stay calm.

"It's never too late to start something new," the young grandmother encouraged. "You have so much to offer at your age, so much more compassion and insight into the complexity of the human mind and body."

"This past year I have had every cold and flu that's gone around, and I even had angina the first six months after the divorce. I thought I was going to have a heart attack, but now I know it was from all the stress."

"Pain in the heart from a broken heart," Tonie agreed, really thinking, "pain in the heart from a pain in the neck."

"I've seen enough illness take root when someone's emotional life is compromised, and I want to bring my experience to help people. I think there is a much stronger mind-body connection than is commonly acknowledged, and I believe, despite my age, I have something important to contribute."

"I think your age adds to what you have to offer," Tonie assured her, then moved on to the real reason she had asked Amanda out for coffee.

"I'm going to be studying in Paris this summer," she announced nonchalantly. "I just received my acceptance letter from the Sorbonne for a fellowship in botany with Dr. Fernand Michaud, who is a leading botanist in the field. This is a wonderful opportunity for me, and my boyfriend will be working at an archeological site in the south of France, so it all works out."

"Paris! Oh how wonderful!" Amanda exclaimed. "I've always wanted to go there! Maybe I will someday, now that I'm free and single again!"

"Why don't you come this summer?" Tonie invited, as if she just thought of the idea. "We are renting an apartment, and Paul will be gone most of the time. You could come for a few weeks and stay with us, or the whole summer if you would like. Maybe you could even shadow a nurse in one of the teaching hospitals while you're there. Hmm, I will see what I can find out about it."

"I was going to take a chemistry class this summer, but for an opportunity like this I might change my mind," the nursing student replied. "Are you sure that would be all right?"

"Absolutely, it would be fun," Tonie insisted. "I'm doing research on the local flora and will spend a lot of time in the field. I'll look into what programs are available. Do you speak French?"

"Not a word," Amanda admitted.

"You have time to take an intensive class. I'm taking a class to brush up because I used to speak it, but it's been a long time. Well, think about it."

"I will. This is very tempting!"

Amanda stared at the young woman in front of her. "My grandmother's name was Antoinette, and your eyes remind me of hers. And my last name is Stevens. I wonder if we could be distant cousins or something? Where are you from?"

"Maryland," Tonie replied, hastily naming the most remote place she could think of.

"Well, who knows!" Amanda dismissed the idea, not wanting to reveal how much it had intrigued her that her lab professor had the exact same name as her daughter—Antoinette Stevens.

The ladies finished up their coffee and bid each other goodbye. Tonie hurried home, thrilled to be a part of Amanda's life again. She had wanted to shout out a hundred times, "It's me, Nona!" Somehow it seemed to her that Amanda, or whatever person, should completely accept her story that she was 240 years old, and be amazed and want to help her figure out what went wrong. But she had learned from experience that no one was going to believe her at all.

When first husband Isaac died of old age, she had pulled up stakes in London and moved to Bath, shedding her old lady clothes and her painted-on wrinkles. She was an orphan, she said, a midwife, escaping the pollution of the big city. After not too many years of living in Bath, she met Lydia, the oldest daughter of one of her expectant-mothers, and they soon became kindred spirits. One day, after telling each other their deepest yearnings and secret loves, Nettie confided to Lydia that she was over a hundred years old and had never died. Lydia became concerned and told her mother, who told her father, who told the minister at church, who had Nettie committed to the insane asylum where she stayed for the next four years enduring the most outrageous procedures to bring back her sanity.

No. Amanda probably would not jump for joy at having her grandmother back, but rather, would run for her life from a crazy woman, she glumly acknowledged.

She also resisted the siren call of loneliness when it tempted her to confide in Paul that she was born before the French Revolution, that she suspected red berries that grew in Paris to be the culprits in her immortality— well, at least to 240 years and counting—and that she had a grandchild who appeared to be twice her age. She seriously doubted that he would be willing to trot his pony in an arena as wacky as hers. Instead, he would shrink back in horror believing his girlfriend had been bucked off her own horse a few times too many. And adding to her confusion was the new nag in the back of her brain whispering that she was a liar and deceiver for not telling the truth to Paul, who, she knew, never held anything back from her.

Tonie thought back to their conversation where he outlined his belief that man had been created and not evolved. She acknowledged that he had trusted her with his views for which she could have judged him crazy. Would it be so different to trust him with her secrets? Yes, it was different, she decided, because she was claiming a seeming impossibility. What he believed went against the current mode of scholarship, but he was waiting for evidence to back him up before he made his arguments. What evidence did she have? A good knowledge of history? That was available in books, it didn't prove anything. No, she sighed, she would not jeopardize her relationship with him over this. He was a seeker of truth and she loved that about him, and knew how very rare of a quality it was. But, some truth is better kept hidden.

Paul had lately been making references to their future together, and Tonie didn't know why she hesitated. She loved him and would be devastated if he left her, but when it came to the commitment her feet grew cold. The dread of the day that she knew with certainty would come—the day Paul would die and she would be forced to move on—stopped her in her tracks. Foolishly, she hoped to stave off the pain by remaining only semi-attached, by loving him only a little bit. But, she was finding there was no such thing, and fear ran cold in her veins. Paul wanted a devotion that lasted forever, the intertwining of two lives that ultimately led to the creation of two halves of a whole. Tonie could never have that intimacy with someone. She could never share that much of herself. Her curse kept her isolated from the emotional closeness her parched soul thirsted for, her only option being a shallow relationship that never progressed into the sharing of her mind and soul.

And now, they were going to Paris together. This year they were a couple. Paul consulted her before accepting the position in Lyon and made sure she would come along. She wished that this was the relationship for the rest of her life like she had dreamed of with André in her youth, but she knew from being married to Isaac, and then Thomas, that it was a stop-gap, a union that eventually would run out of time and she would be left alone again, her heart torn into yet another piece.

But Paris would be new and exciting, taking their focus off of each other and onto the events that surrounded them. It would offer enough external noise to disguise the fact that nothing meaningful exchanged between them, fulfilling Tonie's need to exist without the ever-present clamoring of her loneliness, and distracting Paul from the truth that Tonie never shared anything.

No, she would not divulge her secret to Amanda or Paul. No one could ever understand her plight because no one had ever experienced the hell of living forever. She would keep it to herself, always searching for the answer, and the way out of it, seeking to rejoin the human race who all railed against the agony of death, while she yearned for it.

Chapter Five

A MANDA CLIMBED THE STAIRS TO HER APARTMENT, located in a vast sea of apartments, that had served as her home for the past year. Unlocking the door and entering, she was greeted by her old tabby cat who was nearing fifteen years old. Mr. Merlin bridged the gap from her former life to this new existence in an impersonal, stranger-filled land of asphalt, concrete, and assigned parking spots.

Flopping her book-bag onto the counter, she absorbed the now familiar surroundings to comfort herself after being away all day. Home. It was becoming home. The interior reflected the newly divorced woman's changed life—homey and feminine with new furniture and new décor. Anything associated with Duncan had either been thrown away or sold at her moving-out garage sale. She definitely had not wanted the bed they had shared, nor the couch on which he had parked his cheating behind, nor the art on the walls that mostly reflected his tastes. The piano was hers from childhood and she kept that.

And, of course, Mr. Merlin was hers without doubt. Duncan never even liked her fluffy friend. Yes, Amanda and Mr. Merlin were the unrecognized gold rejected by the undiscerning eye of a fool.

"My little kitty," Amanda baby-talked to Mr. Merlin, scratching him under his chin. "He threw away the wheat and kept the chaff, didn't he?"

Mr. Merlin purred in agreement.

Amanda replayed her meeting with Tonie in her head. Paris! Could she really drop everything and fly off to the other side of the world on a whim? It had taken a year to adjust to her new circumstances, and she still struggled with feelings of uneasiness if she were out in public too long. But when she had stayed after class today with Tonie, all the ragged ends of her worries relaxed as if they were bathed in vanilla pudding. Moving to the city felt comfortable for the first time. She hadn't felt this close of a connection to anyone since losing Mama and Grandma Nona within days of each other nearly seven years ago.

Oh, how she missed them—their unwavering support, their presence and sense of humor. To Amanda, it was no mystery why Nona died the day after Mama's funeral—her life-spring was broken. Losing a daughter before you, when you are that old, just breaks a person.

Nona always loved to walk along the river, and it was suspected that she must have gone there after the funeral looking for solace and peace. Maybe she sat upon the rocks and stared into the water, then walked along it too closely and lost her footing. Even though they never found her body, her shoes washed up on the shore a week later. In the end, Amanda felt at peace with her grandmother's manner of death. She had lived an active life and had never wanted to die in bed with some protracted, painful disease. Although Nona was not a religious woman, she had surrounded Amanda with love and understanding when her baby had drowned. Not like Duncan who, while never openly accusing her, had secretly blamed her.

Amanda was drawn back to that dreadful day. She had played with little Antoinette and four-year-old Jack in the pool until the sun became too hot and they went inside for Antoinette's nap. She closed the gate to the pool as she always did and it should have locked automatically, but she must not have latched it completely. The phone was ringing as they got inside the house and it was Mama, and they chatted for about ten minutes while Antoinette and Jack played, she thought, upstairs. She didn't panic at first when she went to retrieve the little girl for her nap and didn't find her with Jack in his bedroom. The house was child-proofed and as safe and secure as a house could be. Amanda searched the rest of the rooms before her thoughts turned dark and she realized there was only one place left that she hadn't looked. She raced to the pool, found the gate open and her baby floating face down.

Stop it. Stop it. Don't go there, Amanda warned herself. She tried never to relive that time, that horrific moment of knowing, but somehow she felt herself pulled down the river of the past and into the forbidden backwash of painful memories. It must have been her get-together with Tonie, who had the aura of an old friend, that freshened these images from long ago.

The phone rang now, snapping Amanda back into the present. She saw that it was her son calling.

"Hello, Jack!" his mother chirped, driving the heaviness out of her voice.

"Hi, Mom. How is your school work going?"

"It's going well, but I've got lots of homework this week-end. I can't believe all the work. How did you whiz through college and get all A's? I have to study my brains out!"

Jack laughed. "It only looks easy when other people do it because you can't see them paddling their feet furiously underwater like a duck."

"That's true," the student agreed. "I shouldn't tell you how hard it is for me so then you would think I was brilliant."

"I already think you are brilliant, and I am proud of you."

"Thank you for the encouragement, sweetheart."

"Colleen and I will be in town tomorrow and I was wondering if we could drop by and visit for a little bit?"

"Of course, I would love to have you. Why don't you come for dinner and I'll make spaghetti and brownies?"

"Sounds like a plan, Mom. See you tomorrow." Jack hung up, and his mother smiled to herself.

Jack and Colleen had been dating for a year and seemed very much in love. Amanda anticipated that this was going to be an engagement announcement. Her mind jumped quickly to what preparations would need to be done, if indeed a wedding was in the works. She would need to lose fifteen pounds. Jack's father and his new wife were sure to be at the wedding, and she was darned if she was going to let them see her fat and frumpy.

When their baby drowned, Duncan had questioned her minutely on every detail of the last minutes of his daughter's life. Amanda saw it in his eyes that he blamed her, and rightly so—she blamed herself. She had not made sure the gate was locked, although she believed she had, and she had to live with that for the rest of her life.

After three years of grief and despair, the mother of a friend of Jack's approached her while she was waiting to pick her son up after school and invited her to come to Bible study the next day. Amanda hastily told the mother she was busy and wouldn't be able to come, but in the morning, after dropping Jack off at school, she drove to the church, parked the car and walked into a room full of women that she didn't know. The mother rushed over to her, welcoming her and introducing her to the other ladies who immediately included her in their group. At the end, everyone put a hand on her and prayed for a special blessing.

At first, Amanda began to experience a few seconds of well-being every day or two, and they slowly increased. She forced herself to go to the Bible study every week, and after several months she had taken some strides, the episodes of well-being stretching to a couple minutes each day. But one night when Jack was staying with Grandma, Duncan came home late from work and began berating his wife for the dirty house, for her sweatpants, for always making the same thing for dinner. Then he stomped out, saying he couldn't stand to look at her anymore. Amanda broke down and cried and couldn't stop. She fell on the floor clutching her stomach and moaning and screaming. It was the end of the world all over again. Her baby was dead and she had killed her through her own negligence. She hated herself. Duncan hated her. Where was God, did He hate her too? Did Mama and Nona secretly hate her? Amanda writhed under the weight of a thousand demons attacking her, torturing her with her own unworthiness, her unlovableness, her stupidity. She deserved to die, and she wanted to die. Raking her nails into her face, she rolled in convulsions on the floor, screaming out over and over for God to help her. Slowly and inexplicably her oppression lifted and her angst departed, leaving her exhausted, but not beaten.

That night while getting ready for bed, Amanda felt a flood of love and peace wash over her and she knew that her little girl was safe with God in heaven, and that God did not blame her for her daughter's death. Amanda was a human, a fallible human being who had tried to do her best but had erred as all humans do, and she was finally able to forgive herself.

But Duncan was another matter. His judgment and coldness kept her constantly second guessing herself.

"I am going to Paris!" Amanda boldly proclaimed to Mr. Merlin. "I will live backwards as you do, my fun starting now as I approach my middle age. I was brave and took the step to go to college, and I will be brave again and go to Paris! When will I ever get this chance again?"

Giving the purring kitty a quick pat, she told him he would stay with Uncle Jack, and then she got a pencil and paper to start making a list of everything she would need to do before she left. Delighted with her swift decision, she beheld the world opening up to her like an oyster, beckoning her to dive in and revel in its pearls.

Amanda enthusiastically began organizing her ideas, then stopped and pondered. What had taken her so long to seek out joy in life? Why did she stay with a husband who demeaned her and was disloyal? And when they did finally divorce, it had not been her decision—Duncan left her. She had lived in a loveless marriage for twenty years before it ended, and had done nothing to change the situation. She had prayed to God every day for an answer that never seemed to come.

Then a light came on in her head—she needed to walk by faith, and not by sight. Although knowing deep in her heart, years ago, what she should have done, she had never taken the first step because she couldn't see to the end of the road. Fear had paralyzed her—fear of the unknown, fear of failing, fear of disappointing people. Had God been calling her to leave her husband but she hadn't heard His voice over the clamor of self-doubt? God knew her pain and tried to lead her, but she hadn't had the courage to follow.

Thinking about her decision to go to college, she realized that it was a single step, a step made in blind faith not knowing whether she was capable of doing college level work or not, that set her on the path to where she was today.

"God will honor the baby-steps I take, showing me that I don't have to know where I'm going, I just have to show my willingness to go where He leads me. My list is my first step, and on Monday I will tell Tonie, and that will be my second step." On her paper Amanda wrote down, "Number one. Suitcase." For number two she listed "cute skirt." Losing fifteen pounds would serve double duty, she marveled—for her trip and for the wedding. "No brownies for me tomorrow," the excited traveler resolved.

Buoyed by her new-found discovery of trust and her upcoming trip to Paris, Amanda easily grabbed her purse and left the haven of her apartment to go shopping for groceries for her dinner party tomorrow. The usual reluctance and need to mentally prepare for the onslaught of the public world was missing as she breezily descended the stairs into the concrete jungle.

Chapter Six

T ONIE STRUMMED HER FINGERS NERVOUSLY ON the tray table as she gazed out the small, round window. There was nothing to see at this altitude except gray clouds below and bright blue sky above. Her first flight on an airplane, and she was embarking on a journey back to her homeland after an absence of nearly two hundred years. But Tonie was not nervous for fear of flying—crashing could only improve her situation—she was hopeful of unlocking the secret of her immortality and fearful of failure at the same time. If the berries did not hold the answer, then her last six years of study were in vain. Not that time mattered to her, but she would be at another dead end.

What would Paris be like, she wondered? From books and the internet she knew it had immeasurably changed. Baron Haussmann had swept through in the mid-1800s—after she had already sailed to England— mercilessly cutting wide swaths through the city, demolishing crumbling medieval buildings and tenements, and replacing the winding, narrow streets with magnificent boulevards that showcased the city's great monuments. A double coup in one, Haussmann not only routed out the alleyways and impasses that harbored still-rebellious factions from the Revolution, he also modernized Paris into a clean, gleaming, world-class city.

Would she recognize her hometown, would it feel like home, the now-stranger contemplated? Yes, Tonie assured herself. Notre Dame still fastened her watchful eyes over the daily cavorting of her residents. The imperturbable Louvre stood its ground after a thousand years, reminding Parisians of their unshakeable roots. St. Chapelle, St. Sulpice, all her old friends would be there to greet her, and some new friends that she hadn't met yet, but who, she was sure, would join the welcome-home party. Paris might grow, but the heart of Paris never changed—like a friend that has gained a few pounds but still possesses the same soul.

The last time she saw Paris, grief had shaken her the way a dog shakes an old shoe. Her decision to leave France had been born out of the desire to escape herself.

At fifty-seven years old, Nettie has no one. Standing forlornly at Amélie's grave, she says goodbye to her best friend, her sister, who shared with her the progression of sorrows that life hurled at them. Amélie was the strong one though, and Nettie quivers on the shifting sands under her feet. Who will go home with her today when the priest stops talking and cry with her and try to make sense of the day's events? Who will encourage her to eat on this sad day, and who will she encourage? Who will share her memories as the years unroll—of Mama and Papa; of brave Gervais and kind, gentle Jacques, two young men who gave their lives for the dream of freedom; and of the little girls who grew into beautiful young women and moved far away from the hell-pit that Paris became? Who else grieves for little Henri like she does? She cannot remember a minute of life on earth without Amélie, and now they are ripped apart.

Nettie glances around the graveyard with heavy eyes. So many stones with her family's name on them, each one representing a mountain of pain. She doesn't want the priest to stop talking and force her into the vacuum left by Amélie, but at some point he does, and her wooden legs carry her mechanically homeward, alone, time yawning in front of her like a gaping void. When she gets there, she packs her few belongings into a small satchel that was Mama's and, not able to bear the empty house clamoring with the silence of ghosts, leaves in the hope that it isn't really true.

So long ago. Tonie reflected on the month she spent in Rouen after leaving Paris, before deciding to travel on to England and America. Wavering between her longing for the familiar and her need to escape so far away that the torment couldn't find her, she had finally set off for Calais to catch a boat across the channel, never once suspecting the long road ahead of her.

And now, she was going home. She glanced over at Paul who had fallen asleep with his science journal still open on his lap, only five hours into their ten hour flight to Paris. No high stakes for him. He was free to explore and discover and be happy putting together the puzzle pieces of what he found. Whether humans moved into the Loire Valley fifteen thousand years ago or a hundred thousand years ago was exciting, but nothing that affected his eternity.

She savored what a rare breed of man he was in her experience, a man whose thinking was not confined to black and white, one right and one wrong, to extremes. He didn't doggedly keep tracking a scent that led nowhere. He didn't develop a hypothesis and twist all evidence to fit it—instead, he took the evidence and let it shape itself.

Tonie had initially been surprised by Paul's candid discussions on the topic of God. He talked about God like He was an invisible friend with whom he consulted about everything. When Paul told her that the more he studied the fossil record the more he believed that the so-called "missing link" was actually the hand of God, Tonie felt obligated to gently challenge him, not believing that there was a hand of God.

"But what if someone does find a link that proves that people evolved from apes? Would that destroy your faith in God?"

"No!" Paul's eyes lit up. "Because I believe God created humans regardless of how He went about it. I just don't happen to think He did it by a series of fortunate mutations, although He could have, but I don't see any evidence for it. I see science as revealing the handiwork of God, not explaining Him away. And the more I learn, the more bowled over I am by the brilliance and wonder of His creation."

"Maybe. But what would happen if everyone you loved in life died? Would you still think He's the 'magnificent creator?'"

"That's where He shines the best; He is our Comforter," Paul assured her, refusing to be offended by her cynicism.

Paul's curiosity had been piqued in his teen years as he noticed discrepancies in science journals. One year the universe would be described by astronomers as so big and growing, then a few years later it was described as only this big and shrinking. It was the same thing for the theory of evolution—the dating of artifacts changed wildly from year to year. During a visit to a museum one summer, it was explained that a dinosaur had been found to be constructed all wrong, necessitating its rearrangement to fit the current mode of thought regarding which bones belonged to which dinosaur. It boggled his mind that such sketchy, incomplete findings could be presented as fact.

When Paul entered college, he discarded all theories and started out afresh instead of following along with the same hypothesis as the evolution theorists who only had the aim of bolstering their claims. He began his studies presuming nothing, wanting to find what he could stand on solidly as true, and which "proof" may have begun with a kernel of truth, but had become surrounded by so much flotsam and jetsam as to have lost its validity. This approach served him well, exposing many assumptions that could not hold water, but were built on all the same.

Another source of information which Paul found persuasive, but was categorically dismissed in academic circles, was literature. So many events recorded in ancient writings by many cultures were regarded as untrue if no physical evidence could be found to back them up. As a teen, Paul had loved the story of the sun and moon standing still in the book of Joshua. However, this occurrence, which was also described in Mexican, Incan, Babylonian and Egyptian writings, was considered a superstitious yarn with no foundation. Why would so many people go to incredible lengths to write of this seemingly impossible event if it had no merit? These were the kinds of questions that intrigued him and led him into the field of researching the past. With his belief that God was capable of anything, no mystery was too big for this man of God and science to contemplate.

So now the scholars were winging their way Europe-bound to their respective summer projects. Paul was directing a team of archeologists to extricate and study what was estimated to be a modern human settlement, preliminarily dating back thirty thousand years, that had been found by two young boys while digging an underground fort in a small village east of Lyon. Tonie was charmed by this finding of the fossils by the boys because it reminded her of her brothers and how much they loved to build forts and dig for treasure. She delighted in the notion that little boys never change.

Paul was also pleased that his girlfriend would be spending the summer at the Sorbonne so close to his work. He wanted to marry her and considered romantic Paris to be the perfect place to propose. However, it would have to wait a little while because he needed to catch a connecting flight to Lyon immediately upon his arrival in Paris, but he would be coming back every weekend.

Tonie mused at the coincidence that she was ready to search for her berries at the same time that Paul was studying his bones. A rare contentment flowed through her, although she knew it would be temporary. While she tried to resist becoming attached to Paul, she recognized that he contributed to the serenity that flowed through her. Amanda was coming for a month in July, and she was happy for that, too. But the fear that she would lose them both was always nagging, nagging at her.

But right now, today, she was happy and not worried about the future. She had high hopes of finding the berries, finding an antidote, and stepping back into the human race. Then she could grow old with Paul and Amanda, sharing life as it came—the good and the bad, in the same rocky boat with all of humanity.

"Am I a mutant?" Tonie had privately wondered when Paul told her that there was evidence to suggest that some cataclysmic event took place thousands of years ago, suggesting that modern humans arose very quickly, not slowly evolving as had been theorized since Darwin. However, she dismissed the idea that she was the mother of a new breed of humans. Her own child had grown old and died easily enough, so she obviously had not passed on some super-longevity gene. Pretty as her granddaughter was, she still looked in her forties.

The long flight finally drew to a close. Upon their descent into Paris, Tonie told Paul not to worry about her finding her way from the airport into the city, that she would hire a carriage. Paul tried to keep a straight face and not laugh, but his eyes betrayed him.

"What?" she demanded, seeing his amusement.

"Nothing," he assured her. "You just have a way with words that is not exactly typical."

Realizing her mistake, she quickly covered. "I've been reading a book about Mendel's life in the 1800s, and the people took carriages wherever they went. It's very vivid in my mind right now. I'm glad I provide you with a source of entertainment."

Paul pulled her in and kissed her cheek. "I love your idiosyncrasies, that's all. It's part of what makes you you, and I love you just how you are."

Tonie took out her map of Paris and the thrill of going home overtook her now that it was within her grasp. Her heart was aching for these places that she had last seen with her family. Steeled for Baron Haussmann's sweeping changes and modernization of Paris after the Revolution, she warned herself that two hundreds years had turned it into a foreign city and to not have any expectations.

"Be careful," Paul warned, as he left her at the airport to take his flight to Lyon. "You are young and beautiful, and muggers might see you as an easy target."

"This is Paris, not New York," she reminded the small town boy who perceived Portland, Oregon, as a metropolitan city.

"Don't take the metro."

"I won't," she laughed, eager to get away and melt into her past. She felt like she was stealing off to meet a secret lover. Her protector saw her safely settled onto the bus and kissed her goodbye.

Charles de Gaulle airport was a city in itself—the air was French, the background chatter was French and she was home and it felt so good that it hurt. The past two hundred years collapsed into nothingness.

Chapter Seven

TONIE SETTLED INTO PARIS LIFE AS IF SHE HAD never been gone. The city was still essentially Paris, and they shared a bond. She knew Paris "back when," and it knew her "back when," and she was herself again. She had come full circle and trusted without question that Mother Paris would render up the secret of her curse, and she would become fully human again— vulnerable, fragile…mortal. Her tranquility stemmed from the hope that she would soon have an expiration date indelibly stamped on her butt like everyone else.

Walking by Notre Dame on the second day of her return, Tonie noticed a line of people alongside the cathedral extending nearly its length. Wondering what they were waiting to see, she walked to the front of the queue and saw a ticket taker at the tiny door leading to the stairs that wound their way into the inner bowels of the church. All these voyagers were waiting their turn to climb to the top of these smooth, stone stairs polished by feet through the ages, seeking a connection to days of yore. Tonie stopped and stared at the narrow door, and memories sent her reeling into the past.

She is sixteen. She and André are running up these stairs to get out of the rain while Papa delivers a load of cabinets to the home of a noble. They have just promised each other that they will get married, when the gathering storm clouds burst, sending them running for cover in this tiny entrance. They have been friends for years, and every time she comes into the city with Papa she finds him, and they talk and dream together, and this summer they are in love. Making their way half-way up the winding stairway, André stops and puts his arms around her, pulling her close and kissing her for the first time, but they can't stop, and he puts his hands on her breasts and she doesn't want him to stop, it is so delicious. But the thought of Papa searching for her brings her to her senses, and she and André run laughing from their shelter in the stairs, more in love than ever.

"Does Mademoiselle wish to buy a ticket?" the guardian of the door inquired, interrupting Tonie from her reverie.

"Non, non monsieur," she answered back, reluctant to be pulled from the portal of her old life, where she was young and happy and full of dreams for the morrow. She slowly walked away, leaving André and their secret hiding place behind.

A whirlwind week was spent meeting professors, presenting her thesis, and getting settled into her office at the Sorbonne. Every morning she stopped for a coffee and croissant at the neighborhood boulangerie before setting out on the ten minute walk from her apartment to the university.

On her first free day, Tonie launched on her quest to search for the area of her childhood home. She carried no hope of finding her actual house, knowing that centuries had passed, but even finding the street, or a landmark of some sort, would provide the connection she craved. Her family had lived in the St. Antoine neighborhood on the eastern outskirts of Paris, beyond the Bastille and the city wall. The Bastille had been demolished during the early years of the Revolution, so she was not surprised, as she ascended the metro steps, to find a roundabout teaming with cars frantically rushing around a tall column which marked where that prison fortress had once stood.

Faubourg St. Antoine was a village in its own right in Tonie's younger days, separated from Paris by the massive stone city wall, with entrance into Paris gained through the St. Antoine Gate. Now, all those necessary fortifications that once protected the fledgling town from marauding armies had disappeared. Gone also were the fields and orchards that had extended into the hillsides.

The newcomer watched the dizzying array of cars entering the roundabout from the surrounding streets at breakneck speeds, horns blaring, five to six cars deep with no defined lanes.

"Connard!" a driver in the outermost circle screamed out his window at some transgression from another vehicle. Tonie winced, wondering if that still meant what it used to mean. Cars continued to dart around, cutting off other drivers unannounced, flinging themselves through three lanes at the last second when their exit approached. She involuntarily squeezed her eyes shut at the expected carnage, but, like a well-rehearsed ballet, tragedy was impossibly averted at the last crucial second, and the dance went on to the rhythmic blasting of horns and cursing drivers.

Continuing down the rue du Faubourg St. Antoine, Tonie searched for any vestige of times long past. Nothing was familiar, and her head swam from disorientation. She turned back and lined herself up again with the Genie of Liberté which stood on the top of the Bastille column. Rue de Charonne should soon be on her left, she reaffirmed, and kept on walking. Up ahead, the architecture of the buildings changed abruptly, and an old stone fountain came into view. The fountain of Trogneux. Tonie ran to the two well-known lions' heads, still spitting water, where she had filled her bucket for years. It was no longer situated at the edge of a village on a muddy, medieval dirt road, but now resided on a smoothly cobblestoned, building-surrounded, clean city street clogged with traffic. But there it was—a piece of home. Tonie put her hands in the water that gushed from the lions' mouths.

Pretty girls walked by in their colorful summer clothes, cellphones to their ears and expensive purses on their arms, young men eyeing them appreciatively, but Tonie noticed nothing of the everyday life taking place around her. The pavers morphed into dirt and the lustrous buildings mutated into shanties.

She is eight years old and wearing a brown, homespun frock, the apron smeared with mud from the bucket of water she has just lifted into their wooden wagon. Amélie is with her, and they pull the wagon home over the dusty, rutted road—not much wider than a path—happily chattering about the playhouse they are making in the woods behind their house. Really just a clearing between three trees, the two girls have swept away the underbrush, laying branches on the ground to divide the area into rooms, and they have made a baby's bed with moss where their two cousin sock-babies sleep. Now Amélie is telling her that Papa has given her a scrap of board from his shop, and they are in a serious discussion of the unlimited potential of this propitious windfall.

Leaving the fountain, Tonie turned into the hushed atmosphere of the rue de Charonne, off the busy main thoroughfare that had led travelers and merchants in and out of Paris for a thousand years. Instinctively following the path that would have taken her home, she barely noticed the amassing city that had grown up around her village. The muddy lane was now paved with cobblestones, with cars parked so closely jammed together that it looked impossible to un-park them. A formerly grassy cow pasture, also paved over, sported rows of parked motorcycles packed in like dominoes. Tonie quickened her step, the aura of her former life swirling in her mind, past the little path where her friend Marguerite had lived, and finally, the tiny Passage des Ateliers on the right.

Tonie stopped and stared. There it was. Haussmann had not directed its removal. Hitler's tanks had not plowed through it. Time had not pulled it down. Paved over and much cleaner than the last time she saw it, everything had changed, but everything was the same— like a best friend in a Halloween costume where all you can see is their eyes, and the eyes give them away. The eyes were there. Tonie ran halfway down the street and there was Papa's shop, and attached to the side of it, her home. Day after day had rolled by since she lived here— one day sunny, the next windy and rainy; one day with children playing in the dust and the next with soldiers running through the mud shouting and shooting—each day leading to the next until this day arrived.

Vines wildly climbed the corners of the house, winding their way to the roof and erupting in a riotous display of verdure. Bright sun glittered off the mullioned windows exactly as she had last seen them. How Papa loved these windows that showered his shop with light and bestowed the view of the bustling, busy world as he shaped and sanded and coaxed former trees into works of art. Was Mama inside? Was Papa in his shop working? But now the door was locked to her.

Without considering whether she should, Tonie knocked on the door to which she formerly had free access. Over it hung an old wooden sign in the shape of a chair, announcing "La Chaiserie." It was not her father's sign. No one answered, so she peeked through the windows into the dark shop. It looked like an artist's studio. She saw easels and canvases, a table with paints spread out on it, and cans of turpentine and oily rags. There was only one window on the street side into the living area, and it had a curtain covering it. She was sure now that she did not want to see inside anyway. It probably looked like a modern house with running water, a television, a stove, and she would rather keep her memories.

Standing back, she savored the fragrance of the air, soaking in the essence of this street, this house, this exact spot under the sun where love and living took place, and horror and loss, and where one day innocence was replaced with rage. Guessing that she should move on, she quietly took a picture, then continued down the lane in search of the wooded area where she and Amélie had made their playhouse, and where she had eaten the berries. But there were no longer any woods, and soon she was back on a busy city street, leaving the little oasis that was the last remaining vestige of her neighborhood.

Tonie wiped her mouth with a napkin, swallowing the last bite of the croissant. She looked up at Paul. "I think I would like another. Will you still love me if I get fat?"

"I'll have another one too, and we'll get fat together." Paul grinned at her, signaling to the waiter to bring two more croissants.

Paul had come into Paris the night before, only able to get one day off. Summer in the city seldom witnessed any rain, but on this particular Sunday, soft, cool drops lazily fell from the sky, glistening the streets and hushing the noises of the usually bustling sidewalks. But nothing could dampen the enthusiasm of the two lovers so eager for the familiar sight of the other's face amidst a city of strangers.

"What do you want to do on your one day here?" Tonie asked her boyfriend, who she knew was eager to explore Paris. "I've had time to do a little sightseeing, but was waiting for you to make any big outings." Sitting inside the warm café, they sipped coffee, watching the drizzle and the parade of umbrellas passing by.

"Even though it is wet and rainy, I won't feel like I'm really here until I've gone up the Eiffel Tower," Paul responded like a true tourist.

"Me too, I would love to do that! After the Eiffel Tower we could ride in a pedi-cab," Tonie suggested. "I've seen them around, and it looks like a fun way to see the city and absorb the ambiance. They have a canopy so the rain won't matter."

"Sounds cozy to me." Paul took out a map and studied it for a minute. "There should be a bus at the corner in about five minutes. Shall we brave the elements, my dear?"

Tonie laughed, and the happy couple poked their heads out the door as Paul opened up the umbrella.

Huddling under it, arms criss-crossed behind each other's backs, they slowly made their way to the bus stop, oblivious to any ambiance the city of love had to offer.

After much more than five minutes passed, Tonie became aware that the bus had never arrived, or else they missed noticing it, leading the pair to begin meandering toward the river, keeping half an eye out for it. But the strolling became more fun than the goal, their mission soon evolving into a quest to cross every bridge in the heart of Paris.

Pausing on the Pont au Change to admire the tall, spired medieval towers where Marie Antoinette had been imprisoned before her beheading, Paul shivered and mused out loud, "I wonder what it would be like to be locked in there, knowing that you were to be put to death the next day?"

Tonie pondered this question. Dogged by her long life, she had earnestly pursued an answer to be able to end it, believing herself unafraid of dying. But what would she feel if tomorrow, for sure, she knew it would be over?

"I wonder what my regrets would be, and my fears?" Paul continued.

Having always had an endless supply of days, Tonie never examined what she may have done better, what she regretted, or what she would change if she could and strive to do better the next time. But, imagining her head and hands bound, waiting for the cold steel of the blade to rip through her neck, she shuddered. "I think it would be hard to know that people hated you so much that they were willing to purposely do such a horrid thing to you."

Paul nodded and paused in contemplation. "I would want to tell my brother that I love him. We were never close, and, as a teenager, I hated him for making fun of my, my quietness, I guess I would call it. Lucas called it something else. So, of course I fought back, calling him things like 'stupid.' It went back and forth. Maybe I should write him a letter just to talk about what he's up to, and see where it leads."

"That's a good idea, before time passes and it's too late." Tonie liked this closeness with Paul, even though she could not reciprocate. Being that her regrets mostly lay in the distant past, she saw no use in hauling them into the light of day if she could help it.

Forging ahead to the next bridge they laughed and chatted, their bright future unfurling before them like a glittering path, its jewels theirs for the taking. The theme of regret hovered in the back of Tonie's mind however, even as Paul snuggled close under the umbrella that shielded them from the pattering of raindrops.

"The head is out, Mama. One more push!" Nettie tells her mother. Mama bears down, and the baby's shoulders emerge, followed quickly by its entire body.

"A boy!" Amélie announces.

Nettie lays the baby on Mama's belly and rubs his back. He gasps and lets out a little cry, then another, louder, until he is wailing lustily and his face is red.

"Oh," Mama cries. "Is he perfect?" Her eyes glisten with tears of awe. She is still a beautiful woman at thirty-eight.

"Yes," the student midwife reports. "He's already gaining a nice pink color and has good muscle tone. And you can hear his strong lungs." She ties his umbilical cord which has stopped pulsating and lifts him gently. She runs her fingers along his spine and neck.

"Straight back." She then palpates his head. "Fontanelles correct size. A little bruising you can see here," she indicates his forehead, "but not too much molding—you did deliver rather fast, Mama." Nettie looks to her mother for her approval of the examination. Mama is all smiles and nods at her.

Amélie wraps the newest member of the family tightly in a blanket and places him in Mama's arms. Mama tickles his cheek with her nipple, and Henri eagerly nurses at her breast.

Nettie is proud that with the birth of Henri she has become a full-fledged midwife, and will take over Mama's patients now that Mama has a newborn baby. Exhilaration surrounds her as she becomes an equal participant in the caring for her family.

The recollection of Mama's joy at Henri's birth was overshadowed by Tonie's vague rumblings of regret at not recognizing Mama's pain at losing her son. Along with losing Henri that day, Mama also lost a daughter.

The guilt for multiplying her mother's burden came bubbling up through the many layers of denial, bursting forth into her consciousness. Tonie stopped abruptly in the middle of the next bridge, interrupting Paul's discourse on his first car that he had bought for four hundred dollars.

"I would wish that I had been more of a comfort to my mother."

Paul looked into her face, not understanding the reference, but knowing how hard it had been for her to share that private sorrow. He held her close, and she cried into his shoulder.

Chapter Eight

ARRIVING BACK IN PARIS THE FOLLOWING WEEKEND, Paul hopped off the train and studied his watch. He had taken an earlier train from Lyon than planned, and Tonie wouldn't be expecting him for another two hours, which gave him enough time to secretly search for an engagement ring. Marc Diceccio, his colleague at the dig, had recommended an antique jewelry store on the boulevard St. Germain and had given him detailed instruction how to get there on the metro. This would be Paul's first foray into this mode of Parisian travel. He was to take Line One from the Gare de Lyon to Châtelet, transfer to Line Four to St. Germain des Prés, and then the jewelry shop would be down the block on the left.

Armed with this formidable list of French names, Paul descended the metro steps and entered a world of winding tunnels and rushing commuters. A frenetic energy permeated this underground expanse where previously normal, sane, appropriately paced people became madly dashing autotrons who must catch the first possible train at any cost, even though the next one would be along two minutes later. Caught up in this nervous frenzy, Paul spotted the Line One sign and catapulted himself down the tunnel with a horde of similarly minded folk. Reaching the platform as the train came barreling in, he hurled himself on as if it were the last helicopter out of Viet Nam. As it pulled out of the station, he checked the map on the wall over the door and counted the stops until "Châtelet" where he would change trains. Four stops. Paul relaxed and hung onto the pole as the train darted its way along. Soon it slowed for the first stop, and a voice on the loudspeaker announced "Reuilly-Diderot" instead of the "Bastille" that he was expecting to hear.

"Wait a minute," the confused globetrotter muttered, scrutinizing the map. "Oh rats, I'm going the wrong way." Right then the door closed, sweeping him along even farther from his intended destination.

At the next stop Paul was poised to dash off the train the minute the door opened, in search of Line One's opposite direction. He now remembered Marc's insistence of getting the right "direction," which Paul had dismissed as such an easy concept that any fool could get it. Resisting the urge to rush, up he went, climbing a steep staircase, through a long tunnel, and then descended another staircase to the opposite side of the platform.

"Well that's one secret I'll keep to my grave," the revered scientist vowed to himself sheepishly.

Stepping out of the jewelry shop into the softening sun of late afternoon, rush hour traffic already gaining momentum, Paul consulted his map, then bravely set out to follow the winding streets of Paris to the rue de Vaugirard and the apartment he shared with Tonie. It looked straightforward. He hoped he would do better above-ground than he had with the metro.

Paul patted his jacket pocket and felt the ring box. The perfect ring for the perfect girl, he reflected poetically. Tonie was a bit of an enigma to him. She wasn't impressed by money or prestige the way most people were, and she had a curious attraction to the past and an incredible working knowledge of it. She also had an uncanny way of cutting through a smokescreen to find the truth of a matter instead of being blinded by all the bluff that people will put around their arguments to hide their true agendas. When another professor had criticized a paper Paul had written, Tonie surmised that the paper must be stepping on his attacker's toes for a theory he was about to make which would be invalidated by Paul's findings. And, it turned out that she was right— he was attempting to discredit Paul in order to keep his own paper in the running for scholarly recognition.

The soon-to-be husband wanted a ring that would represent her personality, her spirit, and scientist Paul set forth to define these qualities—integrative thinker; romantic tendencies in her less guarded moments; independent, but also very vulnerable. She would hate that he thought that. But she was. He loved her, and therefore he loved however she was. He loved her essence regardless of what talents or quirks or weaknesses may be attached to her. Tonie was Tonie and he loved her. Love is a funny thing, he mused. This is how God must love us. Covered with dirt, whistling clean, stupid or smart—God loves us.

Paul knew that she grew up in Maryland, had no brothers or sisters, and both her parents were dead from a boating accident. She had several cousins that she did not keep up with, and they were her only relatives. He suspected a darker story in there somewhere because she never made any references to her past, but since she hadn't shared it with him, other than the remark about her mother, he was careful not to infringe on her privacy by asking. She would open up to him as her trust grew, he believed, and he was content to respect her silence.

Yes, the ring couldn't be better, Paul concluded. Made in Paris in the 1920s, it had a dazzling, old European cut diamond in the middle adorned by baguette diamonds on the sides. It had belonged to a Marguerite Benoît, designed by her husband-to-be, and worn throughout their sixty-five years of marriage. The jewelry store had only recently acquired the ring through an estate sale upon the death of Marguerite's granddaughter. Not too gaudy for Tonie's less-is-more tastes, but definitely an eye catcher that harkened back to an earlier time, and—Paul was the most pleased with this aspect—the ring had a story, which he knew she would love.

His plan for the evening was to take his girlfriend out for dinner at a chic and trendy Parisian restaurant, then go for a leisurely walk along the river. Then, he would pop the question on the Pont Neuf, the oldest bridge in Paris. He knew she would not want a public display or anything too showy, so that would suit her perfectly. An old bridge in an old town. Perfect.

That evening, Paul leaned forward and smiled at the alluring young woman across the table from him. The alluring young woman smiled back. Dinner had been fun and charming, both parties delighted to see each other again after a week apart.

"Mademoiselle." The waiter set the glass of Lillet on the table in front of Tonie with a flourish, openly appreciating her beauty, and then set one in front of Paul.

"To us," Paul toasted, and the lovers clinked glasses.

"Mmmm, delicious," Tonie admired.

"I heard it's made from orange peels," Paul offered, studying his glass as if to see if any might be floating in there.

"Lovely," Tonie agreed, laughingly taking another sip.

"Tonie, will you marry me?" Oh rats, he grimaced to himself, there goes my plan! He fumbled for the ring box in his pocket. The box was an art-déco miniature hat box. He pulled off the lid and revealed the ring inside. "I love you, darling."

Tonie stared down at the ring, and then up at Paul. "Oh my gosh," she put her hand over her heart. "I...I didn't see this coming." She stared back at the ring. It was beautiful. She had never much liked jewelry, but she loved this. It was her. Paul had to have looked into her soul to have this insight into what she would like, and he must love her very much to have done that. She wanted to marry him more than anything in the world.

"Yes, oh yes. I love you, Paul."

The waiter caught the flash of the ring and the light in their eyes. He motioned to the other waiter. As Paul was slipping the ring onto his fiancée's finger, they were warmly serenaded—one waiter-musician playing "La Vie en Rose" on the accordion, and the other one, all smiley and misty-eyed, singing along.

"I guess it's true that all Paris loves a lover," Paul whispered to his sweetheart and kissed her again.

Sitting in the early morning sun, the newly betrothed couple enjoyed their coffee and croissants before Paul needed to catch the train back to Lyon for work and Tonie would set off in pursuit of her berries.

"This week should give us some more solid dates on the bones," the man of science speculated, taking an appreciative bite of the buttery pastry. "Marc and I have been given a team of students to work the site—to do the more tedious work of unearthing the fossils and cataloguing them. And, we have several local laborers for the heavier work and to help haul away debris. It is turning out to be a very important find, much more extensive than was first believed." He took a sip from the tiny cup of espresso. "What is your schedule like this week?"

"I'm ready to start gathering specimens of the local flora, and then I will assay them for anti-senescent content," the student replied. "That will probably take two to three weeks, and then I will be going to Arles to collect samples in that area. There have been some exceptionally long-lived individuals there, including Jeanne Clement who lived to be 122 years old. She once said that she had had only one wrinkle in her life, and that she was sitting on it."

"She sounds like a feisty gal! Arles, you say. That's in my neck of the woods. You'll have to stop in and see the dig and meet Marc. He's a terrific guy—very knowledgable and easy to work with. I'll rustle up another cot and sleeping bag, and you can stay in my tent. Nothing too fancy, but, we even have a shower tent." Paul winked at Tonie as he stood up to go catch his train. Tonie gathered her backpack and the lovers hugged and parted ways, each on their own quest for the next five days.

Chapter Nine

TONIE SET OUT FOR THE FAUBOURG ST. ANTOINE area to search a little more around her old neighborhood for any signs of wild plants and hopefully the berries. It was a long shot—the old woods were gone, with paved roads and city structures extending in every direction. But, while she acknowledged that it was improbable she would find anything, she had been itching to see her family home again. Finding it had soothed her tremendously and chased away her interminable sense of drifting and lostness. It bridged the "before" with the "here and now" and made her life seems whole and continuous. And shorter.

Memories roiled within her as her house came into view again. She noticed details that she hadn't seen the first time and now inspected. Just like after Henri died and she had stared at a crack in the wall, and the crack became her friend and shared in her grief. Had that stone at the bottom of the wall that she saw now always been broken? Had it endured rain, wind, day and night for

250 years with its jagged edge, and no one had ever noticed, and here it was today? Was it a witness to the horror that happened that night that shook the foundations of the family within and shattered their lives forever?

The morning hours creep in gloomy and cold, raindrops spitting down from the dark clouds. Henri has been sick with putrid throat and fever for three days, and Nettie has watched over him all night, rubbing his chest with garlic and squeezing drops of water in his mouth when he can no longer drink by himself. But this morning his cheeks are gaunt, a bluish hue darkening around his lips. Mama has placed a pot of boiling water to produce steam next to the bed and heats it back up on the fire every time it cools off. Papa paces in the kitchen, helpless, while the other children sleep. He fetched the doctor the day before, who advised them against getting their hopes up, the diphtheria epidemic having already snuffed out the lives of four other children in the village.

Papa prays in that kitchen, where so many happy, boisterous meals have been shared, while now the minutes move like hours. Mama prays too, trying to keep faith in the face of the knowledge that other mothers have not been immune to losing their own beloved children. Nettie prays with the blind faith of the untouched, scared, but believing that ultimately God will heal their precious Henri.

Henri lies lethargic, his barking cough giving way to struggling, rasping breathing, until the breaths come no more. Nettie screams, rocking his lifeless body, frantically patting his back and willing him to breathe.

Mama tries to take him from her, telling her gently that "Henri has gone to be with the Lord." But Nettie doesn't believe Mama and thinks she is giving up too easily.

"Do something!" she implores Papa. Papa stands there with tears rolling down his cheeks, helpless.

"It's over, sweetie," Papa nods in agreement with Mama, and scoops little Henri out of her arms.

Pain scoured Tonie anew as she relived that night, the guilt that engulfed her at the time heaving itself back upon her. She had been going out on Mama's midwife calls while Mama recuperated. She should have never left her baby to go and take care of other people while her family needed her. Had she brought the sickness back with her? Maybe if she had been there all along she would have seen the signs earlier and been able to nurse Henri through it.

But...maybe not, she suddenly thought for the first time, the inkling of a new view taking shape out of nowhere. I did my best. Mama did her best—God knows Mama did. And Papa too. We all did everything we could.

Tonie contemplated the way Mama changed after losing Henri. Not really changed, perhaps, but intensified in her softness. She had always been a gentle, patient woman—loving and kind to her children and her patients—but she became even more so. She became ethereal, she expanded. If there were a wound to be bound, she bound it, seeing in the physical the spiritual. A broken leg to her was no longer merely a bone to be set, but an affront to the soul, an attack on the personhood of the afflicted. She tended to the emotions of others as much as to the injury. She was in tune to the universality of suffering and saw into the souls of those around her, intuitively gravitating to their distress and offering a kindred spirit to their losses.

Nettie had gone the other way. She railed against God and felt that no one in the world had ever suffered as she did. Isolating herself in her misery, she was not aware of anyone's pain but her own, and any attempt to ease her heartache by another was met with stony silence. She hated life, and she hated God. She hated other people whose babies were alive and laughing and happy.

Madame Lacoste has just given birth to a perfect baby boy, to the joy of her mother, two sisters and two neighbor women attending her. He reminds Nettie so much of Henri—the hearty cry, the dark wet hair, the chubby legs—that, for that moment, she thinks he is Henri, and she will do anything to get her baby back. While the happy gathering oohs and aahs over his beauty—and he is beautiful—Nettie notices that Madame Lacoste is bleeding a lot, and the situation is dire. There may be no hope at this point, but, if she doesn't notice the bleeding for another few minutes there will be no hope at all. She hesitates for only a moment—more likely a half a moment she later tells herself—then calls out for a cup of hot water and hurriedly retrieves the herbs from her bag to make a tea that will help the new mother's womb contract and stop the bleeding. But Madame Lacoste is already too groggy to take more than a sip or two of the tea, and Nettie sees that she has died.

Grandmother Lacoste notices too and shakes her daughter, turning to the midwife desperately for help. Nettie grabs the baby from her, saying that he has a heart murmur and that she will take him to her mother for care, then runs out of the door with him.

"Mama!" she calls out as she arrives home with her replacement brother, anticipating Mama's eyes lighting up with joy at the sight of Henri.

Mama looks up at Nettie while stoking the cooking fire under a pot of stew, and her eyes are confused when she sees the baby.

"Mama, his mother died, and he needs a home."

Mama comes over and pushes the blanket away from the newborn's face. "But, Madame Lacoste has family." The alarm in Mama's eyes turns to sorrow at the sight of Nettie's hopefulness. "She has a husband, and a mother and father. And sisters. They will all want this baby." She looks into her daughter's face. "He isn't ours to take… and, he isn't Henri," she whispers, understanding.

Nettie looks down at the bundle with his mouth twitching for the breast, and his weight feels good in her arms, and there is a peace in her soul that she hasn't felt for six months.

"No," she begrudgingly agrees, "he's not, but he looks like him, and I think he will make us happy."

Mama hugs her and holds her close. "Our Henri is with God in heaven, and this baby belongs to the Lacostes."

Nettie stares down at the baby in her arms, and he is suddenly a stranger that she no longer wants, but the loss of the want is as devastating as the original loss of Henri.

She studies the little red face with his swollen eyes, so fresh from the womb, and she hates this child—this interloper who dares to mock her Henri and tries to take his place. She shoves him into Mama's arms and crumples sobbing to the floor.

Tonie trudged away from her old home, guilt riding her like an overweight jockey, the airiness she had worn all week smothered by the reminiscence of the dark times endured in this house. She fixed her mind on her berry mission, scanning cracks in the cobblestones for any opportune shoots trying to sprout in the hostile environment of a city street.

By the end of the week, after searching the many green-spaces of Paris—the expansive Bois de Boulogne; the enchanting Bois de Vincennes; and the botanist's haven, the Jardin des Plantes—Tonie conceded defeat to finding her berries in the urban area. These meticulously maintained and well-tended city gardens showcased the best and the beautiful. Her berries were likely weeds, bitter and poisonous, nothing that would be sought after and exhibited in an illustrious garden. Any brave tendril trying to make an uninvited appearance would be shown the door before the sun could set.

Sitting on a park bench pondering her next move, Tonie absently watched the colorful merry-go-round make its laps, each wild animal carrying an elated child up and down in time to cheerful music. Wild fields no longer existed in Paris, she acknowledged, which necessitated a search further afield. Ideally, finding specimens as close as possible to the original berry bush would provide the best chance of finding the exact species, but since that effort had proved fruitless, the persistent botanist decided to move her search out to the suburbs the following week.

Lingering on the east side of town, Tonie decided to walk through the Père Lachaise cemetery. She had been about thirty years old when Napoleon bought the land from the Jesuits and turned it into a cemetery to ease the over-crowding in the city graveyards—especially the unsanitary Cimetière des Innocents which had served the citizens of Paris since the middle ages. But this new site was situated two miles from town, and nobody wanted to bury their dearly departed so very far away until, with much fanfare, the remains of Héloïse and Abélard were joined and transferred to Père Lachaise. It then became an acceptable, and even fashionable, eternal resting place.

Abélard was a twelfth century priest who fell in love with his student, Héloïse, who soon became pregnant with his child. Héloïse's uncle was so furious when he found out that he broke into Abélard's house one night and cut off the young man's genitals. Héloïse joined a convent and Abélard was sent to a monastery far away, and, although they exchanged letters the rest of their lives, the lovers were never to meet again. This tragic love story had survived generation after generation, so it melted the hearts of the Parisians when the lovers were finally reunited after hundreds of years, their bones entombed together at Père Lachaise.

Tonie wended her way through the maze of paths lined with monuments to the dead—ranging from small, modest headstones to towering and elaborate mini-chapels. Trees swayed gently in the breeze, their branches filtering the sun into winking, dancing lights on the cobblestone paths. The noise of the city receded. Bees busily flitted from flower to flower and birds sang out to each other—announcing finds of worms or seeds, or warning each other of a human intruder. Soothed by this glimpse into the peace of eternity, Tonie begrudged no one their bed of dirt this day.

Seeing the graves, many still lovingly tended, Tonie considered all these people who in life were plagued by their own failures and hurt by the failures of others. Now they lay in sweet repose, oblivious to their worldly pain which no one remembered anymore but which had been a crushing force at the time. "I'm sorry I hesitated, Madame Lacoste," the midwife whispered.

She consulted her map and continued on in the direction of the tomb of Héloïse and Abélard. Growing up French, Tonie was familiar with their sad story, and soon she beheld the ornate grave, its regal canopy covering the reclining stone forms of the star-crossed lovers, protecting them in death from the ravishes of time and elements as if to atone for the lack of protection they received at the cruel hands of life.

"What if it were Paul and me?" Tonie pondered, studying the silent figures of the famous couple. "Would I love Paul for the rest of my life if he were castrated and sent away, and I had to give up my baby? Would I live a meaningful life and write brilliant, thought-provoking ideas as an abbess, or would I wither away and die?"

Héloïse was not that much different from her, Tonie continued to muse. Héloïse lost Abélard, and she lost André. Héloïse lost her baby, and she lost Henri. Héloïse lost her freedom and lived out her life in an abbey away from her loved ones, while she lost her mortality and had to wander alone through eternity.

"I'll bring flowers to Héloïse tomorrow," she pledged, "for she has suffered as I have."

The sojourner felt a kinship with this medieval woman. Tonie remembered running up and down the streets looking for André in the city when she accompanied Papa into town that summer day in 1789 and not finding him, only to be told by some young men in the neighborhood that he had been killed in that very first attack on the Bastille, that initial defiance that led to a revolution, the churning of which would last a hundred years while men overthrew a monarchy and learned, the hard way, to govern themselves.

Nettie jostles in the wagon along with Papa as they ride into Paris to deliver furniture to the home of a bourgeois a few years after the fall of the Bastille. To be exact, Nettie remembers, four years and eight months after her baby died, and four years and two months after André was shot. Rumors of horrific killings taking place in the city run rampant in the streets, and now fear rushes through her veins as she witnesses the reality of it, smelling the stench of fresh blood rolling off the blade of the executioner's new weapon—the guillotine.

Driving past the Place de Grève, she and Papa hear the screams of terror from men and women alike as they are led up onto the platform and their heads are locked between the boards. She hears the pitiful pleading of the condemned, their useless prayers reduced to the raw supplication, "God help me! God help me!" before the blade drops, sending their heads rolling into the awaiting basket.

After making the delivery, she and Papa wait in line for the empty packing materials in their wagon to be inspected before being allowed to exit the city through the Saint Antoine gate. "When I die," Nettie vows, "I will never throw away my dignity by begging some non-existent God to save my life."

Looking at her watch, Tonie saw that she needed to move through the cemetery at a little faster pace. She had a paper due in the morning that needed some finishing touches. Also, Amanda would be flying in this afternoon, and the hostess wanted the apartment to be ready and welcoming.

Approaching the back exit, she encountered some of the older tombs hidden in trees and flowering shrubs, long forgotten by the groundsmen. Wild vines wound around the headstones like a pied piper enticing the dead to rise up from their earthly habitats and follow him into another world of singing and dancing and feasting.

Tonie leaned close to read the dates on a tomb and brushed away a thorny branch dangling over the inscription. She stopped and stared. At the end of the branch was a red berry, resembling a raspberry, but not so closely that she would mistake it for one. But a little girl may have. Pulling out her camera, she took pictures from every angle. Then she retrieved a specimen cup from her backpack and plucked the berry. Several more branches circled around the back of the headstone, and she collected the berries from them too, for a total of six berries. She recorded the exact location in her notebook and took leaves for identification.

She mentally planned her procedures as she hurried out of the cemetery with her treasure. First, she would flash freeze the berries until she could start the assaying process, which would be Monday. She needed to finish her paper, but she was too excited to believe she could concentrate on it. Ducking into the metro station, she sped her way to the Sorbonne, her berries more precious than gold in her possession.

Once back at the lab, Tonie easily identified the berries in the plant identification manual. It was a common berry of the region, bitter with a slight toxicity, with no nutritional value. That completely meshed with her experience of it as a child, although she would have described them as berries from hell, not just "slightly toxic."

Encountering her professor, Fernand Michaud, on his way out of the lab, she stopped him to ask about the berries. "Is this large enough of a sample to do testing on?"

Professor Michaud put on his glasses and took the cup from her. He peered closely at the contents. "No, you will need about three times this many to get accurate results. Go ahead and freeze them until you can collect some more."

Professor Michaud was nice looking, with the unkempt hair of a scholarly man too absorbed in studies to groom it, probably about fifty years old. He was an interested, yet reserved, mentor to Tonie. He had helped her focus her thesis and had given her many ideas for organizing her research, but he remained formal and distant.

"Why do you think these berries would have anti-senescent qualities?" he asked. "They are a common enough berry in this area with nothing to recommend themselves to an inquiry such as you propose."

Tonie was ready with her story. "There is a tale that I was told, by an old woman, about a young girl who accidentally ate these berries and almost died. However, she lived, but after that she never aged. I know that it isn't likely, but I thought that it could be true. Since no one would eat them on purpose because of their bitterness and toxicity, their qualities could go undiscovered. I think they fall within the scope of my study because of anecdotal evidence."

The professor was charmed by this story and smiled at his student over his glasses. "You make a good case for bringing them into your study, Mademoiselle Stevens. Old women should never be doubted. I shall be interested in the results. Have a nice weekend." He nodded his head at her and continued his way out the door.

Chapter Ten

P AUL WAS NOT ABLE TO MAKE IT TO PARIS FOR THE weekend, nor for the following weekend either. A new area of fossils had been discovered very close to the main dig, and he needed to stay to organize the unearthing of this new excavation. Tonie assured him she would be fine in the big city by herself.

Amanda arrived from the U.S. and, between classes, Tonie busily escorted her granddaughter to her growing list of delightful places—to the Marais for falafel and pastries, to rue Mouffetard for its outdoor markets, to the covered passage Vivienne for its trendy boutiques, and especially to her favorite place in the morning—a tiny table at a sidewalk café to have coffee and croissants and absorb the rhythms of the newly awakening day.

"While I'm here, one thing I want to find is a dress," Amanda told Tonie while strolling along the Seine during her first week in the City of Lights. "My son is getting married two weeks after I get back to the U.S."

"Really!" Tonie's ears perked up upon hearing this news about little Jack. Wasn't he just a boy? "Who is he marrying?"

"A very sweet girl named Colleen who he has been dating for a year. She's an artist, and he is an accountant. They're having their wedding in a small Presbyterian chapel in the town where he grew up, and the reception will be outside in the church garden."

Tonie knew exactly where that church was. "So, what kind of dress are you envisioning?" she asked, her mind whirring to think of a way to get herself invited. Her term would be finishing up in the middle of August.

"Well, I want something not old-ladyish. I've been kind of frumpy-dumpy for years, and now I've lost fifteen pounds, and I want a new me to go with my new life."

"Oh, I think Mother Paris can provide! You couldn't find an old-lady dress in all the city if you tried. You'd have to go to London for that!" Tonie snickered to herself, realizing that old rivalries die hard. Then she explained a timeless truth about Paris. "It's because there are no old ladies in Paris. All women are young and beautiful here, regardless of their age. What is the date of the wedding?"

"August thirteenth."

"Oh! That's my...that's my last day at the Sorbonne," she made up quickly, then seized the opportunity to interject herself into Jack's wedding. "Maybe I could finish a little early and come too?" she giggled, as if it were a silly idea.

"Absolutely! That would be so much fun! We would love to have you. August thirteenth is a traditional wedding date in our family. I was married…to the yuck-puck…on that date, and it was the anniversary of my parents and grandparents. I was thrilled when I learned that Jack and Colleen had chosen it, too. And what about you? Have you and Paul set a date yet?"

"Not yet, but we want to get married before we go home. But now, with the new discovery at the dig, Paul thinks he may be here longer than the summer, but I would still need to go back. We've been tentatively planning the end of August."

"Why don't you get married while I'm still here, and I could be your witness, and then you could come back with me to Jack's wedding? I would love that. And we could go dress shopping together—you for a wedding gown and me for my non-old-lady dress!"

Intrigued by this idea, Tonie talked about it to Paul on the phone that night.

"That would give us a month to arrange it," he replied, reflecting on the date. "My parents and brother are planning to fly over, so I'll have to see if they would be able to come earlier. Marc will be able to arrange a day off whenever we decide."

"I've looked into the procedures here, and we first need to do the legalities at the Mairie, and then we can have a ceremony anywhere we want. It takes about a month to apply for the license, so we'd have to hurry. There is a little church in the twentieth arrondissement that I want to show you next weekend," the bride-to-be offered, knowing her groom wanted a church wedding. "It's a medieval church, Saint Germaine de Charonne, and it is so quaint and has gorgeous stone steps leading up to it."

"That sounds wonderful, sweetheart. If you like it, then I know I will like it. I can't wait to marry you, so sooner works for me." Her fiancé chuckled at her choice. Nothing new and modern for his girl. He swore than she could sense the life in stones and pillars.

"You are a hopeless romantic, you know," Tonie sighed with mock exasperation.

"I know, but I'm not sure I'm the only one. Don't make me catch the train tonight and come to Paris to prove how much I love you."

Tonie laughed and said good night. She was not a romantic, she protested to herself. Old places were time machines that rocketed you to the past. She liked walls that have heard the woes and joys and everyday cares that have preoccupied people throughout millennia, and the stone floors that have borne their weight as they walked to the altars with their celebrations, and with their sorrows. These stones were here when she was little, and they would still be here when her current soul-mates were gone.

After a week of exploring Paris together, Tonie and Amanda boarded a train that would whisk them to Rouen. The ladies settled into their seats in the second-class wagon as the train silently and smoothly pulled out of the Saint Lazare station. Tonie had research to do in this medieval town, where Joan of Arc had been burned alive some six hundred years earlier, and where she had come to lick her wounds when her sister died. She was happy that her granddaughter was excited to come with her.

As the train sped along, Tonie reflected on the busy days she had spent together with Amanda so far— exploring centuries-old churches, shopping in little boutiques, enjoying a glass of wine while watching the sun go down. Tonie worked on her research most mornings, but always hurried home to meet Amanda in the afternoons for their excursions. She loved getting to know her granddaughter again and was eager for all the news of the past six years.

The countryside rolled by as if on fast-forward from the lightning speed of the train. Villages appeared on the horizon, promptly loomed up, then sped by in a flash, but not so fast that Tonie didn't notice the church steeples in the middle of every town. Amanda noticed too, and commented on it to her companion.

"Each town has a church in the center and the town circles around it, like planets revolving around the sun."

The humming of the train shrouded them in a snug cocoon, where silence was muted and time stood still. Tonie felt safe and content within the developing friendship between the two women.

After a moment Amanda asked, "Are you a woman of God?"

Completely caught off guard by the question, Tonie stammered, "Oh...um, no...I wasn't raised in the church."

"Neither was I, but, at the lowest point in my life, at a time when I couldn't even get out of bed in the morning and demons howled in my brain day and night, and I thought the only peace I would ever find would be at the end of a gun barrel, God came to me. He picked me up and comforted me with unworldly comfort, and He's carried me ever since."

"What happened that brought you to that point?" she whispered, already knowing the answer but wanting to be trusted with the secret.

"I had a little daughter, two years old, who drowned in our family pool. And it was my fault because I didn't latch the door properly."

Tonie's mind lurched to the thousands of times she had relived Henri's death—minutely going over every detail to ascertain if she had any fault in it. In her heart of hearts she knew she did not, that she had done everything humanly possible, and, she shared the burden of his death with Mama and Papa and the doctor. But here was Amanda, nearly thirty years later, tortured by the knowledge that it was she, and only she, who caused little Antoinette's drowning. How could she stand it? Never for a minute did she and Amanda's mother blame her, and they repeatedly told her so, but to what avail? She blamed herself.

Tears rolled down Tonie's cheeks. "I am so sorry."

"I'm telling you this because it is a big part of who I am, and to not tell would be a deception, and I value our growing friendship. And, I am a woman of faith. God picked me up out of my sorrow and made me whole again. My ex-husband always said that you can't make chicken soup out of chicken poop." She laughed to show Tonie that her misery was behind her, and she required no pity. "But I know that God can! He made chicken soup out of my life."

Tonie looked into her granddaughter's eyes and saw her own mama's eyes looking back at her. She had never understood the peace, the acceptance in those eyes, and here it was again. What makes her think her life is wonderful when God allowed her baby to die, she wondered. And, she's thanking the same God who allowed it. She and Mama. Why?

In Rouen, the ladies enthusiastically embraced their wedding shopping. Just off the vieux marché, they found a quaint boutique situated in an old house from medieval times, with exposed wooden half-timbers and panels of small-paned windows. Here, Tonie found her perfect dress—ivory satin and old lace, hearkening back to the era of her engagement ring, a modern creation with vintage flavor. Flowing to her ankles, it was a dress elegant enough to grace the steps of Saint Germaine de Charonne for a simple wedding, yet unassuming enough to be worn in a restaurant without demanding too much attention.

As Amanda fussed around her and adjusted the headpiece, chattering on about something borrowed, something blue, Tonie had the odd perception of being the daughter that Amanda had lost. With the passing of little Antoinette, gone also were the dreams of her mother for their future together—of ballet lessons and shopping excursions, first dates, braces, and eventually a wedding day and the passing on of the torch. The birth of a child is to have a stake in eternity, and when that child disappears, so does the hope of tomorrow.

Could I give that back to her? Tonie unexpectedly pondered, watching the shining eyes of Amanda as she fluffed the lace around the modest décolletage. She needs a daughter. I am the age of her daughter, and I could give her grandchildren that will look like her, and cousins for Jack's children. We could have big family Christmases and…Tonie's mind raced with the possibilities. She had not wanted children in her new marriage because her heart was through breaking. It was a dreaded conversation she avoided with Paul because she knew he wanted to be a father and assumed he would be. Now, she lost her aversion to the possibility of children as she realized the happiness it would bring to both of her people.

The birth of Emily had ushered in for her, as it does for all mothers, the perpetual inability to not care about the course of the world. She loved Amanda, and Jack, and the children Jack would have, and the children they would have.

She had languished in despair after Emily died and she was forced to leave Amanda and Jack. While time demanded that she move on and change her identity, she loved being back in their lives, being a friend and a part of their everyday existence. Trying to love half-heartedly would not ease the pain of the eventual parting, it just spoiled the joy of each day. The time would come again when she would need an exit strategy, but she decided she would stay in the lives of her progeny and figure out how to manage the rearranging of relationships when the need arose.

Happy in her decision, Tonie turned to Amanda and smiled. "One dress down, one to go!"

Chapter Eleven

T HE SORBONNE ROSE MAJESTICALLY ON THE SIDE of Mont Saint Geneviève, keeping vigil over this ancient city where a young girl had once, over a thousand years earlier, fervently prayed for the protection of Paris from the imminent invasion of Attila and his Huns. This girl of faith convinced the quaking citizens to fast and pray instead of fleeing in cowardly abandon. So, when the Huns abruptly reversed their march and instead directed their destructive efforts in the opposite direction, the townsfolk rejoiced, thanking their unexpected champion and naming this protrusion on the south end of Paris after their faithful Jenny. Over the centuries, a university grew up on its grassy slopes and generations since have marched in these hallowed halls, invaded the libraries and conquered term papers.

Two days earlier one of the latest soldiers of wisdom proudly squired her granddaughter through the myriad of buildings of the grand university, spying in classrooms and forging across crowded courtyards until they finally advanced upon the biology department. Tonie introduced Amanda to the unhappily single Professor Michaud, whose eyes lit up at the sight of this pretty American woman with the very broken French. Tonie saw the first real smile cross his lips since she had met him. Fernand continued Amanda's tour, showing her his work and office, while Tonie was left in the lab to dust the windowsills.

Today, arriving in the lab with the intention of working into the evening hours, Tonie informed the infatuated man, who promptly inquired about her friend, that Amanda would be coming by later to pick her up for dinner. The pining professor stayed late also, feigning to be working until Amanda came, at which time Tonie invited him to come along and then begged out, pleading that she had too much work to finish up—which was completely true. The smiling couple cheerfully left together, giving Tonie the satisfaction of playing the matchmaker. It would serve rotten Duncan right if his ex-wife brought a French boyfriend to Jack's wedding, she smirked.

By 9 p.m. the glare of the white fluorescent lights reflecting off the studious girl's papers were giving her a headache. Their low buzz accented the silence of the room, contributing to an eery, otherworldly dimension which finally pushed her into gathering up the mounds of data and calling it a night.

After hours of sitting at her desk in the lab scrutinizing the results of the multitude of tests she had performed on her berries, she had found nothing, not the tiniest inconsistency that might suggest an ingredient that may halt cell aging. Disappointed, the budding biologist planned her next step—animal testing, probably mice for their short life span. It would not take long to determine if a mouse was living beyond its geriatric possibilities. But there were other factors to consider in choosing the best animal, and she would tackle this new direction tomorrow. Right now, she needed a glass of wine and some dinner.

Night time had fallen when she left the building, but the warm glow of lights in the street was inviting and the sidewalks full of life. She hungrily headed to the corner café to get something to eat and rest her brain. Tonie grinned with satisfaction as she imagined Professor Michaud and Amanda still out here somewhere, dancing and smiling into each other's eyes.

Paul buzzed into town the next weekend, full of enthusiasm over the new dig. Sitting face to face in a back, cozy nook of the restaurant, he regaled Tonie with the events of the past two weeks.

"The whole site is agog," the anthropologist told his fiancée. "The preliminary results have come back on the second dig, and it is confirmed to be Neanderthals, with the exact dating expected within the week, which, of course, you have to take with a grain of salt. But, significantly, the physical evidence is that the two sites are contemporary to each other—the first one is modern humans—and my speculation is that they used the Neanderthals as workhorses for their brute strength. There was definitely a working relationship between the two groups, but exactly what that was is impossible to say yet. There is no evidence of interbreeding, which indicates that their DNA was not compatible and that, more than likely, the humans regarded them as animals."

"What would this signify as far as evolutionary theory goes?"

"What's shaping up—and I wouldn't say it publicly yet—is that this could be the discovery that cracks apart the theory of evolution."

"Really? How?" the skeptic inquired, finding his certainty abrasive.

"Well, there are many evidential features of the two digs that tie them together. This is the only occurrence of both groups coexisting from, what everything so far points to, the exact same time period. Humans cannot have descended from Neanderthals if they already existed side by side. And especially, the fact that their DNA doesn't match shows there is no history of interbreeding, either."

"What is Marc's view of this?"

"I've been surprised how low key he is being, but I think he wants to be cautious not to say anything out of line. I haven't shared my thoughts on it with anyone but him, and now you, but it will be his and my analyses that will put the label on this and be published in the science journals."

"Do you think you could be seeing the findings through the lens of your religious beliefs because that is what you already hold to be true?" Paul's helpmate in life suggested.

A burning red crept up Paul's cheeks and ears. "I can't believe you would say that. I told you before that this is not the first evidence that I've seen for my hypothesis. It is because of my lack of blinders that I see through to the truth. Maybe it is you who sees everything through your lens of atheism."

"Maybe truth is subjective. I have seen an appalling lack of evidence where God is concerned. If a miracle from heaven fell on my head, I don't think I would be so stubborn as to not reconsider."

"And what kind of a miracle would it take? I see God's miracles every day. Would you recognize a miracle if you saw one, or does your lens filter them out, like a good pair of sunglasses filters out UV rays?"

Now Tonie's face was red. "I don't need you criticizing me for my beliefs. Maybe your 'God loves me best' arrogance is a bit of a put off."

"It is you who has criticized me at every opportunity. At first, I didn't think it would matter that you weren't a woman of God but, quite frankly, I have been dismayed that I can't share anything meaningful with you."

A woman of God. Amanda had used that phrase too, Tonie remembered. Her mind reeled from how abruptly their pleasant reunion had turned ugly. She had never seen the usually unflappable Paul upset like this.

"What do you mean? Are you saying that since I don't agree with you on religion that you don't want to marry me?"

"I don't want to say anything that I will regret. I'm tired and worn out from a stressful week. It was hard seeing Marc deny what was so obviously in his face, and now you. Maybe I will get a hotel tonight, and we will talk about it tomorrow."

Tonie stood up abruptly and grabbed her purse. "Maybe that will be a good idea." She turned on her heel and made for the door. That's what she got for being honest, she huffed to herself. Her first husband wasn't like this. Isaac was a Christian and they went to church and he even contributed a lot of money to charitable causes, but they never talked about the Bible or Jesus. She never had to make rude remarks because it was never in her face, she never felt judged, or that she needed to stand up for her views. Society had demanded that people go to church, so they went. Exactly the same thing with her second husband, Thomas. But with Paul, she felt like if she didn't make a contrary statement every time he spoke about God, then she was giving unspoken agreement, and—she justified to herself—that just wouldn't be honest.

By the time the honest woman returned to her apartment, her anger had lost its heat and was crumpling into sadness. She had to blink back tears and remind herself how very unreasonable Paul was being. Amanda was in the kitchen in her pajamas making hot chocolate. When she saw Tonie, her happy face turned to concern.

"What's the matter, honey?" She set down the cup and put her arm around the now openly tearful girl.

"Paul and I had a fight and he's getting a hotel room, and, and, I don't think he wants to marry me anymore," she sobbed, her angst now spilling out like an erupting volcano.

"Oh, that can't be true! I know how much Paul loves you. You just had a fight, that's all. All couples have fights. Haven't you had fights before?"

Woebegone Tonie shook her head, trying to mop up her eyes with a kleenex.

"What did you fight about? Do you want to tell me?"

"No. I don't want to tell you because it is something you might not like me for either, and I don't want to lose your friendship."

"There's not much that would make me stop being your friend," Amanda assured her.

"I'm not a Christian, and Paul doesn't think he wants to marry me for that. But he's always known, so I don't think it's fair for him to all of a sudden decide that it's a big issue. I don't want to destroy Paul's faith, or yours, but I just don't see any evidence for God, and I told him that."

Amanda smiled tenderly at her storm-tossed friend. "You don't have to worry about destroying my faith, or Paul's, because when a person comes to know Christ, He sends His Holy Spirit to live in you, and once you've known the Holy Spirit your faith is a solid rock. I've been to hell, and I would still be there if it weren't for God, and, believe me, I will never go there again."

"But I'm in hell all the time and I can't get out!" Tonie shrieked, collapsing onto the couch.

Amanda held tightly to her. "When you are ready to get out, just ask God and He will pull you out."

"He won't pull me out because He hates me." Tonie hung her head between her knees and moaned. "Oh, I can't stand it anymore, I want to die," she sobbed, rocking back and forth. She clenched her fists and screamed again.

"You're okay, honey. God doesn't hate anybody. Jesus is with you." Amanda stroked her hair, holding her tight, and began to pray over her. "In the name of the Lord Jesus Christ, I command Satan to depart from here."

"I want to die," Tonie screamed again.

"In the name of our Lord Jesus Christ, I command Satan to depart from your body."

"Jesus help me!" Tonie fell to the floor, writhing and moaning. "I can't stand it! I want to die!"

"In the name of the Lord Jesus Christ I command Satan to depart from here!" Amanda's face was ashen, her eyes burning with determination, every nerve taut. She would fight to the death for the soul of this young girl. Tonie's frenzy slowly began subsiding, and Amanda sat beside her on the floor. When she was calm enough, she helped her up to lie on the couch, covering her with a blanket and made her a cup of tea.

Amanda sat with her while she sipped her drink and calmed down. After a second cup, Tonie was sufficiently recovered to be horribly embarrassed. "I'm sorry I got so upset. It was all so sudden—one minute I was happily engaged having a nice dinner, and the next, I was dumped ..." she trailed off.

Amanda sat quietly contemplating for a few moments. "You have reminded me, ever since I have known you, of my grandmother, Antoinette. She had dark hair and eyes like you. She came from England with her husband, Thomas, when she was eighteen years old, and they settled in Oregon during the Great Depression. Thomas had been a city-dude in London, and he longed to have a cattle ranch, so when they came to the U.S. he was attracted to the West with its wide open spaces and lots of land for homesteading. Nona—that was what we called my grandma, my mother's mother—while she seemed content enough, she never shared much about herself and was always somewhat aloof. Mama told me, when I was in my teens, that she believed Nona had a secret sorrow, and surmised that perhaps she had been jilted by a lover and never recovered, marrying Grandpa on the rebound. I remember thinking how awful it would be to live your life in a sadness that you could never escape. You have that same reserve about you. Do you have a secret sorrow in your life, Tonie?"

"The only sorrow I have I just vomited all over you, so it isn't very secret. I'm sorry you had to witness my meltdown." Tonie was mortified by her outburst. She had kept a tight leash on her emotions since she had exploded at God so long ago.

"That wasn't vomit, that was a demon. Do you think it's pretty when Jesus drives out demons? I had a whole herd of them and believe me, I was howling like a banshee. I'm happy you shared with me. We are friends, after all."

"I can't stand the thought of losing Paul, and I feel so out of control." Tonie maneuvered the conversation back to Paul and off her breakdown. "Do you think I owe him an apology? I guess I was pretty rude."

"It's hard to discuss differing viewpoints without becoming defensive. By your own account of the evening, it sounds like you felt threatened and attacked out of fear, so maybe the best thing you could do is be totally honest with him," Amanda advised. Hesitating, she added, "Not that, well, not that you would want to listen to anything I have to say about marriage—you know where mine ended up—flush!" Both ladies laughed at the fickleness of love, and the mood relaxed.

The next few days brought Tonie a lightness of spirit that she couldn't remember feeling since she didn't know when. Every few hours a spark of well-being lit up inside her, a tiny second of happiness out of nowhere that gave relief to the never ending grind of suffocation that had plagued her for so long. It was such a contradiction to her current situation that she especially marveled over it, but didn't want to examine it too closely in fear that it would disappear as quickly as a mirage in the desert.

Paul, on the other hand, was beset with misgivings and fears concerning his upcoming nuptials with a woman that he was beginning to doubt he knew completely, and wasn't liking what he saw emerging.

Growing up in a well-to-do family in the suburbs of Portland, his upbringing had left him lonely. His father spent long hours at work every day and on the phone whenever he was home. His mother loved the social life, being vitally active in causes and teas, and was never available to kiss the booboos or cheer on his childhood accomplishments. Older brother Lucas made friends easily and generally skipped out of the house after school to play basketball, or skateboard, or go driving with his pals. Quiet Paul was left to his own devices, which often meant reading or conducting experiments on plants and rocks around the neighborhood.

While each Sunday found the family dressed in their best and sitting front and center for church—Dad for the business contacts and Mom for the socializing—the love of the Lord never entered into it. Paul's deep loneliness and yearning to connect somewhere led him to join the youth group at church, and there he found a rich new world of thought and acceptance, a breath of fresh air in the stale, stagnant nothingness that pervaded his home life. He became a believer, treasuring his new-found faith as only one can who has known the bleakness of life without God. God became his constant companion. From then on, regardless of happy circumstances or bad, the world made sense to him.

Upon meeting Tonie, he recognized the same loneliness in her that he used to struggle with, and he believed, without deep examination, that his love of God would automatically save her. It would envelop her and she would be a Christian too—the thorn of disbelief removed from her side.

He loved everything about her—her kindness, her sense of humor, her curiosity—and he became attached to her, not even worrying about the spiritual aspect of their relationship because never once did he consider that her lack of religion was for any reason other than lack of exposure. It never crossed his mind that she wouldn't instantly warm to God as she came to know Him. But as time went by, her tolerant attitude toward God and church shifted, until here in Paris she had risen openly antagonistic toward his faith. For the first time, the thought entered his mind whether she would be a suitable life-mate for him, and having once crossed the threshold, the thought became a permanent resident.

Chapter Twelve

T ONIE TURNED THE KEY IN THE LOCK AND ENTERED the animal testing lab. On the left wall, a set of shelves housed the four cages of five mice each that had been approved for her study. She first attached labels to the two cages of control subjects, then eyed the mice in the experimental cages.

"Who knows, little guys, you may get to live forever," she whispered conspiratorially. One critter sat back on its haunches and sniffed at her curiously with its quivering nose. "Berry pie for you tomorrow," she said while trying to refrain from breaking forth into song about a little brown mouse. She attached the labels which decreed their fate. Addressing the first set she apologized, "Sorry fellas, it will be mouse-pellet pie for you." She then left the mice to focus her attention on the process of assaying the berry samples she had collected during her trip in southern France.

As Tonie arranged her notebooks on her desk, she mulled over the past week without satisfaction. While she and Paul had made up and the wedding was back on, her time spent with him at the dig had been reserved and formal. She met Marc, who had been a jerk to her, eyeing her provocatively and asking if she was doing her research so she could "remain a cute young thing forever." The interviews in Arles yielded no insights into longevity beyond the usual attributing of long lives to either chocolate, or not drinking, or to drinking lots, or to having never married. And none of it pertained anyway, because they all had aged, and no one surpassed the oldest known lifespan. Although old Jeanne Clement claimed to have had only that one wrinkle in her life, Tonie had seen pictures of her, and she had aged normally, albeit more slowly than average.

The berries held the best hope—because who eats poisonous berries? For all she knew, hundreds of very, very old people were walking around and not saying anything for fear of being thrown into a mental asylum.

Tonie sighed. After the awkward trip to Arles, she had accompanied Paul to see the oldest cave paintings in the world in the Chauvet Cave in the Ardèche Valley. As an expert on Paleolithic life, Paul had been invited for a consultation regarding a child's footprint found inside the cave, and Tonie was thrilled to have also been allowed in.

Discovered a mere twenty years ago, the cave contained thirty-six thousand year old wall paintings—well, according to current dating procedures, Paul had reminded her. Each year, only a handful of scientists were permitted in the cave in order to protect it from the destructive action of moisture and carbon dioxide emitted from human exhalation which would erode the delicate artwork the same way acid rain eats away ancient Greek architecture.

After donning the required sterile clothing and shoes, Tonie had joined a team of five scientists as they descended a ladder into the dark and mysterious cave that had not seen the light of day for over thirty millennia, the original entrance having been sealed off all these years by a landslide. Beams from their headlamps criss-crossed each other, revealing drawings and etchings stretching across the walls and spilling onto the ceilings, nudged awake from their long slumber by the battery-powered false dawn curiously thrust upon them. Complete darkness pressed in from all sides, the spectator's only reality the glowing circles of light shining on the images in front of them, invoking a hushed reverence at the sight of this flamboyant, unabashed display of man reveling in his own powers of creativity.

As Tonie witnessed Paul in his element, she appreciated his passion for truth. He would never twist anything to fit a preconceived viewpoint. He was attempting to put together the puzzle of life, scrutinizing every scrap of data for its relevance, refusing to chisel any ill-fitting piece if it were not ringing true, no matter how attractive it seemed. Remembering her petty insinuation of his integrity at the restaurant, she writhed with regret, and grasped why her remark had wounded him so deeply.

With this insight, she recognized how she walked the earth thinking she knew everything because of her long life, and how superior she perceived herself to be by not being fooled by God-talk like mere mortals were, with their fears of growing old and dying. "What an arrogant brat I am," she realized, "and Paul, after only thirty-five years, is a solid rock. He deserves much better than how I treated him. I may have nearly 250 years, but empty times 250 is still empty."

Paul walked away from the week of Tonie's visit plagued with worries about their compatibility, his doubts mounting as he considered his life-changing encounter with human history while deep inside the Chauvet cave—and had no one to share it with.

The musty odor of time immemorial had risen up to greet the team as they descended into the cave on that fateful day, ushering these intruders into the forgotten world of their ancestors. As their lights shone on the walls, the cave sprang alive with the spirits of its original occupants. Red ochre handprints announced who they were. Red palm prints creating the shapes of bison and cave bear spoke of their fascination of the animals who shared their world. Sweeping lines of charcoal modeled the forms of sleek horses and charging rhinoceros, their marks as fresh as if the artists had set down their brushes and ran off to hunt a bear and would be hurrying back any minute.

The sophistication of the paintings and etchings surprised Paul. Animals leapt and danced before his eyes, the artist's every brush stroke capturing the essence of the wild beasts—snorting, kicking aurochs; rhinos locking horns in combat; graceful horses peacefully oblivious to the chaos around them. Rushing across the great expanse of the walls, they hung in time, all intervening years snuffed out, the ancient animals as whisper-close to the scholars as to their painters.

Continuing on through chambers and galleries, Paul beheld, at every turn, the beauty and depth of the art, equal in genius to any grand civilization that later would flourish. These were not the paintings of a primitive people who would need thirty-thousand years to evolve into the intellectual peers of their descendants. They were not "half-animal, half-human" as had been postulated by theorists of an evolving, progressing race. They were fully human, as complex and advanced as any to come in the future.

Was he witnessing the early dawn of man's creation? Was this when God bent down and scooped up a handful of dust, speaking their forms into being and breathing a soul into a man and into a woman? How many years was this after the fall—that calamitous rebellion against God that caused Adam and Eve to be evicted from the Garden? Were these the children of Cain? How long had they been toiling in a rocky environment, their close communion with God now clouded by sin?

Rounding a protruding rock in the corridor, close to the original entrance, Paul found himself face to face with the revelation that jelled the vague, rumbling sense of expectation that had haunted him since entering this underground world. On the wall in front of him, a boldly painted red cross rose up out of a bleeding human heart. He stopped and stared, the winds of God's boundlessness buffeting his mind—the decorators of this cave knew the Triune God. The veil was lifted for him to see, and he trembled at the sign of God's tender love for His people, present from the day of their creation.

For the remainder of the week, Paul performed his duties in a daze, unable to concentrate on work, his brain still jostling to process this new-found discovery. Afraid of sharing his epiphany with Tonie and chance having her poo-poo it, he savored it to himself, its immensity bursting inside him. And, he realized that having someone who didn't care about his deepest passions was lonelier than having no one at all.

The weekend following Tonie's visit, Paul dutifully returned to Paris, exuberant with the results of the dating of the Neanderthal fossils but reluctant to share the news with Tonie in fear that she would be less than supportive. But, he had expected these numbers, and he decided it wasn't so soul-touching that he would be crushed if she were disinterested. Privately, he rejoiced at the corroboration of the dates of the fossils in light of the cave paintings.

"So," he concluded over dinner that night, "I have written to Dr. Bonvalet, who appointed Marc and me to head up the team at the dig, and I shared all our findings at the site along with my summary and recom- mendations. I should hear back from him by Monday. This is an incredible discovery and will change the course of future studies of the Paleolithic period."

"Paul, that is wonderful. After seeing the Chauvet cave, I am in awe of how intricate and advanced the paintings are, and how, with that one cave, our knowledge of human history took a giant leap. And, it made me understand your passion for the work you do. I was talking with Dr. Michaud the other day about the cave and the meaning of it, and he seems to believe along the same lines as you, that we are barely scratching the surface in our knowledge of prehistory."

"So, how are Amanda and the good doctor getting along?" Paul inquired, wanting to keep the conversation light, masking his doubts with joviality.

"They are really liking each other, and they go out together every evening. But, if they get married, will they live in France or the U.S.?" Tonie pondered this dilemma. She would not want to lose her granddaughter now that they had found each other again.

"Hmm, that would be a problem all right, but I'm sure they will figure it out. His English is definitely better than her French, so maybe the U.S." He chuckled.

"Oh, be serious! These are important considerations. And, her French has really improved."

Paul playfully rolled his eyes.

"It has," she insisted as he made a face of mock horror.

"Well, since they are adults, and not children, we don't have to worry about it," Paul concluded.

No, they're not children, Tonie half-agreed in her mind, but, she is mine, and she better not stay in France. She shrugged and turned the topic of conversation. "Speaking of weddings, our paperwork has been approved and we can make an appointment at the Mairie to do the civil service, and then we can get married at the church."

"Oh really? Then it sounds safe to say, maybe, two weeks from today?" Paul asked. "I need to let my family know as early as possible."

The bride-to-be perked up, relieved that Paul seemed comfortable making concrete wedding plans. "Yes, that would work. We could visit Saint Germaine tomorrow, if you like. I talked to the priest when I was there last month, and he said to call him when we know our date. Amanda said she could stay an extra few days because it took longer than expected for us to get the license. Then, I'll going to go back home with her for a week to attend her son's wedding, since it looks like we'll have to wait on our honeymoon until Christmas anyway." Tonie smiled and put her hand on his.

"That's true. I will be very busy at the dig for a while. I was hoping to get my part in it finished up by the end of summer, but now I'm not sure. I'll see what Dr. Bonvalet has to say on Monday."

"You mean, you really might have to stay after the start of the school year then?"

"I'm not sure, but I would expect that he will want me to continue overseeing this new site also, in which case the university will be scrambling to find a teacher for the classes I'm scheduled to teach in the fall. But, we'll see. It's a little early to start surmising anything right now."

"I wonder if there would be any possibility that I could continue studying here at the Sorbonne this fall?" Tonie mused. "I haven't applied, but Dr. Michaud might agree to mentor me. I will ask, just to know my options."

"Why don't we go for a walk?" Paul motioned to the waiter for the check.

Outside in the warm evening air, the couple sauntered along the Seine, the lights of the bridges reflecting off the dark, shiny waters. Paul hesitated, then took a quick breath and looked into Tonie's face.

"Tonie, I'm not being honest with you, or myself. I have been thinking a lot about us, and I worry that we are too different to make a marriage commitment. I fell in love with you thinking that it didn't matter that you weren't a believer, in the back of my mind assuming that you would become one once you came to know about God. But, I have realized that you don't have an absence of the knowledge of God, but you seem to have an antagonism toward Him that I don't understand. I can see that it irritates you for me to talk about my faith. I need a life partner who loves God as I do, and I think we will both end up miserable."

Tonie stared down at the ground in stunned silence. "Good old Paris," she silently rued, "pulling the rug out from under me again." She sighed and addressed her ex-fiancé. "It's true. I will never be a believer, and it does bother me when you talk about God because I see it as a sign of self-delusion. So, I guess this is goodbye."

"Yes, I guess it is," Paul stammered, the sudden finality of it slapping him in the face. They both stood silent and awkward, neither one knowing how to take the exit bow.

"I'll send your stuff to you at the dig," Tonie offered.

"Yes, that will be great."

"I'm sorry it didn't work out."

"Yeah, me too." Paul felt tears stinging his eyes so he turned and walked away.

Tonie stood there and watched him disappear into the night and it hurt. She eyed the river, so deep and wide, and contemplated its proven ability to sweep people out of their miseries. But, she knew it would not do this favor for her. What would happen, she wondered, if she hurled herself in? Would a boat mysteriously appear and catch her? Would a fisherman's net rise up, gently scooping her at the last second from death's icy clutch? Should she try? Did she have anything to lose?

Tonie bent over and studied the swirling water alive with shimmering light and icy black depths waiting to welcome her in. It was calling her name. She was born in Paris and she would die in Paris. Climbing up on the waist-high wall she opened her arms and fell forward, the wind from the descent blowing back her hair, and she was free and flying and nothing could stop her this time. "Oh bliss, take me into your embrace, oh cold water, snuff out my life and let me be released." Time moved in slow motion as she felt every second of her fall, cold mist caressing her cheeks as she approached her goal.

Suddenly, her left foot caught on a tree root growing out of the side of the river's retaining wall, abruptly snapping her to a stop and slapping her into the rough-hewn bricks. Her hands caught the wall first, tearing the skin off her palms but saving her nose from being broken, only skinned and bloody. She dangled upside down slightly above the water line. There she hung, skirt up around her neck, with nothing to do but wait to be rescued. Hearing a commotion above her, she knew help would be soon.

"Dear God in heaven," she prayed quickly. "If You are there, I will believe in You forever if only Paul is too far away to hear the yelling and will not come back and see me upside down with my underwear hanging out."

"I tripped!" the unsuccessful suicide shouted up to the gathering crowd. "I tripped!"

Chapter Thirteen

F OLDING UP HER LAST PAIR OF JEANS, TONIE STUFFED them into the suitcase and tugged on the zipper. "There," she stated emphatically. "That is everything except what I will pack in my carry-on tomorrow."

Amanda held up her non-frumpy mother-of-the-groom dress that they had finally shopped for this past week. "How should I pack this to get it back without getting crumpled?"

Her friend inspected the champagne-colored lamé dress with its chiffon overskirt that swooped lower in the back and stylishly shorter in front. "I wouldn't pack that. Let's just carry it in a garment bag and hang it in the airplane closet. It will attach to my roller bag to tote through the airport."

"Great idea," Amanda agreed. "Are you leaving the dress here?" She subtly nodded her head toward the closet where the jinxed wedding dress hung like poison.

"Yep," the jilted bride replied flatly.

"Okay!" Amanda rallied her cheerfulness. "The apartment is cleaned, our stuff is organized for an early breakfast and trek to the airport in the morning, so we are free to spend our last day in Paris doing any outrageous thing we want."

"Are you seeing Fernand tonight?"

"No. We said our goodbyes last night so it wouldn't be sappy." Amanda didn't add that the couple worried that Tonie should not be left alone. They had taken care to include her in every outing since the breakup, not really sure that they trusted the "tripping into the river" story. It seemed a little suspicious to the lovers who, in the grips of *amour* themselves, could well imagine throwing themselves into the river if rejected by the other. Amanda thanked God over and over for the tree root growing through a crack in the bricks which entangled Tonie's foot.

"We are going to write every day, and Fernand is coming for Jack's wedding, and then he will visit me every month."

"That will be nice. I've been wanting to walk around an old neighborhood that I found the first week I was here, and I think you will like it, too. It's past the Bastille in the old Faubourg St. Antoine area. Would you like to do that? There are some really old, quaint houses dating back before the Revolution, and some fantastic cafés."

"Café is the magic word for me! Let's go!"

Strolling with her granddaughter past the house where she was born, Tonie felt the long, silvery thread that wove through her, binding her to all those that had gone before, and weaving all of them into the future—to

Amanda, and to Jack and the children he would someday have with Colleen. She was saying goodbye again, and her heart tugged at the old conflict between her desire to stay in Paris where she was home, and to be away from where so much pain had ravaged her soul. But, as time had proved, she couldn't run far enough away to escape herself. Her mind drifted back to the first time she left her homeland, a time before she knew she would never grow old.

The shoreline of France slowly recedes into the distance, the fog jealously obscuring the town of Calais from sight. The crossing to Dover should take a day and a half. The tides are favorable so they set sail, even though the weather is questionable.

Nettie is disguised as a boy—her breasts bound with cloths, her hair tied back severely at her neck, and wearing breeches and boots in place of a dress. It is dangerous for a woman to travel alone. Despite her fifty-seven years, her skin is without wrinkles and, even with ash dust smudged on her face, she exudes the air of a young boy.

The first night she lies in the darkness contemplating the journey ahead. Not having wanted to spend precious money for the luxury of a room on this short crossing, Nettie sleeps on a cot on deck with dozens of other passengers, the ship rolling and heaving on rough seas.

"Is there a midwife among you?" a worried male voice breaks through the night in stilted French. Silence. "Is there a midwife among you?" the voice asks again. A man makes his way in the dark among the cots. "My daughter is at her time and she is doing poorly," he explains.

The midwife hesitates. Her medical bag is in her satchel underneath the cot, but what will happen if it becomes known that she is really a woman?

"Monsieur, I can help you," she asserts in a hushed voice, her decision made. Once before she hesitated, and a young mother died. Now she must help this man and his daughter to prove to herself that she is not really a devil. The father judges her skeptically.

Nettie grabs her bag and leads him to the stairwell. "I am a midwife," she whispers to him, and sees the suspicion in his eyes.

"A young boy is a midwife? I do not believe you. I will not allow a man to attend my daughter."

"Monsieur, I am really a woman. I had to dress as a boy to get on this ship. If you like, I can prove it to you."

"You are wasting my time, young man. My daughter needs immediate care. Please excuse me." He tries to push past her. They are alone in a dim hallway. The faux-boy directly unbuttons her blouse, and the impatient man glimpses the bands and stops. As the cloths unwind her breasts spill out. Grabbing her chin he turns the changeling's face toward the lantern hanging on the wall.

"Good Lord!" he exclaims brusquely. "Come with me, mademoiselle!" Nettie hurriedly closes her blouse, trailing the bands behind her.

As they rush toward his quarters, the gentleman introduces himself as Mr. Stafford of London, and informs her that the captain has told him they are off course and not expected to make landfall before tomorrow night. His newly widowed daughter, whose French husband was killed in the Paris revolt of the Trois Glorieuses, wants to return home before her baby is born, but she expected the birth to be at least another month away.

"How did your daughter come to be married to a French man?" Nettie inquires while they make their way through the passages.

"Esmé's parents escaped from France during the reign of terror before he was born and moved to London. Last year after he and Flora married, he wanted to return to his family's homeland to do what he could to help establish the republic. It was hard on Flora being so far away, so I came over to bring her home. I think the trauma of Esmé's death and the rough crossing have brought about her early labor."

The midwife hears screaming before they reach the English gentleman's cabin. Upon entering, she sees a girl of perhaps nineteen or twenty writhing on the bed and another girl of the same age attending her. The maid's face is tense, and she turns her fearful eyes pleadingly to her master. Mr. Stafford speaks to her in English, of which Nettie only understands a little, and the maid steps away from the bed, relieved for the appearance of help.

He then addresses his daughter, also in English, gesturing to Nettie, whom Flora eyes suspiciously.

"I'm not revealing myself again," the seemingly male midwife announces belligerently. "If you want my help I will help. If not, then I will go." The soon-to-be grandfather motions her to his daughter's side.

"How long has this been going on?" Nettie asks Flora as she palpates her belly. The baby is very low, and her pains are coming again.

"Since yesterday," she cries out in accented but fluent French. "I want to go home! I want my mother! My husband is dead and I want my mother!"

Since yesterday. By her breathing Nettie surmises she is getting close and her panic has worn her out. "Lottie, moisten two washrags with cold water," she instructs the maid. "Put one on her forehead, and have her suck on the other." Flora's lips are dry and red from dehydration. The washrags give them both a sense of purpose. She strokes Flora's head.

"Wait outside," Nettie directs Mr. Stafford.

She evaluates the laboring woman, determining that everything is advancing normally, and that she probably has another hour. First babies take a long time. Nettie soothes her during the next pain.

"Everything is going so perfectly for you," she reassures her. "Baby's head is down, and your pains are making progress. I wish all my mothers were as lucky as you."

"I thought I was going to die here on this boat."

"No dying today. Our biggest challenge will be finding out if we are in French waters or English waters when this little one is born," Nettie teases her. "Which would you prefer?"

Another pain comes, and the midwife helps her through it. "English," Flora responds raspingly after the contraction eases, hating France for killing her husband.

"Lottie, will you bring me my bag, please, and the bowl of hot water?" Nettie lays out string for the cord and a blanket for the baby.

The midwife turns back to her patient. "You are almost done, Flora, only a couple more pains. On this next one I want you to quit bearing down when I tell you."

Five minutes later, baby girl Esmée comes into the world, in English waters they are sure. After Nettie examines the newborn, Lottie wraps her up and gives her to her mother.

Grandfather Isaac is called in. He is beside himself with joy and pays Nettie ten times her usual fee. After extracting a promise from him to not reveal her gender, she packs her bag and tiredly heads back to her cot on deck, the first hints of pink painting the eastern sky.

The next day, the new Grandpapa seeks out the midwife on the rolling deck. "Monsieur," he addresses her with a conspiratorial wink. "You told me that you are an orphan, trying to work your way to America. I would like to extend an invitation for you to stay with me and my family in London until you have saved up enough money for your passage. There would be ample work in your field, especially if you polish your English. Last night you helped us out in our time of need, and we are forever in your debt. It would do me an honor to be able to help you in this way."

"Oh monsieur, that is so kind." Flabbergasted by this offer, Nettie forgets the pretense and responds in her female voice, then hastily amends her response into the deepest bass she can muster. "Oh thank you, sir!"

Isaac laughs at the joke. "How old are you, son?"

Nettie reddens and doesn't know how to answer. Last night, Isaac made remarks that seemed to indicate he assumed she was much younger than her fifty-seven years. Back home people commented on her youthful air, but people are kind enough to flatter a woman of a certain age, and Nettie accepted those compliments in the spirit of kindness in which they were offered, not as truths about her actual appearance.

"A lady never tells, monsieur," she murmurs, knowing he thinks she is Flora's age.

Isaac laughs delightedly. "When we reach London you may borrow one of Flora's dresses and transform into a young demoiselle again." He looks pleased at the notion. "I just spoke to the ship's captain, and he reports that we should dock in Dover by sundown. I will come by and collect you at that time."

Two years later, Nettie is walking down the aisle in the grand Cathedral of St. Paul in London, wearing an ivory silk dress that skims her girlish figure. Isaac waits for her at the altar, ready to make her Mrs. Isaac Stafford. Ever since his wife died the year before of tuberculosis, the pair have grown closer, and time has flown by since Nettie delivered his granddaughter at sea—in English waters, Flora still loves to recount. And now, that little girl is walking in front of the bride, throwing rose petals out of a basket then stopping to gather them back up again. Her mother blushes and tries to hurry her up, but Nettie is in no hurry. She so loves this man she is marrying that she wants to savor the moment, smiling up at Isaac who made her get naked in front of him the night Esmée was born, but who now gallantly swears he was in such a dither that he has no recollection of it.

Tonie brightened at the memory. Her mood lifted and the world seemed right—lost in the reverie of her security in Isaac's home. But real life tugged her into the present as she and Amanda entered the bustling rue du Faubourg St. Antoine, with cars racing and exhaust rising. To longer preserve her peaceful mood, Tonie suggested lunch at a café on a quieter side street, and the ladies turn around.

Seated at the small round table on the sidewalk, Tonie sighed and lamented. "I just don't understand why Paul would break up with me over a difference of opinion. No two people could ever agree on all things. I mean, good luck to him finding some ninny who'll worship him and hang on every word that comes out of his mouth."

"Well, religion is an important issue in a relationship, probably the most important. Do you want to spend your life irritated when he talks about his faith? Probably not.

So, in reality, you have the same objection to wanting to marry him. Only, it sucks that he came to the realization first."

Tonie stared at her wise granddaughter. "You're right. It's important that I be able to state my opinions freely, too, and I would have always felt stifled." But after a minute, tears slowly started running down her cheeks. "Why I am so sad, then? And I still want to marry him. What about Fernand? Is he a believer?"

Amanda nodded. "He is. He was a Christian in name only until his wife left him for another man, and then he was forced into relying on Jesus to carry him through, and he came to know Him and trust Him. Life tends to put people into that situation. It did with me. And Paul, from what you've told me."

"How can you find comfort from the same God who caused the discomfort in the first place?"

"Oh, honey. God hurts more than we do when bad things happen, but He can turn the worst pain into the greatest blessing. There is a deadly enemy prowling the earth out to destroy God and us, and we are the battlefield. While we are assured of winning the war, there are many trials between now and then, trials that can lead us to greater faith and insight into God's true nature if we let them."

Amanda paused a minute before asking gently, "Do you want to talk about your parents, Tonie?"

"No." Tonie dismissed the offer adamantly. "It makes absolutely no sense to me why pain and misery abound in this world, especially to people who have done nothing to deserve it."

Amanda realized she had hit a sore spot and backed off. "It is true that bad things happen, and I won't pretend I know all the answers, but I do know that God can bring light to even the darkest night. God saved me out of the pit of despair. And that pit of despair is hell, and I never want to go back. My baby is not there, she is in heaven, so why would I hang around the wrong place?"

"My mother said that, too." Tonie softened her stance as she remembered her mother's words.

"Said what?"

"That babies go to heaven when they die. But, I didn't believe there was a heaven."

"If there is a hell, then why wouldn't there be a heaven?"

"I'll have to think about that, because I do believe in hell." Tonie acknowledged, confused by the duality of truths she held in her mind.

Chapter Fourteen

T HEIR LAST NIGHT IN PARIS, THE TWO WOMEN turned in early, setting the alarm for 5:00 a.m. The plan for the morning was to stop for breakfast at the corner café, then get a taxi to the airport. A little after four o'clock, Tonie's phone rang, and with blurry eyes she saw that it was Paul.

"Hello?" she answered groggily, her mind not completely understanding where she was.

"Tonie, I'm in trouble. Can I come over?"

"Um, well, of course. What kind of trouble?"

"I'll tell you when I see you. I'll be there in five minutes."

Amanda awoke when the phone rang and she heard talking. Poking her head into Tonie's room, she whispered, "What's going on?"

"Paul said he's in trouble and he's coming over."

"Weird."

Putting on their robes, they waited for their nighttime caller. Within minutes he arrived and rushed inside as soon as they opened the door. Completely disheveled, with a coat over his pajamas, he leaned against the door frame, holding one arm with the other.

"Paul! What happened?" Tonie helped him to the couch where he collapsed, his strength failing him now that he had finally reached the haven of the apartment.

"I was attacked in my bed. A guy tried to kill me. I don't know if anyone followed me or not, but I doubt it, or they would have got me by now."

"What? Who would want to kill you?"

"Well, I don't know for sure. But, last week I never heard back from Dr. Bonvalet as I should have. And then, out of the blue, I was shunned at the dig by Marc and the others, like I had the plague or something. Then last night I was asleep in bed, about eleven o'clock, and I woke up for some reason, and someone had crept into my room. I lay still, watching a man's shadow in the dark, then I saw him lift a huge rock over my head and start to bring it down on me, so I rolled to the side and it caught me in the arm and sent the cot crashing to the floor with its force. He missed my head but he got my arm, and I think it's broken."

Paul rubbed his arm gingerly. "I snagged him by his ankles with my other hand and pulled his feet out from under him and sent him flat on his face, and I picked up the rock and smashed his kneecap as he turned over to get up. He lay there screaming, and I grabbed my wallet and the notebooks with all my data and I ran out. I think I recognized the man as the laborer who runs the forklift."

"Oh my goodness, Paul! But why? Was he trying to rob you?"

"Could it be that the university doesn't like your pronouncement regarding the meaning of the modern humans and Neanderthals living side by side?" Amanda tossed a knowing look at him, having heard the findings from Fernand.

"That's what I'm worried about, Amanda," Paul grimly agreed. "I doubt it was the laborer's idea. I'm sure he must have been paid by Bonvalet to kill me and destroy my records. I suspect they will keep looking for me, and that's why I didn't want to take the time to go to the hospital for my arm. I hitchhiked here and got a ride with a trucker who drove right through."

Amanda tended to the wounded arm, which relieved Tonie because she was finding it awkward to be close to him.

"I think it's broken, all right," the nurse reported. "My son broke his arm once and it has the same look, all swollen and red. It's going to need to be set."

"I ache all over. I'm going to need to rest first, plus, the more I think about it the more I'm sure they probably guessed where I would go. I will rest and then sneak out of here somehow." The weary man's eyes drooped until they were closed.

"Well, it can't be set until the swelling goes down anyway. I'll call Fernand in a couple hours and see if he can help. He's a biologist, and I know he'll know what to do."

Paul half-opened his eyes and glanced around the room. "Are you leaving today? Everything is packed up. I don't want to interfere with your plans."

"Oh, I can afford to wait one more day, so we can cancel our flight. Wouldn't you say that's okay, Tonie?" Amanda turned to Tonie for approval, and she nodded in assent. Glancing back at Paul, they saw that he had fallen asleep.

At seven o'clock, Amanda determined that Fernand would be up so she gave him a call to explain everything that had happened. He said he would be over as soon as he could. Arriving less than an hour later, he brought a bag full of supplies that he had gone by his office to collect.

Tonie offered to run out and get coffee and croissants at the café since the cupboards were bare. She took along a plate to put the tiny espresso cups on to carry back. Paul was just waking up as she left, and Fernand was eager to discuss the night's events with him.

On her way back from the café, balancing the four cups on the plate and carrying a big bag of croissants, she was almost home when she heard someone call out her name.

"Tonie!"

Surprised, she turned and saw Marc Diceccio crossing the street and coming toward her.

"Have you seen Paul?" he asked as he drew near. "He was missing from his tent this morning, and we are worried about him."

"I guess you haven't heard the news—we broke up."

"Oh, yes, I did hear about that. I'm sorry. So, who are you taking all those coffees to?"

"Well, not to Paul, if you know what I mean. He's not my favorite person anymore."

"Can I come in for a visit? I've come a long way, and, it would be nice to catch up with you."

"Sorry. I have friends over for breakfast. You sure got to Paris quickly for having just noticed he's missing. Did you say this morning?"

"Um, well, yes, a guy was heading out to work early, very early, and thought he heard a scuffle so he was worried."

"Maybe you should check the tents of the female students. I think that might be a much more logical place to start your search."

"Oh, yes, good idea. Well, if you see him tell him to give me a call."

"I'll do that."

Tonie turned her back to Marc and entered the digi-code on the door to the building, making sure that the rotten old cur couldn't see the number over her shoulder. She walked through the courtyard, entering another digi-code at the gate, and then arrived at her apartment, using the key to get in. Pretty safe place, she considered, alarmed by Marc's appearance.

Inside, Fernand was finishing wrapping a splint on Paul's arm, whose face was white from having to bear the biologist's manipulations of the bone without the benefit of painkillers.

"Ah, c'est ça, that should take care of it just as well as a cast," the makeshift physician admired his work. "A bit clunkier, perhaps, and you'll have to keep it dry as you would a cast." He turned and greeted the bearer of the coffee as she came through the door. "Oh la la, bonjour! I would love a cup of that right now!"

"Paul!" Tonie blurted out. "Marc is outside the building, and he questioned me about your whereabouts. He said he is looking for you because you were missing from your bed this morning."

"What did you tell him?" Alarm crossed Paul's face.

"I said we broke up and that I hadn't seen you."

"Did he say anything else?"

"He wanted to know why I had four coffees."

Fernand turned and nodded his head at the invalid. "Ah, oui, you are in trouble, my friend. They seem to be definitely after you, non? Marc must have set out for Paris shortly after you did. It sounds like he suspects strongly that you are in here. And, that it is Marc who comes tells me a lot. He must have a stake in this too."

"But is it really worth killing a person over a research dispute?" Tonie asked, trying to make sense of the situation. "Wouldn't Bonvalet only have to say that he doesn't agree with your assessment regarding the meaning of the two finds, and that he supports Marc's theory? This seems like an overreaction to the severity of what's at stake."

"Even though Bonvalet knows it isn't true, it is to his benefit to support Marc's conclusion that the Neanderthal site is much, much older than the human site," Paul asserted. "And, I know Marc doesn't believe it either. They're as crooked as an old man's back."

"They want to destroy your evidence to advance their own theories," Fernand spit out. "Quels connards! I see this all the time in the academic world."

"I think the two of them are in cahoots to say that the Neanderthals slowly mutated into the modern humans that we find next door to them. It doesn't step on anyone's toes and it upholds the current theories. It seemingly adds to the pile of evidence of evolution. Bonvalet will be the genius behind understanding the meaning of the two digs—giving him prestige and the monetary rewards of a higher position. Supporting me would bring a blast of criticism from around the world."

"Ah, yes, that is devious." The botanist continued to realize the implications of the move. "Marc will get credit for adding an important contribution to the theory, maybe even heralding it as the 'missing link.' It will guarantee that he will be honored and, quite possibly, the dig named after him. He will most certainly enjoy an elevated status in the archeological field. There are huge financial rewards for scientists who discover."

"This attack makes it clear that Bonvalet and Marc want to destroy my findings, and me," Paul grimaced. "They have to get rid of my data and the lab results that verify it. And, if I'm dead, then I can't cast any doubts on their claims and shroud their glory."

Fernand nodded. "They will never have to stand against the onslaught of a thousand furious naysayers who will fight to their last breath to not be humiliated that their theories are wrong."

"Yes, just look at me. Two of those naysayers have already tried to kill me. The scientific world will never admit to anything that suggests that the universe is orderly, created with a specific goal in mind. Although the most basic law of science states that everything tends toward disorder, which means that without God, all life is impossible. Yet, this seems to be completely ignored in the race to explain the universe."

"What do you mean?" Tonie asked dubiously.

"Life is incredibly organized. All systems in the human body work together with unimaginable precision. Same with trees, flowers, animals, everything living. Have you ever seen order come out of chaos without an intervening, intelligent hand put to it? A mutation is a breakdown, a step toward disorder. What would make anyone think it could guide life toward an improved outcome? It's like throwing a hammer through your computer and expecting it to work better."

The doubter tried hard to think of a refutal but couldn't.

"The evidence is right in front of our eyes. All the findings at the dig support that humans have been fully human since their appearance on earth. The art I saw at Chauvet let me see into these people's minds, and they were as fully thinking and feeling as you and me. Neanderthals were animals that went extinct a long time ago, as have many other animals throughout history."

Paul reached for his bag and pulled out some notebooks. "I should make copies of all this. This is everything. If it gets lost or stolen I will have absolutely nothing to back me up." He held them out to Fernand.

"I am happy to take them to my office and do this for you, if you are comfortable giving them to me. It is a good idea, and also, I will scan them and email them to you so there will be additional backup."

"I'm sure my email has been hacked, so send it to yours. Thank you for doing this for me. It is nerve-wracking knowing the lengths they are going with this. I never imagined Marc would turn on me, even though he's been unnecessarily antagonist lately—and the weirdness of this past week."

Fernand stood up and started cleaning up the bandages and gauze he had used in wrapping Paul's arm. "I have an idea to get you out of here. You should wait until tomorrow because you are much too weak to travel today, n'est-çe pas? Amanda and I will leave together now so Marc can see us as a couple, and later she can return home alone with lots of shopping bags that will actually be full of extra clothes of mine. Then, this evening, I will pick her up, and we'll go out for dinner, and after, I'll bring her home—to condition any voyeurs to seeing us together. Tomorrow, I'll come over for dinner and stay the evening, and then you will dress in my clothes and leave with her after dark as if you're going out for, say, a glass of wine or the opera. If Marc has been watching, he will assume it is Amanda and me, and then you can get away, and I will leave shortly after you and meet Amanda somewhere."

Paul mulled over this plan and nodded. "I like it."

"And, I will send along a hat to help disguise the fact that, ahem, you are a bit younger than me." Fernand chuckled good-naturedly. "Have you given thought to where you are going to go?"

"I was thinking that I will take the train to London. Then I can fly to the U.S. from there. I don't want to fly directly out of Paris because I'm afraid that may be watched, but Marc, and whoever else is with him, can't possibly watch all the airports in every bordering country. I could just as easily go to Rome or up to Amsterdam."

"Bon, that sounds like it should work well. You will stick out with a broken arm but, hmm, let me think. I will get an extra large coat to go over your arm, and it won't be nearly as conspicuous. It is useful that you are left handed."

"And, I'll let a mustache grow, and that will be a small distraction. I kind of feel like a spy." Paul tried to see the humor in his situation.

Fernand turned to Amanda. "Chérie, is it going to work for you to wait two days until you return home? If not, we will come up with another plan. There is more than one way to skin the dog. That is what you Americans say, non?"

Amanda laughed. "Cat. More than one way to skin a cat. And yes, I can delay my departure two days and still get home in time. I'll call my son and let him know, and I'll call the airline, too. The wedding isn't for a week, but there is cake to be made and flowers to be arranged. I will be very organized and efficient when I get there, and Tonie will be helping me."

With the departure of Fernand and Amanda, Tonie was left uncomfortably alone with her ex-boyfriend. She cleaned up the coffee cups, then picked up her purse and announced to Paul, "I'll go get some groceries to make lunch and dinner. We don't have any food in the house

NETTIE AT THE WELL

since we were planning to leave this morning. Do you need anything before I go? Maybe I will do a little browsing in the shops too, so I won't look like I'm on a mission."

Paul was just as ill at ease. "No, I'm fine. I'll lay on the couch and watch T.V. I'll be okay; don't worry about me." He hesitated a moment. "Tonie, I am really grateful to you for taking me in after what we've been through. I knew you would. And I'm sorry I've made you miss your plane."

"No problem at all. Well, I'll be back in an hour or so. Don't let anyone in."

Paul grinned. "Don't worry."

Not wanting to hurry back, Tonie decided to go by the Sorbonne after she shopped to see if she could help Dr. Michaud make the copies. Her summer projects were finished—final analyses written, mice experiment terminated, no conclusive evidence of anti-senescence properties in the berries or other plants she had collected. She wasn't completely convinced the mice data was accurate—the darn things wouldn't eat anything associated with the berries. She tried to dismiss her growing doubts that the answers would be found in those little red balls that had made her so sick as a youngster.

However, she was no longer a drifter. Having taken up the reins of the berry mission, she had confidence now in her ability to find the answer. There was an answer, she was sure, and another idea would present itself, and she would pursue it, no more floating through time waiting for God-knows-what to solve her problem.

Chapter Fifteen

T ONIE GLANCED AROUND NERVOUSLY AT THE
guests at Jack and Colleen's wedding reception. She
had known many of these people as old Nettie, and
Jack's first comment upon meeting her was that he
believed she must be a long lost relative because of the
family resemblance. Amanda's friends sought her out and
greeted her warmly, asking about their trip to France
together. Tonie also sensed a curious interest toward her
for bearing the same name as Jack's lost sister, although
it wasn't mentioned. She tried to steer the conversation
with the guests to her summer in Paris with Amanda, and
away from where she was born and grew up—in case
anyone knew Maryland more intimately than she did.

Duncan ambled over to Tonie, his face in a pinch,
sour over seeing his ex-wife so lovingly doted on by her
new French boyfriend.

"So," he addressed her gruffly. "Jack says you spent
the summer in Paris with his mother. I hear the French
are pretty rude."

"Oh? No, we never experienced anything like that at all. They are very warm and friendly...as you can see." She gestured over to a smiling Fernand, giving his girlfriend help with putting pieces of cake on plates.

The ex-husband grunted, ignoring the reference. "Yeah, I could have gone several times, but I didn't want to go spend my money just for rude people to try to rip me off at every turn."

"Well, maybe it helped that Amanda and I speak French," the native Parisian offered patiently.

"I have a friend who speaks seven languages, all of them fluent, and he hates the French."

"Maybe he can go to hell then, and so can you." Tonie smiled sweetly and moseyed off. Duncan avoided her the rest of the evening, clinging to his young wife who appeared to be over the infatuation.

Amanda sparkled—face radiant from love, figure svelte and sexy in her Parisian dress, confidence soaring as she had taken hold of her life. Her grandmother was very proud of her, so happy that she was rid of that odious Duncan, and that she had conquered the adversity that life had thrown at her.

Colleen wended her way through the crowd to say hello to her new mother-in-law's traveling partner. She was a pretty woman, strong and capable looking. Tonie remembered Amanda telling her that Colleen was a water colorist, and that she recently had two of her paintings selected to be displayed in a local gallery.

"I'm so happy you could come to our wedding," Colleen welcomed when she reached Tonie. "I've heard so much about you through Jack. What a terrific opportunity for Amanda to spend the summer in Paris. It sounds like you two had a wonderful time!"

Tonie liked this girl who seemed like a perfect fit for Jack. Her wedding dress was…how would she describe it? Eclectic, she decided, like only an artist would wear.

She hugged the newlywed. "Yes, we had a great time. Amanda is a lovely person, and it made the trip extra special to have her come over. I love your dress. Did you make it?"

"No, I just remodeled it a little. It was my mother's wedding gown." The bride pointed to the woman who was chatting to Jack by the punch bowl. "But she never had it put in one of those, you know, little sealed boxes for posterity, so the top of the bodice had been chewed by mice when I went looking for it, and the sleeves were a bit mildewy. I remade the bodice and put this beaded collar around the neckline, and I removed the sleeves and made shoulder caps out of lamé to compliment the shininess of the beads. And, since I'm a little bigger than Mama was, I reshaped the back neckline into a deep vee, and then opened up the waist in the back and added the layered peplum all down the length of the dress, and, 'voila,' as they like to say in France!" Colleen made a half twirl to show the back, which, of course, Tonie had already viewed as the bride walked down the aisle of the church earlier.

Tonie was charmed by this delightful girl, practical and fanciful at the same time, to whom it was of such utmost importance to wear her mother's dress to her own wedding that she tapped into her creative genius to make it work.

"How brilliant! It is truly stunning. Be sure to put it in one of those boxes for your own daughter someday." She winked.

After discussing the couple's honeymoon plans to Mexico, Tonie sought out Jack to wish him well. It had been wonderful seeing him again the past couple days. Time had melted away, and he was the same enchanting Jack, but now a man, strong and confident. And, just as she had with his mother, Tonie reminded herself to remember her new role as a stranger and not be too intrusive.

Colleen's bridesmaids gathered all the single women together for the throwing of the bouquet, which was caught by Amanda to many whoops and whistles. An ardent Fernand rushed in and kissed her for all to see, taking this harbinger of marriage as divine truth, to the delight of all but one. Then, the newlyweds were off amidst showers of rice.

With the wedding over, the French trio drove back to Eugene. The professor had the next two weeks off until "la rentrée," the beginning of the new school year in Paris, when Amanda would also start again on her nursing studies at home. Grand plans were in the works for showing America to Fernand.

Tonie hovered undecided on her own course of action, not wanting to be in the same department at the university as Paul, but not really wanting to give up her work in biology. Now that he obviously was not staying on at the dig, he would be back to teach his classes this fall. She debated going back to the Sorbonne with Fernand and studying with him, but didn't want to be that far away from her family now that she had a relationship with them once again—and not a strong hold to be a part of it if she let the ties fade.

Once at Amanda's apartment, Fernand revealed some troubling news during dinner.

"I didn't want to say anything before the wedding and rain on the merriment, but the day after you two left Paris, Paul's picture was on the news as a wanted man for attempted murder. They are saying he tried to kill Marc to steal his findings, and that he assaulted a laborer who tried to stop him, then fled with Marc's records."

Tonie stared at Fernand. "What a lie! How can they say this? Well, thank goodness he got out of France. Is he back in the U.S. yet? I have been wondering, but I didn't know if you would know. I thought he would have let me, well us, know, since we were a part of helping him."

"It gets worse, mon amie," Fernand continued. "Paul called from London and said he is on the news there as well. He hasn't decided exactly what to do yet, but said he will keep me informed."

Tonie turned to Amanda. "Do you suppose it would be on the news here, too? How will he come back if he will be arrested as soon as he does? We haven't seen the news in days because of the wedding."

Amanda rose from the table and retrieved her computer. She typed in the news address and didn't need to search Paul's name. "Yes, here it is—'American professor wanted in France for attempted murder.' It goes on to say that Paul Delaney tried to kill Marc Diceccio with a rock, and when a passing laborer stopped him, Delaney attacked him and ran. They are claiming the exact same thing that they did to Paul."

"He will not be able to get out of the U.K. without being arrested," Fernand interjected, "and, if they get him, he will be extradited back to France. He's going to need money because now that there are criminal charges, the police will be watching his bank account. And, he can't use his phone because it will be traced. He said he will call in a few days from a pay phone and let me know his plan."

"What if I came back to Paris to study with you, and I could take him money. I can go in and out of England on the train or ferry. He must be sleeping on a park bench by now," Tonie offered, without considering the ramifications.

"If you are going, then I'm going!" Amanda chimed in, determined not to be left in America if everyone was going back to France.

"Oh, ma chérie! That makes me so happy!" Fernand proclaimed. "I have been depressed at the thought of leaving you here. But, this might drag on more than a couple weeks, and what about your studies? Are you sure you are willing to take some time off?"

"If that happens, then I will take French classes at the Sorbonne for electives. And, Sabine, who I shadowed at the hospital, told me they would accommodate me for volunteer work if I stayed, which I believe could transfer to credits in the U.S. if I get it approved here. Therefore, I would still be moving forward."

"My only doubt, now that I think about it, is if Paul will want my help," the jilted girlfriend voiced her probable unwelcomeness. "But, I would be willing to support you, doing whatever is necessary to get him cleared of these charges."

"Well, he did come straight to you when he needed help," loyal Amanda pointed out. "However, it may be true for your own emotional protection not to get overly involved."

"You women know nothing about a man's love," French Fernand declared. "When a man loves a woman he never stops loving her—not because of a quarrel, or a difference of opinion, or even a raging fight. That has nothing to do with it. Even if the moon fell out of the sky he would not stop loving her." He scowled at Tonie as if giving her the most important lesson she would get in life. "Ma belle, I know Paul still loves you and still wants you. He wanted to marry you, and then his intellect made him analyze his relationship with you because that is what scientists do. They analyze with their brains in matters of love, and then they make mistakes. But that is not the heart." Fernand thumped his hand on his chest a few times for emphasis. "His heart still wants you, still aches for you, he cannot sleep at night." The great lover turned to Amanda and stroked her cheek. "I know this because this is how much I love ma bien-aimée."

Tonie made every effort not to roll her eyes, currently gripped in the bitterness of unrequited love. Good Lord, she sighed to herself—leave it to a French man to get carried away on the wings of *amour*. However, she wondered if it were true? Did Paul really still love her? He had come to her when he was in trouble, but the man had absolutely no where else to go, and he was in a foreign country. What else could he do?

He probably hated having to ask her for help after dumping her like that. Well, it was useless worrying about it, she chided herself. The ball was in his court as far as his feelings toward her were concerned. But still, a pit gnawed at her stomach for worry of his plight.

Fernand's phone rang, relieving Tonie of chasing her love dilemma in circles like a dog chasing his tail.

"Ah, I'll bet this is our jailbird right now." He showed the long string of numbers on the front of the phone, starting with the U.K.'s country code. "Hallo?"

The curious ladies listened to the conversation in anticipation of clues to what was going on. After a few minutes, Fernand hung up and gave the full report.

"Paul is in Bath, on the west coast of England, staying at a youth hostel under the name of Braden O'Riley. He says he has enough money for a couple of weeks. Before he left London he called his parents, and they have contacted the U.S. Embassy in Paris. They called a lawyer who advised him to stay in hiding until this can be resolved, because he will otherwise be arrested and remain in jail until it goes to trial. Paul's brother is going to see if he will be able to go to France and snoop around the dig, hopefully finding the worker who tried to kill him, and see if he can get him to say who put him up to it."

"Couldn't he come home and get a lawyer then fight it from here?" Amanda asked.

"No," Fernand explained. "A person is subject to the laws of the country where the crime, or alleged crime, was committed, and that country has the right to try the accused in their court of law, according to their own standards. His parents have a lawyer so they will decide on what steps to take next. I gave our offer to help, and Paul was grateful and said he will be in contact if he needs anything."

In Bath. Tonie shook her head. She hoped Bath would work out better for Paul than it had for her when she went to live there after Isaac died. She felt herself washed into the river of time, swept backwards against the current, her mind pulled to when she lost Isaac, and her curse drove her to move on, on into the black forest of loneliness once more.

Bells toll mournfully from the tower of Saint Paul's, escorting the widow as she leaves the same cathedral in which she married Isaac years earlier. Flora and Esmée flank her sides, the shock of death making the three of them huddle together, trying to keep life's storms at bay by hiding their vulnerable underbellies from fate's capriciousness. Nettie never gets used to death's sting— the sickening finality, the crashing helplessness, her impotence to rewind the clock and restore order.

How lovely it had been being married to Isaac, to be swaddled in a family's warm arms again and be able to forget, for the time, her worries and sorrows. He was a kind and attentive husband, their home a mansion filled with parties and friends with never any concerns about money. She and Flora flitted around like sisters. She knew Isaac expected children and believed she was young enough to produce them for him, which was true—the monthly way of women was still with her even at her advanced age—but never would she be unfaithful to her sweet Henri, the only baby she could ever love. There were ways, she had learned in her years of midwifery, of stopping the seed of a man, and she used these secrets without letting Isaac ever suspect, and so they remained childless throughout their marriage.

As time rolled on, her lack of aging finally became worrisome to her. Wrinkles appeared on Flora's cheeks, but not on hers. Flora's hair was graying, her waistline thickening, while Nettie's hair was dark and glossy, her figure trim. Flora's hips got stiff, and her bones ached, but Nettie sprinted like a gazelle in springtime. She had taken to rubbing ash in her hair and dabbing coal dust under her eyes to age herself in order to deflect suspicion that she might have made some pact with the devil. That was before she knew her curse. But, as she entered her eighties, fear gripped her with the realization that she was an old woman trapped in a girl's body. Years earlier, people had confused her for Flora's sister, and then it became Esmée who was perceived to be her peer, and now, even that young woman was beginning to look like an older sister.

With Isaac's passing she is no longer under a man's protection, and she constantly worries about being accused as a witch. Even though witch hunts are rare these days, they are not unheard of, and several concerns beyond her youthful body begin to hound her. In her midwifery practice her maternal and infant mortality rates are much lower than the other midwives—Mama taught her well—which, while it puts her in demand, it has also led her to being labeled "charmed"—one word away from "possessed." A third factor which could be used against her is that she has supplied quite a few women over the years with the same pessary of cotton wool soaked with acacia decoction that she used to inhibit conception. Not only illegal, it is considered by many to be the devil's potion.

With heavy heart, she at last decides she must leave the people she loves—Flora, a true and faithful friend; Esmée, who has loved her like a grandmother, who she delivered at sea and watched grow into lovely womanhood. They don't understand why she is leaving, and she doesn't either, other than she knows it won't be long until they wonder how she has lived so long. And what will she do then? She loves them, and her heart is breaking, but she must go. She tells them that now that Isaac is gone she wants to go back to her homeland, but it is a lie.

Her plan is to go to the west of England, to Bath, and start again. Bath is a thriving, growing community with many newcomers, and she will fit in easily. She will take off her veil, wash her face, and once again become a young orphan girl. At eighty-two she can't have many years left to live. So she goes, and she cries, and she hopes she will die soon.

But another thirty years go by, and she is the same, and that is when she becomes friends with Lydia, confiding her secret to her. It is true there are no more witch hunts, they have evolved into "lunatic" hunts, and her jail is an asylum where she is tortured for four years to bring back her sanity. And it works. She becomes sane enough to know she will never again trust her secret to anyone.

Now, hearing that Paul was in Bath, homeless and alone, Tonie pondered whether she would be willing to go there, to take him money. No, she decided. He doesn't want her anymore and has other people to help him. She will move on—as she always has.

Amanda and Fernand drove Tonie to her old apartment after dinner, carrying her bags to the door.

"Are you sure you'll be all right by yourself tonight?" Amanda asked, reiterating her offer for Tonie to stay with her.

"Yes, I'll be fine, and I've got so much work to get done to move out in two weeks. This will give me a chance to start getting organized."

"Okay. Good night. We'll see you in the morning for coffee." They hugged goodbye, and Tonie walked alone into the apartment that she hadn't seen in three months since leaving it to spend an exciting summer in Paris with her boyfriend. Its silence mirrored the silence of Chauvet cave, dormant energy leaping up to greet her, welcoming her home and looking past her as if to ask, "Where is Paul? Where is your friend?" His tennis shoes, still parked by the door draped with socks, wanted his feet in them, not hers. His books and notebooks lay in stacks on the end table, waiting for his eyes to find them and his hands to caress their pages. In the bathroom lurked Paul's first gift to her—a toilet plunger tied with a pink bow, proudly stationed beside the biffy. It startled Tonie with the strength of emotions it evoked.

Wanting to get the melancholy task of moving out over with as soon as possible, Tonie began collecting each remembrance as it leapt out at her, tossing some of Paul's things into the trash and some into a box that she would send to his parents' house for his eventual return. From all dismal accounts, no one expected him to be out of hiding anytime soon. She was surprised at how many of his belongings had slowly migrated over to her home from his.

Sighing, she sank into the couch, not having the motivation to further tackle the job tonight. They had left so happily for Paris together with dreams of their future, but she had returned alone. It felt like a death to her, but maybe easier because there would be no sentimentality. He hadn't died—he had just quit loving her.

Tonie heaved herself up and continued on her mission to devoid the house of Paul's essence. On the coffee table she found his Bible lying where he forgot it before they left. She opened it and studied the inscription. This must be the one he received as a teenager when he joined the youth group, she reflected. Paul had told her what an important event that had been, how God's love had dissolved his loneliness.

Flipping through the Bible she stopped at a verse that was highlighted: Psalm 27:1. "The Lord is my light and my salvation, whom shall I fear? The Lord is the strength of my life, of whom shall I be afraid?" Was Paul thinking of that verse tonight, so far from home with evil people plotting against him? She started to toss the Bible into the box, but then decided to take it with her to Paris. He would need it now more than ever, and she could send it with Fernand to give him when they returned to their French home.

Chapter Sixteen

T INY SNOWFLAKES SILENTLY FELL OUT OF THE DARK sky, landing on Tonie's nose and eyelashes as she hurried home across the Pont Neuf, arms brimming with shopping bags filled with Christmas gifts, and wine and chocolates for tonight. The snow sent her mind spinning back to her childhood when she and her brothers and sisters would leave their shoes in front of the hearth on Christmas Eve in hopes of a visit from Père Noël, who never disappointed. In the morning, each starry-eyed child would find a chocolate bar with their initial imprinted in the chocolate, wrapped in white paper and left in their shoe. Hers would have a fancy "A" for Antoinette on it. She would eat all the chocolate from around the initial until the "A" was all that was left, and then she would slowly savor that last part. What deliciousness! And in her memory, it always snowed on Christmas and the house was warm and cheery, festively lit with extra candles and sprigs of mistletoe adorning the doorways. She resisted the urge to run to that little house right now, knowing that, in reality, there would be no welcoming candles in the windows for her. But the closeness of it made the memories all the more vivid.

Lights from the bridge shimmered on the river, reflecting a cozy glow. With every tree and lamppost wrapped in glittering white lights it was almost as light as day. Paris was indeed a shining city. The giant, gleaming tree on the parvis of Notre Dame was a testament to the spirit of Noël, with holiday shoppers scurrying about, intent on the serious business of finding that perfect something for their special person.

Chocolates in her bag and snow in the air—how wonderful to be home for Christmas. Tonie lifted her face to the sky to welcome the tiny dots of coldness caressing her cheeks.

"Mamzelle, s'il vous plaît," a low voice addressed her as she passed a bastion mid-bridge.

The bag-laden shopper turned and came face to face with an old ragged beggar, holding out a cup for money. Rearranging her parcels to access her purse, she pulled out a euro and dropped it in his cup.

"Merci. God bless you." The beggar gazed straight into her eyes, sending a piercing jolt through Tonie's body. She perceived a vague something, but she didn't know what. Intelligence shone in those eyes, a knowing, a longing. Did he see the real her and know her secret? The beggar's eyes held her transfixed for several seconds, then she forced herself free from their pull and rushed away into the night.

Who was he? Her mind spun. Did she recognize his face from somewhere? She filed through her mind trying to place him. There was an oddity about him, something that belied his lowly station in life. Was he a spy, she wondered, stalking her in hopes of finding Paul? She glanced back to his spot as she reached the other side of the bridge, but was not able to distinguish him in the darkness.

That night, Tonie recounted the story of the mysterious man to Amanda and Fernand, who listened attentively.

"What did his beard look like? Do you think it was real?" Amanda asked, following the premise that the beggar may have been a spy.

"It seemed real. It was a full beard, long and gray and scraggly. I didn't study it closely, but yes, I would say the beard was real."

"Well, it couldn't be Marc, then," Fernand deduced. "He wouldn't have had time to grow a beard that long in four months, and, it wouldn't be gray."

"No, it wasn't Marc. But this guy seemed to know me. Oh! Maybe it was the laborer that tried to kill Paul. Maybe Marc showed him pictures of me that were in Paul's tent. He has a good reason to want him dead because Paul can identify him."

"But why would he call out to you and reveal himself?"

"I don't know. Maybe he didn't know it was me when he reached out and was surprised to see my face," Tonie speculated. "The guy definitely seemed to recognize me."

"Yeah," Amanda agreed. "He could be here following you and trying to make a few bucks at the same time by begging, now that he doesn't have a job anymore."

Fernand thoughtfully mulled over all the information. "How old did he look?"

Tonie closed her eyes, concentrating on the details of the beggar's face. "At first, I guessed him to be a very old man—from his demeanor and the long beard and hair. But, when I saw his face and his eyes, there was a youthfulness to him. His skin wasn't wrinkled, and his eyes were sharp. It was this incongruity that caught my attention and made me aware that more was going on than just a beggar wanting money. And, the way he fixated on me. Beggars don't lock eyes with you. I really had the impression that this guy knew me."

As she made this description, Tonie was startled to realize that she was describing herself during the times that she tried to pass as an old woman—gray hair but no wrinkles. Her first assessment of him rolled back over her—he knew her secret. He was no spy. He must bear the same immortality as she did, and somehow recognized that in her. She had to find him again.

"Well, begging for money is a sly way to get to see someone up close," remarked Amanda, still on the trail of a spy.

"My opinion is that you should look for him again tomorrow, in the same place at the same time," the professor suggested, "and proceed from there. He probably wants to see you again, too, since he showed such interest. Beggars have their areas and jostle for them in the streets. If he is a common beggar, he should be in his territory again at the same time tomorrow."

Tonie laughed, wanting to lighten the conversation now that she suspected there was a different agenda going on with the strange man. "It sounds like we are in a bird watching club. 'The common woodpecker can be found in his usual tree just after sunset,'" she mimicked.

They all laughed, and Fernand raised his glass. "To finding the woodpecker," he toasted.

The ladies raised their glasses and echoed, "Finding the woodpecker!"

The next afternoon, Tonie did exactly what Fernand recommended. She shopped in a few stores—which she needed to do anyway now that Christmas was only five days away—while keeping an eye out for her mystery man. Shortly after sunset, her search began in earnest. She headed home across the Pont Neuf as she had the evening before. It was no longer snowing, but the night was colder than the previous one, with patches of snow still lurking in untrodden corners. The hopeful immortal nestled her scarf up tight around her neck, but not too high to hide her face and not be easily recognizable.

She scrutinized every man she saw—whether he was standing, sitting, or lying in a sleeping bag—but none were her beggar. Upon reaching the end of the bridge with no luck, she turned back to retrace her original path. But again, nothing. Her woodpecker was not in his usual tree tonight.

Disappointed, but not defeated, she continued on home with a mission. She must not be the only one with the affliction, she rejoiced. Surely this man had it too, and she had only to find him again to hear his story and compare notes of their long lives. At long, long last, she would have someone to talk to, to confide in, to go through eternity with. Even if they couldn't find the solution, she would not be alone. The relief rocked her like an earthquake. She would not be alone. She was not alone. This hope fueled her and drove her. Her mind soaring in every direction, she fancifully wondered if there were even more. Why not? If it happened to her, it must have happened to others. This thought occurred to her before, and now it took root as not merely possible, but actually probable.

Then the doubts attacked. Was she reading too much into this? Maybe he really was a spy. It had been dark, his form shadowy and mysterious. Had he only seemed young to her later because he wasn't as old as she first thought? No, she declared. Something had been odd, and she would search for him until she found him. Whether a spy or an immortal, he had sought her out, and she would find out why.

Since coming back to Paris after Jack's wedding, life had settled into a predictable routine. The two ladies shared the same apartment they had during the summer, where Tonie's wedding dress was still hanging in the closet upon their return, a mocking tribute to her unlovableness. Amanda taught English at the Sorbonne, volunteered at the hospital and spent her evenings with Fernand. Tonie continued on with her work at the university, but no longer with the zeal that had possessed her at the beginning when she was certain of finding a remedy for her immortality in the berries.

Tonie had no doubts that her granddaughter was here with Fernand to stay. And, while Amanda's relationship with Fernand grew and strengthened, Tonie nursed her broken heart, but found it immensely easier to cope with the support of her loyal friend.

She still found herself surprised that Paul turned out to be so small minded in the end. But it hurt all the same, and while she did not think he deserved the betrayal he got at the dig—and she wished him well—she did wonder if his trust was shaken in his God now that he was in such a mess and all alone. And homeless. And potentially facing spending his life in prison. Did he wonder why God turned His back on him? Was he ready to renounce Him yet, as she had done?

But now, with the arrival of the beggar, Tonie exulted in the unexpected turn of events which gave her renewed hope of escaping her torment once and for all, and also helped take her mind off of Paul. She was determined to find this woodpecker, figuring if he appeared once, then he would appear again. The next few days found her feverishly plotting her course of action on a map, circling the areas most conducive to begging and crossing off her unsuccessful forays. She formulated a plan to engage other mendicants, asking their habits and most lucrative locations. For a euro and conversation, she anticipated, they would be happy to spill their secrets. She would ask them about the old-young man with the long gray beard. For all she knew, there might be a community of beggars who all knew each other, who met and played cards under a bridge somewhere at the end of the day.

Having seen her beggar in rags, dependent on the generosity of strangers, Tonie thanked her lucky stars that she had never desperately needed money again since the time of her marriage to Isaac. After his death, she had carried her satchel full of cash to Bath with her to live on until she could set herself up as a midwife. With each life change after that, she always had her replenished satchel to see her on her way. Later, when she married Thomas and moved to America, there had been some lean years during the Great Depression—as it came to be known— but they had never known the cold, gray pit of want as so many others had. She always knew where her next meal was coming from, and, she always kept the satchel current. It was full right now with a mixture of euros and dollars.

From thoughts of the beggar's poverty, her mind flitted to other details of his life. How old was this man? Was this his first old age, or his tenth or more? Why didn't he let his youthful face show since he was an anonymous man on the streets with no need of fooling anyone? Had loneliness and despair taken their toll, depriving his mind of its sharpness? Had he eaten the poisonous berries as a child? While not encouraged by her berry experiments, she wasn't convinced that she had learned conclusively from the mice that the berries were not the answer. Her time had simply run out on them. When she would finally meet this old man, she would reinstate the berry study if it turned out that he had eaten them, too. But first, she must find him.

It was three days before Christmas, prime begging season, and she would search every day. Tomorrow, she planned, she would once again look around the cathedral of Notre Dame, which tended to be surrounded with beggars, especially this close to Christmas when folks were feeling generous.

Chapter Seventeen

AFTER CHECKING INTO THE HOTEL IN BATH AND dropping off his suitcase, Fernand wound his way through the quaint town to the boarding house where Paul was renting a room waiting out the time until his case could go to trial. Scarf flapping in the bitter wind of late December, the visitor shivered and pulled his cap lower over his ears. On his shoulder he carried a backpack containing Christmas gifts, letters, and cash from Paul's family to cheer and sustain the refugee over the next few months, until the allegations against him would hopefully be resolved. Paul's brother, Lucas, had made his second trip to Paris the day after Christmas with these items, but again, following the lawyer's directive to not deliver them himself for concern of being followed, he transferred the items to Fernand before heading to Lyon to meet a woman who claimed to have some information on the case.

Fernand was happy to make the jaunt to England to deliver these care packages and to see how the fugitive was faring. He had made the trip twice before, bringing news from home and taking back Paul's greetings to his family. Interest ran high in academic circles, with most taking the side of Marc, mainly because he was the one crying foul. Fernand found the case intriguing, not only for the intrinsic interest of a fellow academician finding himself suddenly submerged in the classic "stealing ideas" plight, but also knowing the full reverberations when the truth would finally be known. The dilemma of ideas being stolen was one faced by all research scientists, which many times led to the premature publishing of conclusions not entirely based on facts, but on presumptions, in order to be the first to take the credit.

Another problem inherent in the race for publication was "publication bias," where the promotion of certain research depended less on the quality of the work, but more on its nature and direction. And this bias was exactly what Fernand and Paul believed was happening in the field of archeology. While most research showed no correlation between humans and apes, the five percent that did was presented as the entirety, and heralded as brilliant discoveries, disregarding the other ninety-five percent that showed none. Marc's objective was to trumpet his accomplishment as a major find in this latest dig and throw yet another twisted "fact" into the hat named evolution, blackballing Paul's overwhelming evidence that would prove the contrary.

Paul, alias Braden, met Fernand as soon as he walked up to the door at the boardinghouse, and they strolled over to the park to be able to converse in private. The two men sat on a bench on the leeward side of a tree which, despite its barren branches, partially blocked the winter wind. Paul was unrecognizable. Four months of beard growth on his face and unkempt hair on his head erased the polished professional air he had worn before. But, more than the surprise of his physical grooming, the thing that astonished Fernand the most was the peaceful, relaxed aura surrounding this hunted man who had lost everything. Home, family, and profession had been torn from him the same way that a bear would rip out an opponent's viscera, but Paul had the demeanor of the richest man on earth.

"Bonjour, mon ami," Fernand greeted his friend, kissing him on both cheeks. "How are you doing? You look well. Life on the run must agree with you."

"I have gotten over my sadness. This is my life now, and it's the road God has chosen for me, so I must find the value in it because I know it's there."

"Yes, that is true, but sometimes it is hard to see the light when you are in a dark tunnel."

"It's not so dark anymore. I've made some friends, and we get together here in the park for Bible study every day. These guys have all fallen on hard times, just like me. I haven't explicitly shared my problems, but we are here for each other. And recently, a few more people have been stopping by and listening, and actually, we have quite a few men, and some women now, who join in. It's like a family, and we have a connection with each other. I don't know how to explain it, but I feel a sense of belonging like I've never felt before."

A shiver shook through Fernand's body, but not from the cold. "That is the hand of God on you. You can rest assured that you are exactly where God wants you to be, and that He is holding you. I am in awe to see Him work this way. I have worried for you and for your safety, but now I know that I need not, for you are truly in God's arms."

"Now my concern is that when this all comes to an end and the allegations against me are disproved, I will go back to my life as it was before, but I'm not sure I want that. Not that I don't want to be exonerated—but I don't want to ever become complacent to other people's pain. I don't mean to jump the gun, because who knows really how it will turn out, but I can already see the good in it. I wouldn't give up what I've learned here for anything."

Fernand studied his friend's face, so changed since he last saw him when grief and stress ravaged his features. Now, Paul had crossed his valley of death and was on the other side, where the peaceful waters of the Savior flowed, his dark night fought for him with unseen hands.

"So, what is the news in Paris? I hope Tonie is doing well?" the nomad asked casually.

"Oui, she is plunging ahead with her studies at the Sorbonne and becoming quite a talented botanist under my tutelage, if I may brag on myself. She has been afraid this past week that she is being followed and wonders if it might be the laborer who tried to kill you. Would you happen to remember what he looks like?"

"He's an Algerian man, and I suspect he probably returned home to get away from being questioned. I doubt Marc would send him after me again, but who knows how an evil mind works. He was dark-skinned, tall with a strong build, maybe thirty years old."

"Non, non, that cannot be him, then. This man looked very old from afar, but young up close, and had a long gray beard. He was posing as a beggar, and she only saw him the once when he asked her for money. Tonie is certain there is something very strange about him and has made it her mission to find him again, but has had no success yet."

"I hope she is being careful and keeping herself safe."

"Oh yes, she seems to be a prudent young woman. And I have news, also. Amanda and I are engaged to be married."

"Congratulations! You and Amanda are a match made in heaven. I'm sure you will be very happy together. When is the date?"

"In early summer, after the school year is over. I'm hoping you will be a free man by then and able to be my witness."

"Yes, I would love to be there, and surely all this nonsense will be over by then."

"Lucas said the French police have finished their investigation and are waiting on your lawyer to provide your defense. He has taken off for Lyon to meet with a woman named Astrid, who called him and said she may have information against Marc. Do you remember her?"

"Oh, yes. She is an intern working on her Ph.D. I wonder what she could know? She was very thorough and methodical in her work. She oversaw the daily direction of the student volunteers, teaching them field methods and assigning their tasks. Hmm, that's interesting that she called Lucas." Paul considered this news.

The two men, who had formerly only had the association of knowing each other's girlfriends, were fast becoming good friends themselves. They spent the day together discussing problems near and far, only parting after dinner when Fernand returned to his hotel and Paul to the boarding house. The visitor would catch the early train to London in the morning, and then the train via the Chunnel back to Paris. Paul told Fernand he would call in two days to see what news his brother might have for him. Every few days Paul took the fifteen minute train ride to Bristol to make phone calls to keep them from being tracked, so there was no other way to talk to him other than wait for his call.

Heading home to the boarding house, Paul mulled over the news brought to him today. He was always glad for news of Tonie, but he knew he wouldn't be if he heard she had a new man in her life. To put it more precisely, he was always glad for the news that Tonie was still single. He didn't understand her animosity toward his faith, and he had not noticed it until after they came to Paris. Was she stressed about something? Did her work at the Sorbonne agitate her? Then an awful thought burst into his consciousness—had she hated being engaged to him? Was she looking for things to pick at once she had promised her life to him?

That's ridiculous, he countered the argument in his head. They had been together for two years and were happy the whole time. Was she merely going through a freak-out and would have calmed down? He wished he hadn't been so hasty about breaking it off with her.

On the other hand, he reflected, she had never expressed the least interest in his faith, which he freely shared, at first anyway, and she had never joined him at church—always claiming a deadline or a commitment. And she openly attacked him at the end.

"Women," he sighed the age-old lament of baffled men everywhere. Tonie was his first serious girlfriend, the only time he had been engaged, and he knew he should forget her. Maybe he would have already if he wasn't stuck in this no-man's land where time stood still, he told himself.

He was learning something here, however, something deep and comforting, outside the realm of circumstances. An unshakeable faith was taking hold in him, a rootedness that defied the world, that losing any earthly thing could not upset. It was because of his circumstances that this transformation was able to take place, he was sure. Not that he wasn't ready to go home, back to his work, but he knew without doubt, that even if he went to jail, he had an island of peace inside him that could never be shaken.

Back in his meager room, Paul picked up his accordion and warmed up with a slow Irish ballad. None of the men complained when he practiced, and several always gathered around, singing along to his tunes. He began learning to play the instrument a few days into his sojourn in Bath after he had encountered a man on a street corner playing songs for the coins that passersby would toss into his open case. In the four months he had been on the run, Paul made enough progress that on the weekends he would find a spot on a busy street and set out his case for "tips," learning the disgrace of being denigrated by strangers.

At first, mortification swallowed him whole and shame burned within him that his life had come to this. But then, slowly, he gained an appreciation for every beggar that had gone before him—the lame in the Bible sitting at the city gates of Jerusalem; the widow-women who couldn't feed their children; the demon possessed; all the despised of society who, for whatever reason, did not fit in and were without the necessary talents to make a living. He didn't merely recognize the ordeal of outcasts throughout time, he lived it. The disgust he saw in the eyes of those who beheld him as they hurried past stabbed through his heart like a knife, but most of all, his invisibility in a world of which he was no longer a part shattered his sense of worth.

Every day was a test of faith, a leaning on God, with no assurance of anything past the current day. He, Paul Delaney, was now the despised of the earth, and there was nowhere in the world where he could run and be free. His legs were not lame, but he was crippled just the same, dependent on his daily manna from God. This state of being opened his soul and his spirit soared. His prison provided freedom in a way that he had not experienced before, and he could never go back to live in a stifling box again, oblivious to his neighbor's pain, scrapping to make it in a dog-eat-dog world.

Chapter Eighteen

L UCAS DELANEY JAUNTILY HOPPED OFF THE TRAIN in Lyon, consulting his map to find the café where he would meet with Astrid. The promising intern had excitedly called him three days earlier reporting that she had information, possibly damaging information, about Marc, which she believed could tip the investigation in Paul's favor. He had envisioned this French beauty often since he met her on his previous visit to the archeological site, and he was looking forward to seeing her again. With Astrid's call, Lucas was happy to learn that her surreptitious task of obtaining evidence was accomplished, leading him to leave his wife and kids home alone at Christmastime to rush to her—all for the sake of his poor, lonely, falsely accused brother, he had assured his angry spouse.

On his first pilgrimage several months earlier, Lucas had snooped around the dig hoping to find some clues which could be used against the corrupt Professor Diceccio. Asking questions of the workers in the camp had rendered no clear answers, for the events of that fateful night were not known past what Marc had recounted to the police and the rumors he purposefully whispered into a few ears. Team members had eyed Lucas skeptically, denying any knowledge of the attempted murder. Marc had remained aloof, refusing to talk to him. The laborer who had wielded the rock no longer worked there, and a name was not forthcoming. Although amiable Lucas had a knack for chatting with people and usually got what he wanted, he was striking out until he struck up a friendship with a female intern working on her Ph.D. Astrid had been more than disgruntled at the running of the dig ever since Paul disappeared and Marc was put in charge.

Lucas had taken Astrid out for drinks at a small pub in a neighboring village to discuss the matter out of the prying eyes of the other team members. The wine loosened her tongue, and she soon was spilling her woes on his sympathetic ears. While she was not privy to any insider information, she did tell Lucas that she could not imagine for a minute that Paul tried to kill Marc. She warned him that Marc was underhanded and lecherous and that he had been, for some time, subtly undermining Paul's credibility. Astrid's own observations led her to agree with Paul's theory of two contemporary settlements, and she believed Marc wanted to get rid of Paul to destroy his data.

Also, she had reported, since Paul's absence the lecherous professor was making unrelenting sexual advances toward her which she silently, though furiously, endured for the sake of not wanting to seem a malcontent and difficult to work with, for she was hoping to be hired at a big university upon completion of her internship. At the abrupt departure of Paul, her hope for a recommendation evaporated along with him, her only hope for one now dependent on Marc.

Lucas had commiserated with her plight, and after a steamy night together, Astrid agreed to try to secretly obtain Marc's records and make copies of them. There were also artifacts supporting Paul's conclusions, and Marc wanted all that data destroyed in order to present his findings without any controversy. With the botched rock attack, and Paul's presence of mind to grab his notebooks on the way out, Marc's tactic changed to depicting his nemesis as a religious fanatic who went off the deep end when he lost his girlfriend.

Now, finding the café, Lucas entered and found the lovely Astrid already seated at a small table in the corner. She stood up when he came over, and they exchanged double kisses. With all activity at the dig suspended during the holiday season, Marc was gone, as were most of the workers, giving Astrid and her American lover plenty of time and privacy to themselves.

"Thank you for coming," the pretty redheaded woman welcomed in charmingly accented English, smiling at Lucas. "I have been able to get some information for you, although it has taken longer than I would have liked, but Marc is not a person that I want to cross. I have not found out anything more about that night, but I do know Paul, and he would not try to kill anyone. And, I also know Marc, and I wouldn't trust him any farther than I could throw him."

"Yeah, I can't believe Paul would hurt anyone, and he is not a glory-hound. From talking to his ex-girlfriend it sounds like he didn't agree with Marc's assessment of the dating of the sites, and it would have been more likely that Marc wanted to destroy Paul's findings than the other way around."

"Yes!" Astrid agreed emphatically. "That's exactly what I have found. I started searching through Marc's files when he would be away for the night—I learned how to pick locks from my brother who worked his way through college by retrieving keys from locked cars. Last week, Marc's computer was open and I got into it. I found some letters between him and Dr. Bonvalet discussing how to discredit Paul and get rid of his data."

"Did you get copies of them?"

"Yes," the clever investigator replied, digging in her purse and pulling out a USB flash drive. "I copied the original records showing the initial findings and dates which corroborate Paul's data, and the bastardized files reflecting the new report he wants to publish as his big discovery."

Noticing a flicker of reservation in her face, it crossed Lucas' mind that there might be a price for this information. Studying her closely he asked, "Are you going to go to the police with this evidence?"

"No, I give it to you. My only stipulation is that I do not want to be tied to this case in any way—it would be a disaster to my career. You can say you came across it however you want, but it wouldn't hurt," she hinted, "if Paul showed his gratitude by a recommendation."

Lucas smiled appreciatively at this woman who had just saved his brother's life. What a gem and what a beauty, he admired. They left the café together, arm in arm, the flash drive tucked safely in his pocket. But first, before lawyers, before Paul knowing his new fate, he would certainly bestow his gratefulness to this woman in a big way—showering Astrid with showy dates in Nice, and romantic nights in luxury hotels.

"Taxi!" the victorious man called out. "Gare de Lyon-Part-Dieu!"

Lucas resurfaced in Paris three days later bearing the evidence that could end his brother's nightmare. He sent copies to Paul's lawyer in the U.S. and gave copies to Fernand to take to Paul in Bath. Then the wheeling-dealing brother jetted home to his weary wife and his job back in Oregon, blowing into town just in time for the New Year.

When Fernand sought Tonie out in her office that afternoon and told her the news, Tonie quickly offered to take the papers to Paul herself, knowing that Fernand and Amanda had plans to dance in the New Year in Austria. Since there was a chance that she and Paul might bump into each other back home at the university, Tonie reasoned that this meeting would ease the awkwardness should that event occur. Fernand gladly accepted her offer since he had so recently made the trip, and he gave her all the papers that Lucas had copied off the flash drive.

Leaving the Sorbonne for the day, Tonie made a tour of the Sacré Coeur on Montmartre in the lightly falling snow, inspecting the masses of beggars huddled for warmth in the doorways of the church, but with no success in finding hers. During the long metro ride home she tried to plan her next strategy since more than a week had passed with no success finding the woodpecker. Fighting off discouragement, she counted the things that were going right. If the beggar were a spy, then she probably would have seen him again because he would be following her. Since she hadn't, chances were he wasn't a spy. That was good. Something about him resonated with her. She had a gut feeling that he might have the answers—if only she could find him.

Amanda reached under her bed and pulled out a suitcase. On her left hand sparkled the diamond ring Fernand had surprised her with at Christmas, and now they were preparing to celebrate their engagement by waltzing in the New Year at the Sylversterball at the Imperial Palace in Vienna. The newly betrothed couple were going with some married friends of Fernand's who had been to this most illustrious gala before. The wife described it all to Amanda, including the tip to rent a ball gown in Vienna for the event, as it was prohibitively expensive to buy one. Even more importantly, she advised, was to buy the most comfortable fancy shoes she could find that would stand up to an entire evening of dancing.

Amanda reflected what a strategist Fernand had been, realizing now why he had suggested ballroom dancing lessons right after their return to Paris in September. He was such a romantic, his devoted fiancée mused. He loved moonlight walks, cozy corners in restaurants, and even going to a grand ball. Amanda reveled in this love of a gentleman who always looked after her needs and protected her. Never in her wildest imagination had she dreamed she would be this lucky in love, or that such an incredible man existed.

The only shadow on her happiness this week was leaving Tonie alone in Paris. While her friend had seemingly recovered from the break-up with Paul, and had made strides in putting her life back together, there was still a loneliness surrounding her, a hauntedness, which alerted Amanda that all may not be well.

Witnessing a change in Tonie since that night when the demons were driven out of her, Amanda noticed that she occasionally referred to God now, although taking it back when she perceived her slip, but it was there. She had also lost her despair, softening and relaxing in many of her ways. But Amanda deemed that there must be one unclean spirit left, one that only Tonie herself could expel, and she needed to accept Jesus' love to be able to do this.

Amanda understood loss and the temptation to blame God who possessed the power to spare you pain but for some inexplicable reason chose not to. She thanked her loving God every day for the believing women who intervened for her when she needed it after Antoinette died—picking her up for church and Bible study every week, combing her hair and helping her dress on the bad days, giving her their strength when she had none.

She had experienced full, rich, unconditional love from her mother, her grandmother, and these faithful friends. Loving hands had carried her along, unwilling to leave her behind, soothing her, accepting her, hurting with her. She had seen the face of God in these women. She would be this for Tonie, until she was able to recover from whatever her woes were and enter into the grace of God.

Amanda's friendship with Tonie had so many coincidences, their lives so many similarities, that she believed God had led them together for a reason. With Tonie, Amanda found a kindred spirit, their souls enmeshed as if they had been together throughout time. Tonie was a smart, deeply thinking woman, and to toss God off without thought did not ring true. It was this duality that revealed her true nature to empathetic Amanda.

She also pondered about Paul and his decision to tell Tonie he could not marry her because she was not a Christian, especially after being together for two years. Didn't he recognize that his fiancée was a passionate person who would be an inspirational force of God's love in this world once she delved into the heart of her issues? Was he right to reject being "unequally yoked" to a woman who apparently considered she had ample reasons to deem herself betrayed by God? How could he not see that she needed support, not condemnation?

There was no doubt in Amanda's mind that Tonie was a Christian, definitely an angry one, but surely a Christian. Her anger at God oozed from every pore in her body. The question wasn't whether she believed in God—it was why she was angry with Him. A true atheist wouldn't rail at a God she didn't believe in any more than she would search for fairies in the garden. That Paul was not able to discern this baffled Amanda, and she concluded that her friend was better off without someone so legalistic that he couldn't recognize true value when it was in his hand.

Good-hearted Amanda's reverie was interrupted by Tonie's return.

"Hellooo! I'm in the bedroom," she called out upon hearing the door open.

"Are you packing already?" Tonie asked as she entered the bedroom and saw the work in progress.

"Yes. We're leaving tomorrow so I'm getting everything organized."

"Fernand told me that Paul's brother called him, and he was able to obtain all Marc's work records and also some damning letters between Marc and Dr. Bonvalet talking about wanting to get rid of Paul. I offered to take them to Paul since you guys are going to Vienna tomorrow, so Fernand gave me all the stuff." Tonie offered this news with a casual air, expecting Amanda to be disapproving.

"Are you sure? It could wait until we get back. A couple days won't matter, and it is the holidays so nothing will come of this until next week anyway. Fernand said Paul called yesterday to see if he had heard from Lucas yet. He might call again tonight or tomorrow. I don't want you to be uncomfortable." Amanda eyed her carefully.

"No, it's okay. I need to make it normal to be around him since there's a good chance I'll end up running into him sometime once he's cleared of the charges. I don't know what his plans will be, but I don't want to have to avoid him from now on, especially if we get a job at the same university."

"Well, only if you're sure. It really wouldn't matter to wait a few days."

"I've always wanted to see London, and since I'll be in the neighborhood after I deliver the papers to Paul, I thought I could spend a few days there on my way home. I'm an avid Shakespeare fan, and I'd love to see a play at the Globe Theatre."

"That does sound fun. And you could tour the Tower of London and see where Richard the Third's nephews were imprisoned before he murdered them," Amanda proposed enthusiastically.

"And where Anne Boleyn's head was cut off," Tonie added cheerfully.

"All sorts of fun things!" They both laughed.

Tonie pulled her small roller bag out from under the bed and started packing alongside Amanda. In addition to having a good excuse to see Paul again, she mused, she would also have a chance to visit London where she had lived for so many years. She would look for the house where she lived with Isaac, and there would be no pain associated with it. All her memories of London were good. She would remember Flora and Esmée and walk around the places they used to go. She had assumed, then, that she would die within a few years. Maybe something in London held the secret to her destiny. You never knew what you would find when you snooped around a little bit.

She had found it immensely comforting to rediscover her family home here in Paris. Somewhere along the course of the past six months, she realized, her memories of Henri had softened. Instead of the searing pain of his loss, she remembered his sweet smile and baby laugh. She became thankful for the time she had with him instead of mourning the time that she would be without him. Maybe she would find a new direction by taking a trip into the past, if not the answer itself.

Chapter Nineteen

A CROSS THE CHANNEL, A YOUNG, BEARDED MAN stood on a park bench preaching to an eager crowd pressing in on him.

"The Bible teaches us, in Micah 7:8, to admonish the devil for gloating over us when we fail—'Do not gloat over me my enemy. Though I have fallen, I will rise. Though I sit in darkness, the Lord will be my light.' Friends, we have all fallen, and we will fall again, but we will never stay down because of God's immense love for us. He picks us up. He picks us up every time, no matter how many times we fall, because He loves us and will never give up on us."

Paul pointed directly at an unkempt man whose abode for years had been a sleeping bag under the bridge. "Jesus loves you, my brother."

"Amens" were heard throughout the crowd for the words of this compassionate, modern day John the Baptist who saw to the depths of their weary souls. Word had spread throughout the town of this fiery speaker who understood the trials of outcasts, misfits and poets, those who had endured the cruelties and fickleness of the world and were starving for the word of God. Each week, more and more of society's ugly ducklings thronged to the park to hear this man boldly proclaim that their Creator loved them, despite their sins and shortcomings and inability to measure up.

Along with the outcasts, professional men and women and everyday citizens, to whom the organized church offered up only a weak tea of Christ's teachings, all flocked to hear Paul's sermons. Those who had lost their faith with the passing of baskets, rock music performances, and blindly signing a check each month to be sent only who-knows-where, this man of God brought vitality to the meaning of Christ's sacrifice on the cross and revealed a purpose to their lives which had long been lacking.

On this particular Sunday the congregation was especially large. Paul walked through the people giving words of encouragement and hope. Some of the men tried to press money into Paul's hand, but he refused it, telling them, "I have enough to eat today, help the next man. You are the church. The church is the body of Jesus' followers. Go and spread the gospel of God's love."

Louie, Paul's friend from the boarding house, rushed up to him and said there was a rumor that the television news was on the way wanting a story on the phenomenon that was happening in this park—the growing crowds, the soup kitchens which had been set up owing to new-found faith, clothes swaps for the poor, doctors setting up free care in donated space. Paul glanced around and, spying a news truck, knew it was time for him to make a hasty departure.

These prayer sessions had started with Paul getting together with Louie and discussing life and God and the Bible. Louie had been a surgeon, fresh out of medical school, when he lost his first patient, a three year old boy with a metal shard impaled in his brain from a car accident. Louie had operated on him for hours and believed the tot would recover, but the little guy's brain became infected in the days that followed, and he died. Louie took the death hard, sure that he had not been careful enough to prevent the infection. Falling into a depression, he lost his nerve to see patients, eventually leaving the field and going bankrupt, losing his house and his wife. Infused with atheism all his life, the only prayer he had ever uttered was, "Oh God," when getting stopped at a red light. Paul's talk of Christ's love and redemption was a breath of fresh air for this drowning man, asphyxiating on his own guilt.

Then another man started joining in the conversations, and then another, until it became a daily appointment that brought meaning and focus into their lives, giving them a reason to get out of bed in the morning. Before long, Paul found himself planning talks around specific Bible passages to guide the group as it grew to twenty people, then fifty, and now probably two hundred or more on Sundays. Many of them were men down on their luck as Paul was, and a hitherto unknown world appeared before him—a slice of society coexisting alongside normal everyday activities, yet invisible if you weren't a part of it.

While Paul had formerly described himself as having endured hard times because of his lonely childhood years, his eyes were opened to a new level of pain. The pain of being perpetually the outsider, of never having been loved or having had opportunities. Paul grew up with food on the table, was provided shoes and clothes, and was taken to the doctor when he was sick. He had been expected to finish school. His parents loved him, maybe not as demonstrably as he would have preferred, but he was solidly supported.

Most of these men had lacked the basics of human existence as children—a loving voice waking you up in the morning, someone making sure you got to school every day and your homework done at night. In addition to missing the niceties of life that made a person feel safe and secure, many had also been heaped with abuse. His new friends spoke of spankings, shamings, cigarettes burned into their legs and their genitals violated. Paul knew he could never go back to his pampered life after having witnessed this devastation of the human soul. Only God was capable of restoring their sense of worth, and Paul knew it was his mission to share the love of Jesus with the town's rejected.

He had long pondered Tonie's remark about being arrogant. At the time, he judged her pronouncement as mean, that she was lashing out because they were in a fight. He had not realized the truth in it until the false accusation by Marc had led to his exile. How could this happen to him, he wondered, he who loved and served God? Wasn't he exempt from earthly trials, at least the big ones, by the fact that he was a Christian? But, with the staggering charges of attempted murder, his perception of life changed in an instant. Was his adversity any less fair than having a mental illness, or being born into an abusive family, or having a physical limitation? He joined the ranks of the world's unwanted, and his former inability to see them as whole people made him ashamed, and the minute he felt that shame he knew that indeed, God did love him, enough to reveal his sin of arrogance to him so that he could repent of it.

Paul exited the park through a back gate. A few scattered people hung back from the general throng. He turned to go down a side street to escape the media attention and ran straight into Tonie. She didn't recognize him with his tattered clothes, full beard and straggly hair. Should he say something? He hesitated for only a second.

"Tonie?"

She looked directly at him, confused. "Paul?"

"Yes, it is me. This is my disguise. I've grown my hair and beard to hide my identity. Did you come to see me?" He realized how strange he must look to her, while he viewed himself as more closely mirroring his true essence than ever before.

Tonie scrutinized him closely, making sure it really was him. Was this her beggar? She looked into his eyes, examining his beard. No, this was not the woodpecker. This was her Paul. These were his smiling eyes, always on fire with enthusiasm.

"Yes, I came to see you. I have news from your brother. Is there somewhere we can talk in private?"

Paul led her several blocks away to another park to be sure they were away from the news cameras.

"Your brother brought copies of letters and records that could clear your name. I have them here, and Lucas sent them to your lawyer in the U.S. It's possible that you can come out of hiding as early as in a few weeks. Fernand and Amanda have gone to Vienna for the New Year so I brought the news myself, so that you could know as soon as possible. How is your arm? The last time I saw you it was broken." Tonie knew she was babbling but felt compelled to fill the silence.

Paul took the papers and thumbed through them. "Oh, thank you. It is very kind of you to bring them to me. It looks like there is a lot of information here that will be helpful."

"I'm going to London for a few days, so it was easy for me to make the trip to Bath on my way. It was an enjoyable train ride over here. I'm going to look at the Roman Baths before I leave tomorrow."

"Well, it wasn't exactly on your way. I really appreciate it," Paul murmured, still reeling from the suddenness of seeing this woman he had dreamed about these past long months.

Tonie stood up to go. It was funny that there was much less to say than she imagined. She didn't know what she expected—maybe a friendlier greeting, an apology, maybe a look in Paul's eyes that she didn't get.

Paul rushed to say something before she left and he lost his chance. "Don't go yet, Tonie. I've wanted to talk to you for all this time, but I'm obviously not in a position to ask anything of you." Taking her arm, he seated her back on the bench.

"I'm very sorry about how things ended between us. I think the answer would have been to talk about our issues instead of getting in a huff like I did, and getting caught up in labels and following the letter of the law instead of the intent. You have a much more kind and loving heart than I do. It is easy for you to naturally do the right thing, and I've had to struggle with trying to follow rules. I measure myself by going down the list of the Ten Commandments and ticking off whether I succeeded or not, but I have learned that I don't have to be perfect—I just have to do my best."

Tonie sat stunned at Paul's description of her as having a kind and loving heart. She knew she had a hard and devious heart, and she squirmed under his obvious misperception of her.

Paul paused a moment, then continued. "Since having these accusations made against me and having to leave everything I love, I have come to the realization that God wants so much more than I ever conceived of. He is complete love and will not stop trying to refine me and make me whole. Not that I'm even close, but I now have a better concept. I love you, and my fear is that you will think I'm saying this because of my lonely situation, but it's not. Because of my situation I have learned and matured incredibly, and I want to see you again. Maybe when this is all over, we could have lunch together and talk about things that are important to us and get to know each other on a deeper level."

Tears rolled down Tonie's cheeks. "It is me who should apologize to you because I was wrong to criticize your faith. I don't know why I felt threatened. I wanted to hear about things that were meaningful to you, and then I would go and shut you down. I'm very sorry."

"No, it's me. I can be very bullheaded, and I know that I would become more aggressive when I thought you weren't agreeing with me, which was not fair to you, and then you needed to push back. I think that is what was happening."

They both laughed at their apology competition. Tonie knew it was vital to tell Paul the truth about her. To withhold it at this point, she feared, would be an unforgivable deception. She took a deep breath.

"I have a big secret, one that I always wanted to tell to you, but was afraid to because I was sure it would ruin our relationship, but since there is nothing more to lose, I will tell you." Tonie paused, trying to get her nerve. "It is hard to say it out loud because I think you will be horrified."

"Try me, Tonie," Paul gently reassured her.

"You have to promise to never tell anyone."

"I promise."

"I have a little brother who died…and I flipped out, and…and I loved him so much." Nothing condemning in that confession. A tiny step.

"And you blamed God?"

A bigger step, but she had boarded the train and its steaming momentum drug her half-willingly, half-helplessly, along. Tonie nodded. "I also have a daughter who died."

"I am so sorry. I didn't know."

"I also have a granddaughter, and you know her."

Paul's eyes grew confused.

"Amanda is my granddaughter. I am old, Paul. I was born in 1773 in Paris, and for some reason I have not aged or died. I am studying botany to try to find the answer in some berries that made me sick when I was eight years old. That was my whole reason for coming to Paris, to find those berries and find out if they contain anti-senescent properties, but they don't as far as I can tell."

"Does Amanda know this?"

"No. I'm afraid she'll think I am crazy, just as I am worried you will. But at this point, I don't want anything between us and, if we are going to be friends, or more, you need to know this, and it is you who will need to decide if you want to be with me, and whether you believe I am a crazy woman or...a very old woman."

Paul sat and digested this new information. He glanced at Tonie to see if any amusement danced in her eyes, or if she were on the brink of admitting it was all a joke, but she was crying.

"The only person I ever told was a girl," she continued, "actually here in Bath a long time ago, and I was put into a mental asylum for four years. It's funny that here I am in Bath admitting this again. There must be something in the air here that makes me confess."

Paul pondered for a few more minutes before he responded. "I need time to think about this and figure out what's going on. But I do know that, whatever is happening, I want to help you. This is a lot to take in all of a sudden, and it shakes up my reality, but I will help you."

"Thank you. It is so freeing to be able to share my secret with you. I feel like I'm in a dream, and when I wake up I will be alone again with myself for eternity."

"No, I will never leave you, believe that," promised Paul, whose head was swirling in incredulity.

These claims were beyond belief. His mind reeled in the juxtaposition of sane, sweet Tonie, whom he had known for two years, with the woman sitting in front of him wildly asserting she was hundreds of years old. He had never seen anything in Tonie that would make him believe she was mentally unbalanced. Beyond his first reaction of disbelief at seeing someone who lived and coped intelligently in the world leap into making outrageous claims that appeared to be complete lunacy, he experienced the feeling that this explanation made all the puzzle pieces regarding her tumble perfectly into place. But it couldn't be. His mind decisively rejected any reality of this being true, yet, the next minute he found himself considering its possibility.

"Let's take a walk," Paul suggested, hoping to restore some sense of normalcy to the crazy turn the conversation had taken. A man whose mind had the originality and audacity to challenge the accepted scientific view regarding the advent of humans on earth was not one to shy away from an equally mind-boggling allegation that humans may really be able to live far beyond the current life expectancy.

Chapter Twenty

P AUL RETURNED TO HIS ROOM THAT EVENING STILL perplexed whether he believed Tonie's story or not. Wandering through the town that afternoon, she had related many specifics of her long life. He had heard somewhere that you can tell when a person is lying because they will have too many details about an event, and Tonie certainly had incredible details. But, he argued with himself, since she expected her claim to be disputed, she therefore supplied as many as possible to add to her credibility. He hated that he didn't believe her, but it was too strange of a tale. Was she mentally ill from the trauma of her brother dying? She functioned in every other area of her life, though. Wouldn't he have noticed something else at some point? There was nothing in his experience to compare her assertions against.

Throughout the night he argued back and forth, examining both sides of the dilemma. Tonie did not seem crazy, but the revelation was crazy. Had something happened to her in the five months since they broke up? That was the most plausible, he decided. Yet, Fernand had never mentioned a fall or a hospitalization or anything that would have hinted at a problem. But Fernand was her friend and would be loyal, not willing to spread gossip to an ex-boyfriend.

By morning Paul was still not able to think his way through to an answer. Then the idea struck him to talk to a priest. They often had knowledge of old anecdotes, of old cures and potions, especially in these medieval churches where boxes of ancient writings lurked untouched in basements for centuries. If Tonie had lost her mind, then a priest may likely have a solution to bring her back to sanity. If she had a physical malfunction where her body no longer aged normally, then it had to have happened before, and who more than a priest would have heard these stories? They were the keepers of the wisdom of the ages. Scholars and doctors relied on new information and new discoveries, their feathers ruffled when it was suggested that an answer may lie in the past. Paul was an expert at finding old truths buried below the surface, of knowledge built on the shoulders of those who had gone before, and he decided that seeking out a priest would be his best source for a wealth of information without bias.

A man with a mission, Paul showered and trimmed his beard, pulling his grown-out hair back into a neat pony tail at the nape of his neck. He put on khaki slacks and a collared, tartan plaid shirt for the first time since his former life as a professor. Gone was the scraggly street preacher, and in his place emerged a handsome, well-groomed man. He walked the mile across town to Bath Abbey, remnants of which dated back to the 700s, but rebuilt and added on to throughout the years into the magnificent Gothic cathedral that it was today.

"You say that, according to her, she hasn't aged since she was eight years old when she ate some poisonous berries?" Father Damien reiterated, after listening to Paul's relating of Tonie's plight.

"Well, that's what she thinks may have caused the halt of her age progression. She is twenty-eight now, plus a couple hundred years, but looks and acts twenty-eight and says she will never look any older. Actually, she looks more seventeen. She's a young looking twenty-eight."

"And the greatest trauma of her long life is when her baby brother died when she was seventeen?"

A vague pit knotted itself in Paul's stomach with the correlation of Tonie's body age to the death of her brother. Father Damien wasn't taking the track that Paul was expecting.

"Yes," he focused on the question. "She said he was like her own. She was a midwife who delivered her own mother's child, and she did the majority of caring for him, and thought of him as her baby. When he died of diphtheria, she lost her faith in God."

"Did she blaspheme Him?"

"I don't know. I didn't think to ask such a question. What would that have to do with anything?" Paul was irritated. He had expected the short answer to be that Tonie was confused and needed a special prayer to be healed.

"I have only heard of one person before living perpetually on this earth," Father Damien avowed.

Paul's hopeful ears perked up.

"When Jesus was bearing his cross to the hill of Golgotha to be crucified, He stopped to rest for a minute on a wall in front of the house of the shoemaker, a Jew named Ahasuerus. Ahasuerus forbid him to rest there, and Jesus condemned the man to roam the earth, without dying, until His second coming. He is referred to as the 'Wandering Jew' in some circles. Many people deem it only a legend, but there are enough references to him throughout the ages that some, including myself, consider it to be a possibility that he wanders yet."

"This sounds pretty mystical. And Ahasuerus didn't blaspheme Jesus," Paul pointed out, "he begrudged him rest. Aren't the two things different?"

"He denied Christ. Did your girlfriend deny Christ? It sounds like she still does."

"Do you think that if Tonie blasphemed God when her brother died, that she is condemned to eternal life on earth? That would be," Paul stumbled over the words, "that she is in hell."

"Does it not sound like she is in hell?" the old priest queried. "If what she is describing—wandering this world aimlessly without purpose and without God—is not hell, then what is?"

Paul felt sick to his stomach. "Would there be no hope for her, then? What about Ahasuerus? Is his sentence finite? Will he be able to die once Christ comes again?"

"The legend is that he has, since that time, acknowledged Christ as the son of God, and he will be able to die when Christ returns, with the full rights of a child of God, one presumes. Over the years there have been several sightings of Ahasuerus...none at the mall though." The priest chuckled at his own joke.

"A lot of people must blaspheme God during their darker moments," Paul insisted, ignoring the joke. "If every one of them goes to hell before they die, as a still living person, then there must be all sorts of people walking around with the same curse as Ahasuerus, and, supposedly, Tonie."

"Many people do blaspheme God in the darkness of their despair, but most repent within a few minutes, or days at the most. Ahasuerus has had two thousand years to come to his senses, your Tonie a mere two hundred. No one else has ever come to me with this question. I will pray on this and study what I can to find out more. This is very interesting, yes, very interesting." Father Damien rose from his chair to inspect the books on his shelf. "There must be something here somewhere. I will talk also to the Bishop. He may know more than I do on this subject."

"What should I tell Tonie?" Concern furrowed Paul's brow.

"She needs to confess and be exorcised of her demons. Nothing can help her until she bows down before our Omnipotent Father. God is merciful and wants more than anything to receive a penitent soul back into His embrace. It would be my opinion that if there wasn't a chance for her then she would have lived her normal life, died, and then gone to hell. God wants her back in the fold and is giving her every chance. Every soul is as important to God as every other."

Paul left the meeting feeling uneasy. He knew Tonie would never agree to consider this a spiritual issue. He wasn't sure himself. Although, the priest didn't bat an eye—having an answer and an example. He never suggested that Tonie wasn't right in her head, or having delusions. He went straight to that she had denied Christ and was living in hell.

Walking back to the boarding house he pondered the alternatives and felt more stymied than before. Poisoned, crazy, or damned? Or a mutation? Just because Tonie's daughter had died, and Amanda had aged to nearly fifty years old so far, it didn't mean that it couldn't be a recessive mutated gene. That was easy enough to check. She could get a complete genetic screening to rule that out. The scientist side of Paul found this reason to be the most palatable, and he decided that he would broach it to Tonie when he met her later this morning. He didn't want her to think for a minute that he harbored any suspicions that she was crazy, although, the truth be told, that was at the top of his list.

Paul reveled in how good it felt to be dressed and neatly groomed again and feeling like his old self as he walked sprightly to the train station to meet Tonie. They were going to spend two days in London together. He carried a small backpack containing his toiletries and the all-important notebooks, and the papers that Tonie had brought to him yesterday. His eyes lit up when he saw her running towards him.

"Whoa, mister. You sure clean up nice." She smiled approvingly at the change in his persona. "I can get used to this."

Paul kissed her on the lips and half picked her up around her waist. She looked so normal that all his fears and trepidations of the long night, and priest's dire warning, evaporated at the sight of her. This was his Tonie, and he loved her regardless of what was happening in her life. He would find an answer for her.

They turned toward the station, arm in arm, laughing out of the happiness of being together again, the winter sun glinting off Tonie's shiny hair.

"Paul Delaney?"

Paul turned at the sound of his name, to find two men in black suits right behind him.

"You are under arrest for the attempted murder of Marc Diceccio," one man announced, while the other pulled the fugitive's arms to his back and slapped handcuffs around his wrists. The first man took his backpack and they led him away, leaving Tonie standing there stunned.

"Wait a minute," she yelled, running after them. "Where are you taking him?"

"To jail, Miss. This bird is finally getting his wings clipped, thanks to you."

Paul turned his head as the policemen lowered him into the back seat of a black car. "Tell Louie at the boarding house what has happened to me," he called out. Then the door slammed and the car sped away.

Shocked at the suddenness of this development, Tonie realized she must have been followed all the way to Bath. Marc had probably been camped outside her apartment all this time. How could she have been so blind, she castigated herself. Then a new thought entered her mind...the beggar! This must mean that her woodpecker really was a spy after all and not an immortal. The lost hope of finding someone just like her flooded over her and she felt duped, and disappointed. No wonder she could never find him again—the whole time she was trying to find him he must have been following her. It explained the contradiction in his appearance. He was watching her all this time, and now she had led him straight to his target.

Furious with herself, she set off to find Louie and explain to him that his friend had been arrested. She had heard Louie's story from Paul, and, upon meeting him, was struck by his conscientious and gentle nature. He had a poet's vulnerability, and she understood why losing his little patient would have broken him.

Louie suggested they go to the park to talk, as there was no visiting area in the boarding house, and he didn't think it proper to have her in his tiny bedroom. Tonie shivered, not used to doing most of her living outside in the elements.

"I will check on him at the jailhouse this afternoon," Paul's loyal friend promised when they had seated themselves on a freezing bench. "They will have to do all

NETTIE AT THE WELL

their paperwork, and I doubt he will get a visitor, but I will find out how they plan to proceed."

"Thank you. There is new evidence in the case, so it is my opinion that he probably will be released very soon."

"I don't know if Paul told you anything about me, but I wanted to let you know that he helped me in the darkest hours of my life, and led me out of despair and into the healing of my spirit. Every Sunday I watch and listen to him preach to the crowds, and I see folks who were without hope come alive. He has changed lives and helped so many people."

"He preaches to crowds?"

"Yes," Louie inspected her like she must be an alien from outer space to not know of Paul's super-stardom in the small town. "I met Paul when he moved into the boarding house, and we started meeting in the park every day to discuss life. Then other guys started hanging around, guys who had had some bad breaks in life. Our group became larger and larger with people clamoring for Paul to teach them about God, and he rose to the occasion. They call him the Park Preacher."

"He has a name?"

"Yes. The media came looking for him yesterday because he is getting to be well known, but he snuck out the back before they found him. I guess it didn't do any good because the police caught him anyway."

Tonie stood up to go. Louie shook her hand and thanked her for telling him about his friend's arrest. She pondered the new life Paul had created here. Instead of wallowing in self-pity at the unfairness of fate and living in fear of the future, he had done something meaningful. He transformed other people's lives and helped himself at the same time. Was that the difference between her and him, Tonie wondered? What had she ever done to help anyone but herself?

Running to catch the afternoon train to London, she knew there was nothing else to be done here and decided to go on back to Paris, not having the heart to tour around London now that Paul was in jail. The emotional upheaval of having divulged her secret also weighed heavily on her and she wanted to go home.

Paul's lawyer would be notified, and he would be extradited to France. Her only consolation was that the information gathered by Lucas should serve him well when this went to trial, therefore hopefully limiting his jail time. She kicked herself for her part in Paul's arrest. Since Fernand had safely visited the banished man several times, she had overlooked that her connection to him was known, while the professor's was not. It didn't help that she had been ruled by her heart instead of her head, blinding her to the danger of making the trip herself.

Once on the train, a new worry hit her. Would Paul think she had deliberately sabotaged him and led the police to him? What if he presumed that this was her way to get even with him for breaking up with her? But, she calmed herself, there would be no point to bring him the very papers that would prove his innocence and bring the law at the same time. As soon as his attorney received the papers after the holidays they would work on having the charges dismissed, and he would be free. Holding on to that assurance, Tonie relaxed and enjoyed the passing scenery, confident in Paul's positive reaction to her secret.

Chapter Twenty-One

T ONIE, AMANDA AND FERNAND WAITED EXPECTANTLY outside the courthouse until a triumphant Paul emerged smiling, and, catching their faces in the crowd, waved to his loyal supporters. Microphones were thrust in his face, reporters asking how it felt to be exonerated of all charges and finally be a free man, and whether he would be testifying against Professor Diceccio now that Marc was the one in custody charged with attempted murder. Paul did not slow down to answer, but made a beeline toward the face of the one he loved best. Picking Tonie up, he twirled her in a circle and kissed her, then hugged his friends who had stood by him throughout his ordeal.

Handsome and distinguished in a tailored black suit, he still wore the beard and pony tail, giving him the aura more of an artist than a scientist. Mr. and Mrs. Delaney and brother Lucas pressed through to greet him, the men slapping him on the back, Mrs. Delaney crying while dabbing carefully at her eyes with a kleenex to avoid smudging her makeup.

Missing from the crowd was the new head of archeology, Dr. Pascale, who was taking Dr. Bonvalet's place while an investigation was pending to determine his part in the murder plot. Paul did not note this omission until later, then pondered over the meaning of it until he finally concluded that the new director may have wanted to begin his tenure by avoiding all political affiliations.

A celebratory dinner at an expensive restaurant was enjoyed by all, paid for by the liberated man's ecstatic father. After the hoopla died down, and Paul's family retired to their hotel, he and Tonie walked along the Seine, hand in hand, relaxed and content in each other's presence. During the month that passed since her confession to Paul, Tonie began having misgivings about telling him her secret. There had not been time for her to assess his true reaction, and her fear was that he may have decided, with no balancing information, that she was nuts. But now his apparent pleasure to see her was comforting.

"I've been contemplating your dilemma all this time, trying to figure out the best route to solve whatever is going on," Paul offered.

"And you don't think I am crazy?" Tonie teased, afraid of the answer.

"No, I think you are wonderful. Is Amanda home tonight?"

"No. She and Fernand are going to the opera. La Flûte Enchantée is playing at the Palais Garnier."

"Can we go to your apartment and talk? We've got lots of catching up to do."

In letters to each other during Paul's incarceration, the couple had promised to take things slowly when they were eventually reunited, and that Paul would stay with Fernand while he looked for his own apartment. So now, upon entering his former home scoured of any hint of his presence, his room feminized with Amanda's belongings, a wave of nostalgia came over him. He sat on the couch where he had last lain with his broken arm after the attempt on his life. Tonie brought them cups of hot tea from the kitchen.

"Tonie," Paul took her hands as she sat down beside him. "Let's get married tomorrow. Our paperwork is ready and waiting. My family is here. What are we waiting for?"

"Well, I don't have a dress anymore," Tonie admitted.

"You don't need a dress," Paul insisted. "We'll get married at city hall, and we can have a church wedding in the summer when we will have time to arrange it. My life has been on hold for too long. I want to marry you and I always have. One lesson I've learned these past few months is that life is too short and too fickle to put things off until the timing is perfect, because no timing will ever be perfect." Paul put his hand in his pocket and pulled out the art-déco miniature hatbox. "Here, I still have the ring."

Charmed, Tonie let him put it on her finger. "You are a hopeless romantic, you know."

"It's because I'm in love with you, and I'm not letting you get away again."

Two weeks later, the new husband sped along on a train to Marseille for a meeting with Dr. Pascale to discuss the organization of personnel at the dig, leaving his sweet bride alone in the apartment they had found just a few blocks away from their old one. Paul was antsy to get back to work, hoping the months he was gone had been well managed and that no artifacts had been lost. He trusted that Dr. Pascale would be a man of integrity who would not easily be hoodwinked.

A secretary ushered Dr. Delaney into a plush office with windows overlooking the sparkling waters of the Old Port of Marseille, seating him across from Bonvalet's replacement at a polished oak desk, ornate with two computers.

"I'm sorry to say that we will not be sending you back to the excavation," Dr. Pascale got right to the point. "There are too many factions and alliances surrounding you and Diceccio, so I'm of the opinion that it would be prudent to assign completely new people to lead this dig. I've talked to the dean of your university, and he is offering you paid leave until next fall, when you will resume your teaching responsibilities. I do believe there is a settlement package to compensate for your hardship and suffering during the time you were falsely accused. You will need to contact them for the details. I want to thank you for your excellent work on this project. From all I've gleaned from your colleagues, it was your insight that led to the discovery of the second settlement. I appreciate the scholarly hypotheses you contributed regarding the dating of the two sites. It's always good to have someone who thinks 'outside the box,' as they say." The dean was brusque and fast in his speech, and seemed like he considered this the end of the conversation.

"Those were the dates that came back from the lab, and there is substantial evidence supporting them," Paul felt the need to defend himself. "They later came to be changed in Marc's data, but the original numbers are easily obtainable from the lab."

"Oh? I did not realize that. I will look into it." Dr. Pascale rose and reached his hand out to Paul. "It has been very nice meeting with you. I am sorry for the inconvenience you have been put through. Hopefully the courts will sort things out."

The fired professor walked out of the building, his face burning. "I've been brushed off like a buzzing fly," he disbelievingly comprehended. "Brushed off and bought off. He has no intention of ever publishing the truth." There would be no checking dates with the lab. The lab had probably already changed them. His mind slowly grasped the extent of the cover up. Pascale acted like this was a spat between schoolboys and that he was as much at fault as Marc.

Paul stomped through the streets of Marseille back to his hotel, frustrated with the direction of his life for the past year, disgusted with the academic world, disgusted with rigid minded pseudo-scholars who couldn't see past their arrogant noses. An ugly side of life was rearing its head…again. He preferred to think people were basically good at heart, but in the last year, time and again, he had witnessed a darker side to humanity. First, Marc trying to kill him—he would never have guessed that—then the horrific lives lived by so many of the men he preached to in Bath. And now, Dr. Pascale. Paul's world once again turned upside down, just when he deemed he had reestablished his equilibrium.

During his time in Bath, Paul had itched to get back to work, eager to continue enticing the past to relinquish its secrets. Now, stumbling in confusion, he wondered where God was leading him. How could it not be God's will that he reveal what he learned from the two fossil communities, proving God's hand in the history of the human race? This would lead thousands, if not millions, to Christ. Through the years, so many people had been led astray and away from God by the error of the theory of evolution, and now here was evidence of its fallacy, and he was blocked from spreading its truth.

The disgruntled professor picked up his suitcase at the hotel and walked to the train station. After that record-setting short meeting there was time to catch the afternoon TGV back to Paris and no need for a hotel after all. Paul had come with the expectation of a lengthy conversation outlining his new leadership role, of conferring with Pascale over dinner the significance of the startling findings at the dig, an in-depth discussion of the direction of the research and then spending the night and going home the next day. Paul had imagined telling of his six months in exile and his profound self-discoveries. But now he felt like cussing just to improve the taste in his mouth, reeling from the lengths that the scientific world was willing to go to protect their ability to manipulate the beliefs of the population.

Back home again, the unemployed man ranted to his wife about his frustration with the path of his professional life.

"I don't understand. This discovery is huge. Why wouldn't God want the information out there, even if there are corrupt people in positions of power trying to keep it hidden? I'm not sure what I can do now. Anything I publish on my own will be disregarded, and I would probably be fired from the job I do have if I contradict the formal account. I really felt that it was my mission to tell this truth. I was put in the right place at the right time, to prove what I have believed for years, and now it has come to nothing."

Tonie listened intently to Paul, then inserted her thoughts. "From my point of view it would prove that there was no mission; the fact that you were almost murdered and then were fired from your job would show that it was nothing all along, however ..."

"We agreed to keep our religious opinions to ourselves," Grumpy Gus interrupted.

"First, you are not keeping your opinions to yourself," Tonie shot back. "How many times have you said the word 'God' in the past ten minutes? Second, I wasn't finished talking, but now I'm not going to tell you my ideas because I think you are rude." She irately folded her hands across her chest and quit talking. Since his return she had noticed that their agreement to be respectful of each other's opinions was sadly one-sided.

"I'm sorry, you are right. Go ahead and give me your opinion, and I'll be quiet."

"If you are going to roll your eyes at me, then I'm not saying anything. But I'm not listening to your god-talk anymore, either."

"No, really, I'm sorry, and I realize the error of my way. I confess that I was asking you to consider something you don't believe." Paul dramatically made a flowery show of his apology.

"You may not 'confess,' you may 'admit.' That's just more god-talk."

"You are a hard woman to bargain with, Tonie. Okay, I admit I was forcing God down your throat and hoping you wouldn't notice."

"Thank you," she accepted, slightly mollified. "To continue what I was going to say, from my understanding of your God, back when I did believe there was such a thing," Paul rolled his eyes again but kept quiet, "is that God wanted people to believe in Him through faith, not by sight. Wasn't it Thomas who said he would not believe Jesus had come back to life until he touched the scars on His hands? And Jesus said something to the effect that blessed are those who believe and have never seen?"

The man of God stared, stunned, at this woman of little faith who had just preached truth to him. He wavered for a moment between pride and humility, not wanting to accept a Biblical insight from a heathen, especially one who had just called him on his overbearingness. But his honest side won out, and he was overwhelmed with the clarity of the situation.

CHAPTER TWENTY-ONE

"That's exactly it, isn't it?"

"Could be. Not that I know anything about God's ways," Tonie sniffed, not wanting to seem to be promoting God.

The new wife was now realizing the source of her former resentment toward Paul when he touted his religion. She was expected to nod and agree, but was never allowed to give her view of a world without God. Amanda had said this, and it was true, and she was beginning to fear that their incompatibility was truly insurmountable. Marrying hastily after Paul's acquittal, their absence from each other seemingly solving their differences, the couple were now coming face to face with their original core of contention.

With Tonie's remark regarding why his discoveries were covered up, Paul realized the truth of it and knew with certainty that they would never come to fruition. Physical proofs never lead to faith, and without faith one would never know God. The magnitude of the importance of faith to God shook him. Everyone, including him, struggled with the why of God's methods, not understanding that when things went wrong and seemingly didn't make sense, they were judging the situation using a human yardstick, while God used a different standard. Paul's faith took a giant leap as his mind opened to the overarching purposes of God. Glimpses into His true nature winked on and off with blinding light, too unfathomable to completely grasp.

Tonie's insight of why he kept hitting a brick wall with his discoveries also led him to the idea that maybe the root of her time issue was that she had cursed God like the priest suggested. She would not have this much knowledge of the Bible, and such insightful application, if she had not at one point been faithful. Paul did not believe she was older than twenty-eight, but surmised, perhaps, that there was a likelihood that she had quit believing when her brother died and was slowly becoming mentally ill from her defection. It occurred to him that she may not be an atheist at all—just angry, and now on a downward path to hell with her determination to deny God.

With this new analysis, Paul set out to find a good psychologist. In addition, he would share more of his faith with her, he determined, not less like he had been trying to do in order to avoid offending her. He would show her how his hardships this past year had caused him to grow into a stronger person, and how she could let her brother's death change her for the better, into a more intimate relationship with God, like his ordeal had for him.

Her husband launched into his mission to find help for his spiritually lost mate with all the zeal that he had formerly applied to his work. With nothing to do all day—for the first time since his childhood—this new project brought him a sense of purpose and direction. He finally had a theory that was acceptable to him after unsuccessfully flailing about for answers to Tonie's ailment. He was determined to save her—she would be healed and they would live happily ever after.

Chapter Twenty-Two

S TANDING IN THE BATHROOM, TONIE STARED AT the stick in her hand as she watched the plus sign gain in prominence. A knot tightened in her stomach. After missing her second monthly period, it slowly dawned on her that she might be pregnant. How could this have happened? She, the former midwife who had been so very careful throughout the years with her potions and acacia pessary, had thrown caution to the wind that night after the festivities of her impromptu nuptials to Paul, and now stood facing the consequences of her abandon.

She had been increasingly regretting her decision to tell Paul her secret. His eyes betrayed that he did not believe her, and his tone toward her anymore, while caring, was condescending. The worst thing was that he had become completely obnoxious about his faith, wearing a superior air in every conversation, dripping with Bible references and wisdoms the same way that some women drip with diamonds to demean a friend in her fake pearls.

Pregnant. To tell or not to tell. She would be bound to him forever if he knew of this child. Well, for the next twenty years anyway. As things stood, she didn't care to spend another twenty seconds with him. But, in spite of the entanglement of a baby in an unstable marriage, a tiny tickle of hope bubbled up inside of her, too small to define, a mysterious something.

When baby Emily was born she had tried to resist, without success, becoming attached to her. While wanting a baby for Thomas's sake, throughout the pregnancy she had locked her heart with a heavy chain, determined that no imp of a child would ever steal it again. But, even with all that resolve, she had fallen in love at the first sight of her red and squalling newborn. And now, instantly in love from only the testimony of a line on a stick, her biggest fear was that Paul would claim she was mentally ill and try to take her baby from her. Maybe he should have an accident, Tonie ruminated in the darkness of that thought. She had killed before and wasn't opposed to killing again if the need arose.

Finally released from the Bath asylum, Nettie tears out of town like a mad woman, only stopping long enough to retrieve the satchel full of money that she buried in the woods years earlier. Safely back in London, she becomes a young girl again and tries to establish her midwifery practice. However, times have changed, and she must now become certified to be allowed to work as a midwife in the city, so she hastily enrolls in a formal training program. Upon completion of the program, the headmistress is impressed with her natural talent and asks her to become a childbirth trainer for the school. This new professional career enables her to keep regular hours for the first time in her life, and she takes on fewer patients of her own. It also allows her to become an "old maid" acceptably, with a career replacing a husband and family.

One night while sleeping in her bed, Nettie is awakened by a man banging on the door and shouting that he needs a midwife. Grabbing her bag, she follows the gruff, silent man to his small farm on the outskirts of town. Once there, he leads her inside to a young girl, explaining that his wayward daughter has gotten herself in trouble and is such a whore that she doesn't even know who the father of her baby is.

Nettie sets to work caring for the girl, banishing the man to the barn for the duration to escape his tirades and judgments.

"What's your name, sweetie?" the midwife asks tenderly, at once discerning that the mum-to-be looks awfully young to be a whore.

"Elsa," she timidly answers.

"How old are you, Elsa?"

"Thirteen."

"Do you know who the father of your baby is?" Nettie knows that many unmarried women in the later stages of labor are easily coaxed into divulging the name of their lover.

Fear shows in the girl's eyes, but she slowly nods.

"Can you tell me his name?"

Elsa shakes her head no.

"Is it your beau? I promise I won't tell anyone. I had a beau when I was your age."

"I can't tell you. I'll get beat."

A warning bell sounds in Nettie's head. "Why?" she gently encourages.

"It's my father," Elsa whispers, staring at the door to make sure it stays closed.

"Your father is the father of your baby?" Nettie asks to affirm that she heard right.

The girl squeezes her eyes shut to hide her shame and nods.

"How long has he been doing this to you?"

"Since I was eight, and now he hurts my little sister, too. I tried to protect her, but he beat me."

"Where is your mother? Can she do anything to stop him?"

"She went away when I was nine."

"Did she know that your father hurt you like this?"

"She came around to the back of the barn one time when he was doing it, and she screamed at him, and then the very next day she ran off with another man and left all of us, and we ain't never seen her since."

Nettie asks no more questions, but soon delivers Elsa of a tiny, but healthy, baby girl. The new mother cries and asks how she will be able to protect her daughter as she grows. Grandpa-father comes back in and eyes the infant, calls his daughter names again, then stomps out.

Nettie packs up and leaves, after promising the new mother that she will be back in two days to check on her.

The furious midwife uses those days to make her plan. At the appointed time she returns to the farm, glancing surreptitiously around the property for a hidden grave before going in the house. From years of hiding buried money, she knows the art of making dirt mounds blend in with their surroundings, and, lo and behold, down beside the creek is a barely perceptible human-sized grassy mound covered with thick blackberry bushes. Once inside the house, she notes a gun mounted over the doorway.

Nettie swears she will stop this despicable man who rapes his daughters and murdered his wife when she caught him, and who now has an endless supply of little girls with no one to come between them and him—except her.

Approaching Mr. Harvey in the front room after examining Elsa and the baby, the midwife lies, "Elsa is having unusual pain, and I fear that it may be childbed fever. I want to take her and the baby to a doctor in London."

"She was fine yesterday," the old lout grunts.

"That is the nature of puerperal fever," Nettie patiently explains, using the formal name of the disease to add emphasis. "It comes on in one to two days after birth, and it kills quickly, usually within the week. There is a hospital that will treat her without any cost to you, and without any prejudice toward Elsa for being an unwed mother."

"T'would serve her right to die."

"Now, Mr. Harvey," she gently admonishes. "Young girls fall in love easily, and these things happen. In my profession we see a lot of it. I'll take them in my motor car. Would you like me to watch Effie also, so you will be able to work without worrying about her? It will be no trouble at all, and she would be a comfort to her sister. As soon as Elsa makes improvement I will bring all the girls happily home again."

"Keep the lot of 'em for all I care. Girls ain't nothin' but trouble." Grandfather Harvey walks outside, letting the door slam behind him.

Nettie settles the children into the buggy, having instructed Elsa to clutch at her stomach and look pained, then drives off.

With the three "sisters" safely installed in her home, the next evening Nettie walks the mile to the Harvey house to pay a visit to their father.

After giving Mr. Harvey a fictitious update on Elsa's condition, she offers to make a cup of tea for him, which he gladly accepts in his lonely state. A few minutes later his eyelids flutter, he develops a glassy stare, then he falls right off his chair with a dead thud onto the floor.

"Hmm," Nettie sniffs, "I think the poor man had a heart attack." She gathers up the potions into her bag, rinses out their cups and puts them back in the cupboard. Glancing around to be sure she is leaving no trace of herself, she closes the door behind her and walks home in the dark.

Elsa, Effie and baby Emma become Nettie's nieces and live with her until Elsa marries six years later, at which time the new Mrs. goes to live with her barrister husband in central London, taking her sisters with her.

Remembering that wretched man, Tonie regretted her ominous thoughts toward Paul and scolded herself for projecting such dark motives on him. Paul was a good and honest man who would never do anything to hurt her. Then, it struck her that her husband would be horrified to know that she had intentionally killed someone, however much it was deserved. That was one event that she had kept secret from him even in her overwhelming hunger for closeness.

How different their lives were, she brooded. He could never understand the small concessions to dishonesty and indiscretions that an abnormal life such as hers necessitated. If he were to know the real her he would run screaming into the night, and, that he would pry and prod until everything came out she was sure. True intimacy would never be hers. She had revealed her secret for nothing but condemnation. Again.

Tonie retreated to the murkiness of skepticism rather than face the bright, bold spotlight of shame highlighting her unlovableness. If God couldn't even love her, how could Paul? How much better to deny them both before being washed out in a tide of rejection. Isaac and Thomas loved her because they didn't know her—only the persona she had created and presented to them as the real her. But Paul wanted something more and kept digging for it, and she had mistakenly revealed too much.

Tonie's mind flitted around the circuitous path of her worry, finally deducing that with Paul's failure to be able to mold her into a suitable partner, he would quickly grow dissatisfied with their marriage, then leave and take her baby with him.

With what she viewed as his impending desertion, the weary spouse devised a plan to leave her husband. Offended by his constant efforts to push his religion on her, she decided she could not tolerate it anymore and must confront him. First though, she would discuss her plight with clear-headed Amanda. Amanda loved her as she was, while she felt like Paul needed to shape her to his liking in order to love her. Having no notion how much her husband bent to accommodate her searing disapproval of his faith, she ascertained only her own discomfort.

With her decision made, Tonie threw the pregnancy stick into the trash and called Amanda to meet for lunch. Her granddaughter arrived, cheerful and chatty, filling Tonie in on the wedding planning that was steaming full bore ahead. Tonie listened with enthusiasm and proposed going wedding dress shopping soon. Then she told Amanda she needed to discuss an important issue with her.

"Of course, sweetie," Amanda replied, having noticed that Tonie seemed agitated lately. "I hope everything is going all right between you and Paul?"

"No, it's not. We don't seem to get along anymore. I would leave him except for the fact that I'm...well, I'm pregnant."

Amanda's eyes opened wide. "And you want to leave him? Have you told him that you're pregnant?"

CHAPTER TWENTY-TWO

"No. I'm not sure I want to tell him if I'm going to divorce him."

"But why? You've only gotten married. You two need to adjust to married life, that's all. He will be a good father. While I don't necessarily believe a child needs two parents if one is unloving or abusive, I do think two loving parents are a plus. Don't you think Paul will be a good father?"

"I do think he would be, but I'm also worried that he will try to take the baby away from me if we divorce, and I don't want him insisting we stay married just because I'm pregnant."

"Why do you want to divorce him?" Amanda reiterated, still not understanding.

"I know that, in his heart, he holds that I'm defective, that there is something wrong with me that he needs to fix, and I don't like that. I snip back at him, and then I don't like myself. I'm tired of all the turmoil—from his disapproval of me to my disappointment in myself. I think we bring out the worst in each other. He is a wonderful man for someone else. I wanted to leave him before I found out I was pregnant, and now this adds a complication. We got married in the excitement of being together again after the trauma of his exile and trial. If I don't tell him I'm pregnant and we separate, then he will go back to the U.S. I'll stay here and he will never know. Isn't that better than having to share a child across the continents?"

Amanda pondered this skeptically. "Why would he think you're defective? Have you talked to him about how he treats you, and that you don't like it?"

"We fight about it, but it seems to add fuel to his condescension toward me. I shared a dark secret about my past with him, and now it's being held against me. I should have never shared it, but with our marriage talk I wanted everything out in the open."

"Oh, fiddlesticks. Everybody has done things they are ashamed of," Amanda nodded her head indicating herself. "Everybody. And even him. Have you tried sitting down together and having an honest conversation, explaining that his judgment is hurting you?"

"Well, maybe I could talk to him calmly and explain my issues, but still not tell him I'm pregnant, and see where we get. I don't trust him enough to tell him. Maybe I would be more objective if I didn't feel so trapped."

"I think that's a good idea. You've got a little while before you'll need to say anything about the baby. And Tonie, it really takes a lot of adjusting at the beginning of a marriage." Amanda paused a moment then focused on the new little person who would soon be among them. "Can I tell Fernand that you're pregnant? I'm so excited!"

"Yes, you can tell him if he absolutely promises to not tell anyone." Tonie smiled in spite of herself, happy that someone was glad for her. "I'm two months along."

Amanda hugged her. "Everything will be okay, Paul or no Paul. Fernand and I will be Grandma and Grandpa, and we will take care of you."

Tears rolled down the expectant mother's face. "Thank you, sweet Amanda. These are tears of joy, really. I'm surprised, and overwhelmed, and, well ..."

"You're pregnant. Pregnant women cry and don't know why," Amanda laughed and hugged her again. "You will be a fantastic mother!"

Chapter Twenty-Three

S ITTING AT THE TABLE WAITING FOR PAUL, TONIE inhaled the soft, courage-laden air of spring, searching for its strength to carry her forward in the dreaded conversation that lay before her. She glanced around at the happy couples enjoying lunch together, imagining that their most pressing concerns were what to have for dinner, or where they would go off to for the weekend, or whether they should move to the suburbs now that they had kids. No one appeared to be discussing any earth-shattering woes that had just landed on their doorstep.

A week of indecision and second-guessing herself had weakened her resolve to talk to Paul about their differences, but she knew she must. She shuddered, knowing there would be a final decision made from this conversation. For as much as she had sworn she would not get attached to Paul for fear of eventually being abandoned by his death, here she was, emotionally abandoned, which hurt just as much. One more loss to add to the heap, Tonie bitterly assessed. Would she have to bury her baby someday? And Amanda? She would be destroyed and couldn't stand it, but if she dwelled on it she would go insane. Anguish and immortality locked arms against her as she desperately tried to choke back her rising despair.

Paul breezily walked up and kissed her before he sat down, deepening the schism in Tonie's mind between what his real feelings were and what were merely her fears. Before she could lose her nerve, the fearful wife dove into the churning waters of her turmoil with the unformed hope that Paul would somehow solve everything for her.

"Paul, I have felt that ever since I confided my longevity to you, that you have changed your mind about wanting to be with me. I sense your disapproval keenly, and I want you to know that you are free to go. I do not blame you at all. I believe you are a loyal man who would stand by a woman with the normal gamut of problems, but I am way beyond that and to ask you to stay is more than you bargained for." She paused, waiting for his passionate denial of her fears.

Surprise crossed Paul's face. "Whoa. Your monologue reads like a 'Dear John' letter. Are you wanting to get rid of me?"

"I'm tired of being dealt with like there is something wrong with me. It's your behavior that is making me think that you want out, and if you want out, then I don't want to keep you here."

Paul reeled in the blast of this unexpected declaration, trying to regain his bearings. He finally raked his hands through his hair and answered.

"I have tried everything I know to help you. I have talked to priests and psychologists. The psychologists think you need therapy; the priests think you need God. I've researched mutant longevity, but you already know the answer to that. You push me away and resent any help I try to suggest. I don't know what to think or to say anymore. You don't seem to like me, everything I do irritates you. I'm not sure what you want."

"I want to live my life, get old, and die like any normal person, and for some reason that is denied me. I don't expect you to solve the problem for me. I just wanted you to love me without having to keep this god-damned secret another minute." Anger flashed hot through her veins. Paul's frustration was palpable, and it scared her.

"You tell me that you are hundreds of years old, and then we're supposed to carry on like nothing is wrong? I happen to agree with the priests and psychologists—you need help. But you are hell-bent on denying God and won't even entertain the idea that maybe ..."

"Plenty of people don't believe in God, and it doesn't mean they are crazy."

"No, but none of those people claim to have been born before the French Revolution."

"So, you do think I am crazy? You said you didn't."

"I don't. I think you are possessed by demons that make you believe you are that old. I think that the death of your brother derailed you, you got mad at God and turned your back to Him—leaving you ripe pickings for the devil. My opinion is that all mental illness stems from a wrong relationship with God, but my hope would be that with therapy you could get close enough to reality to recognize your spiritual issues. Won't you at least talk to someone and try?"

"What kind of double-talk is that? That would mean I'm crazy."

"I mean that I think that you don't have to be this way. The devil is messing with your mind."

"You think I'm possessed by demons, but you're saying I'm the crazy one?" Tonie sighed. Why oh why did she ever tell him?

"Do you want to know what the priest at Bath Abbey said when I went to talk to him after you told me? He said you were damned to hell. I asked him, isn't there any chance of your salvation? And he said only if you turn to God. I can't make you do that, Tonie, and heaven knows I've tried. I am with you, I want the best for you, but you are pushing me away." Paul searched her face pleadingly.

Tonie struggled to maintain a calm demeanor, the priest's pronouncement clanging in her ears.

"Of course a priest would say I'm damned to hell, but what about you? Do you think so too? I'm crazy, and I'm damned?" This was beyond the crossroad that she had dreaded. She had been hoping somehow she was mistaken in her assessment of their relationship, but here were Paul's true feelings—even worse than she imagined.

"Tonie, I'm willing to help you, but you've got to be willing to help yourself. I'm at my wit's end. Won't you see a psychologist?"

"I'm through with this conversation, and I'm through with you." Rising from the table, she stormed off in a huff, overcome by fury. Déjà vu swept over her. Hadn't they just done this? This time she would not try to throw herself in the river, but she felt like throwing him in. She knew he would go straight to the bottom. She congratulated herself for having had the insight to not trust him with the information of her baby. At least she had learned something in her long life.

Fuming through the streets of Paris, Tonie ranted in her mind about what an unreasonable man Paul turned out to be, and berated herself for ever trusting him with her secret. Demons! What a religious fanatic—and he was calling her nuts. The memory of her breakdown in front of Amanda seared its way to the forefront of her mind. Amanda had said that she had been released from demons. And it was true that she had felt much better for a long time after that—even though she still knew how old she was.

It struck her in a flash. She was crazy. She stopped walking and held her head. She was crazy and didn't know who she was. Moaning, she sank to the ground by the Place Dauphine. Who was she? Her past was not her past, and she did not know who she was. She was not Antoinette, born in Paris a long time ago. No wonder she couldn't figure anything out. She was a crazy woman full of wild stories. Had she escaped from the asylum and imagined all these years in her head? She rocked herself back and forth, moaning and crying. People stopped to help her, and soon an ambulance siren warbled in the air around her. Her world was black and she could not see. She threw up into the grass and wondered if her pregnancy was real or a part of the crazy. She swirled down into a world of darkness and agony.

Amanda raced into the hospital, stopping at the front desk to get Tonie's room number, then hurried up the elevator to her floor. All the nurse had said on the phone was that Tonie had been admitted to the hospital Hôtel-Dieu next to Notre Dame. Amanda's first thought was of the baby and feared that Tonie was having a miscarriage. She was met at the elevator by a nurse who took her aside and explained what had happened.

"What about the baby? Did she lose the baby?"

"We were not aware she is pregnant. She didn't say anything about that, but she was incoherent when they brought her in. We gave her sedatives and she is quiet now. She has not had a miscarriage since she's been here," the nurse assured her. "You may see her."

Amanda peeked into the room and saw Tonie lying quietly on the bed. She walked over to her and stroked her hair. "How are you, sweetie?"

Her afflicted friend turned to her with tortured eyes. Tears streamed down Amanda's cheeks at the sight of her. "What happened, sweetie? Can you tell me? Is it the baby?"

Baby. Tonie latched on to that word. The baby must be real then, and she recognized her granddaughter, well, who she had believed was her granddaughter.

"What's my name?" she rasped out.

"You are Antoinette Stevens. My sweet Tonie, I call you." Amanda tried to smile through her tears.

"That's not my name. I've been lying to you."

"What is your name?"

"I don't know. That's why I think I say it is Tonie."

"Did you have a fight with Paul? What happened when you met with him today?"

Paul. Tonie tried to place which story he was in. "Is Paul real? He told me I was crazy, and I didn't believe him, but now I do. But I don't know which stories in my head are real and which aren't. I can see that you are real, and the baby is real. But how do I know that is true, either?" Tonie became agitated and started moaning loudly, trying to get up.

"You are not crazy, sweetheart," Amanda held her. "You've had a shock, and you'll be all better in a little bit. You've just had a shock, but you are fine. I'm going to sing you a song that my mother used to sing to me whenever I had a bad dream. You are having a bad dream is all, and soon you will wake up and be fine." Amanda quietly sang the familiar lullaby, soothing her, and she soon drifted into a half-sleep from the drugs.

Amanda stayed with Tonie the rest of the day, calling Fernand when she fell asleep. Not wanting to leave her alone in the hospital for the night, Amanda asked him to bring her overnight things.

A psychologist was consulted and came in every day, but Tonie refused to talk to him, ignoring all his questions. Amanda chatted to her about everything, all the little goings-on of daily life—her wedding plans with Fernand, the little black cat that had adopted them and hung around looking for food, interesting stories from her volunteer work at the hospital. Little by little, Tonie recovered her sense of reality and became more responsive, knowing her age and her past, and which information not to divulge.

A week later, the patient was deemed stable enough to go home, and Amanda escorted her to her apartment where she prepared Tonie's old room for her. Amanda attributed the nervous breakdown to the changing hormones of pregnancy coupled with Paul's harsh treatment. Of course, he didn't know about the baby, she supposed, but to tell Tonie she was crazy and damned to hell was unforgivable, and she hated him for it.

"I guess I don't do too well here in Paris," Tonie offered as an embarrassed apology, settling into the couch with a cup of tea made by her loyal friend. Then a horrifying thought crossed her mind. "Paul doesn't know about me flipping out, does he?"

"No," Amanda quickly assured her. "Fernand said that Paul left a message for him saying he was going back to the states. That was three days ago, so good riddance. I was afraid Fernand might kill him when I told him about what he said to you. Maybe that's why he got out of town so fast—he might have got the word."

"If there's any killing to be done I'd like to be the one doing it—that would be my best therapy," Tonie ruefully joked. "I don't think he was good for me. I've never been a complete nut like this before in my life, but just hearing he's gone I feel a thousand pounds lighter."

Amanda retrieved a pad of paper and a pen from the drawer in the kitchen and sat next to the mother-to-be. "We need to get going on your prenatal care. Let's see, number one—find a midwife. Number two—vitamins and fish oil."

"Fish oil! What are you talking about? I have to take fish oil?"

"Of course," Nurse Amanda laughed. "It's good for you and the baby."

"How about if I eat broccoli every day?"

"Number three—broccoli. But you still have to take fish oil. Plus, it makes your complexion young."

Tonie snorted to herself. Yeah, don't need that.

"I took it every day during my pregnancies and my babies were beautiful. Speaking of which, Jack and Colleen are coming for the wedding. I was wondering if I could bunk with you and give them my room for a couple nights?"

"Of course, you weren't exactly expecting me back. Have you talked them into moving here yet?"

"I'm still trying. I know Colleen would love it, but Jack pleads that he doesn't know French and couldn't get a job. Minor point, I say." Mama Bear giggled.

"Let's go wedding dress shopping tomorrow," Tonie suggested, trying to be perky. "We could look on rue des Francs-Bourgeois for something gorgeous for you. I need a dress that expands since I'll be almost four months by then. And, we could stop by the Monoprix and get the fish oil. I want a beautiful baby, too!"

Amanda shook the pen to make it write, but it was out of ink so she popped up to get another one. When she came back she stopped and stared at Tonie, transfixed.

Tonie noted her funny expression. "What's wrong?"

CHAPTER TWENTY-THREE

Amanda's eyes were dazed, and she stood there staring for another minute.

"What's wrong, Amanda?" Tonie worriedly jumped up and rushed over to the mesmerized woman.

"Tonie," Amanda scrutinized Tonie's face as if she had changed. "I think I just had a vision. As soon as I came into the room I could hear you calling me from far away, but I couldn't find you. I kept following your voice until I came to a grown-over spot in the woods, and I started clawing through mounds of old growth and bushes, and I found an abandoned well shaft, and you were stuck down it. You kept calling for me to help you. I pulled on your hands, but couldn't get you free because your feet were caught on something. So you kicked and kicked and I kept pulling, and all of a sudden you came shooting out. You flew into the air and stretched out your arms, and you had wings of gold. Gold feathers covered your head and body, and you soared into the sky, the sun glinting off your wings, flashing as you turned and swooped, free and exultant."

"All that happened in the two seconds that you stood there?"

"I don't know how long it was. I think it was fifteen minutes."

"No, it was only a few seconds."

"Tonie! I know it was a vision from God. I don't know what it means, but you are going to be fine! You are going to be free and triumphant! Maybe the shaft represents your attachment to Paul, that you are stuck and feel like the life is being squeezed out of you, but once you get over him you will be free and will soar like an eagle!"

Tonie's head spun from the implications. She knew exactly what it meant. Her feet were stuck in the past, but soon she would be free. Did she dare get her hopes up? But how could Amanda possibly have any idea about her past unless it was a real vision. And judging from her amazed reaction, something monumental had occurred.

Amanda sat down, her face radiant. "It was like I was there, like I actually went through it. Oh, Tonie! I have peace that passes understanding! You are going to be free, my sweet girl. I've been so worried with everything that's gone on, and now I know without a doubt that you will be free."

"But why would God do this for me when I've been so ugly to Him? And you don't even know the half of it," Tonie timidly asked, wanting to confirm that Amanda was certain that she was the promised beneficiary of the vision. The vision itself was without question—Amanda's description so vivid, her reaction physically shaking her.

"It doesn't matter what you've done—He has a plan for you. The weaker the vessel, the greater God's glory when He works in you."

Tonie pondered these words and took them to heart. She understood the message—she would be flying, free from her curse. The description of the well shaft was so exact, so fitting of the devouring suffocation that enveloped her ever since she knew she was trapped in her earthly body with no escape.

Reassured that she was on the right track and would find the answer, she vowed to renew her efforts to search out more information about the berries and their predecessors. In the over two hundred years since she had eaten them they may have lost some potency, Tonie speculated. Amanda's vision opened up a new goal for her. Instead of focusing on city berries, she would travel further afield and search out wilder berries, berries that had not had to adapt to city life with its pollutions and ever-encroaching annihilation of their territory.

This new goal calmed her. Her fear of being crazy relaxed, and the trembling in her bones ceased rocking her still-fragile psyche. A solution right around the corner, and it was her job to find it.

Chapter Twenty-Four

T HE COUNTDOWN TO THE STEVENS-MICHAUD wedding was advancing apace. At one week until the day, Jack and Colleen flew into town, sending the bride into a frenzy of wanting perfection in every corner. Her wedding dress hung ready in the closet, flowers were ordered, each nuance of the big day already arranged so that she would have time to devote to showing her son and daughter-in-law around Paris. Stocked with an array of delicious cheeses, buttery breads, freshly ground coffees, sweet pastries, and white and red wines, the pantry was a glowing testament to French cuisine. The visiting couple's bedroom was furnished with a new duvet, French shaving cream, perfume, hair mousse.

As Amanda had rushed from shop to shop earlier in the week with Tonie, purchasing supplies to make her guests comfortable, she assured her expectant friend that children never grow up in their mother's mind—they were yours to worry about and fuss over for the rest of your life. Then, into the basket went a deodorant, shower gel, washing mitt and toothpaste. "You never know what kids will forget," the happy mother justified.

"Yes," Tonie had answered. "And, coming from a third-world country like the U.S., they probably can't buy toiletries there."

The shopaholic laughed and tossed in a couple lavender sachets.

Amanda's gown graced the closet where Tonie's used to be. The ill-fated dress had still been lurking there when they returned after Jack and Colleen's wedding, so Amanda made it disappear one day and nobody ever asked about it. Now instead, there floated a dazzling silk pink-champagne colored dress, with lace overlay and a chapel length train. Keeping company beside it danced two apple-green organza silk gowns adorned with fuchsia flowers, the one dress an empire gown with soft folds of fabric flowing in gentle gathers above the waist line, and the other one slenderly fitted.

Over dinner that night around a large table in Restaurant Guillaume's, Colleen reached into her purse and pulled out some old photos. Turning, she offered them to Tonie. "Jack showed me these pictures of his great-grandmother, and he thinks you're the spitting image of her." The black and white photographs were faded, but the smiling features of a dark haired woman could still be made out.

Tonie's heart thudded as she leaned forward to inspect them closely and saw herself looking back. Hopefully the old fashioned hair-do and dress were distracting enough to draw attention away from the striking resemblance. "Oh, does she look like me?"

"Yes. Jack noticed it right away at our wedding and hunted up these photos. We are wondering if you might be a long lost relative to have the same name and face as Jack's great-grandmother." Colleen laughed, not believing in actuality that it was a possibility, but enjoying the fun of the speculation.

Amanda peeked over Jack's shoulder at the pictures that Colleen was showing. "I haven't seen those in ages. Let me see." Jack handed them from Colleen to his mother. She peered closely and exclaimed, "Oh, you do! I've always thought you have a family resemblance. You're from Maryland. Hmm, I can't help but wonder if Nona had a sister who settled in the East? Tonie! We should compare our ancestries sometime. Wouldn't it be fun to find out we're distant cousins or something? I've always felt a kindred spirit with you."

"That's amazing," the poser agreed. "My family never kept track of such things so I have no idea."

Tonie perceived Jack eyeing her dubiously. She had found him somewhat standoffish at his wedding in August, inspecting her a little too closely for her comfort, but she had nothing more substantial to base her opinion on than that. No words had been spoken that were even remotely out of line, so she had dismissed it to her own jitters of seeing people she used to know as old Nettie.

Tonie reassured herself that Jack couldn't possibly believe she was his dead great-grandmother, and if he did he must think he was dealing with a ghost. However, he had searched out the photos and prompted Colleen to ask about them.

Conversation turned to other topics, and Tonie's stomach slowly settled down. Rotten invention—the camera, she sighed to herself.

Fernand launched into his own family history, captivating the group with the exploits of his great-grandfather during the Paris Commune and the burning of the Tuileries Palace in 1871. Fernand's father argued that it was in 1872, which led to a discussion of how old Grand-Père was at the time and when he was born. The ladies quickly lost interest and turned their talk to the wedding, as did Jack who couldn't understand a word of the father's French.

Tonie nodded along, still stressed out by the pictures. What a dangerous game she was playing, she concluded. Why was she making intimate friends with people she had no business being close to? If she was found out to not be who she claimed she was, they would hate her and she would be ostracized. For the first time, the thought invaded her mind what pain her dear Amanda would face if she discovered Tonie was an impostor. And Jack, and Colleen—whose happiness now was interwoven with her husband's. As Tonie fake-aged, would she look more and more like the grandmother that Amanda remembered, causing her turmoil and self-doubt? She was playing fast and loose with their senses of well-being and reality. It wasn't all about her needs.

Then the soul-searcher again remembered Amanda's vision and clung to it. She was going to be normal soon and escape this scourge that had held her captive for what seemed like eternity, so none of this would matter anymore. Perhaps even now her body was aging and she would go home and find a gray hair. Using this justification, she rejected the idea that she should move on and let Amanda and Fernand build their new life together without her. The vision came from Amanda, so she knew it was true. Amanda must have been given the vision from God, and therefore, it meant that forgiveness was a possibility. Tonie became nervous at this point. She had always known she had crossed the line of forgiveness, had screamed right over it a long time ago. What was left to her but hell, as Paul had so succinctly put it. How much safer it was to deny God, and therefore hell.

"I'm sure Tonie would love to give you the guided tour."

The pondering girl heard her name and saw everyone looking at her.

"Of the church?" she offered, hoping she had guessed the right topic of discussion. "Of course, but I don't know as much of its history as Fernand. He's the one who chose it for the wedding."

"No, the Père Lachaise cemetery," Jack corrected. "Mom was saying that you have visited it quite a few times."

"Oh, yes, I do love it there. It is a city in itself, only its residents are very quiet." Tonie tried to cover by joking. "I found some plant life there for my research that I couldn't find anywhere else in the city. We can tour through it tomorrow, if you'd like. I thought you were talking about the Chapel of Notre Dame of the Consolation where your mother is getting married."

"That place is a jewel," Amanda launched in enthusiastically. "It was built as a consolation to the bereaved on the exact site where a charity bazaar caught fire and killed 130 people in the late 1800s. It is absolutely beautiful, and a wonderful sentiment to reach out to the families and loved ones who bore such loss. Fernand knew of this church and has gone to mass there many times."

Charmed by this story, Colleen philosophized, "And in extension, what a marvelous conviction to remind ourselves that we, too, as the temples of God, may offer consolation and comfort to the brokenhearted of the earth."

The whirlwind week rolled on, gathering momentum, erupting on Sunday afternoon in an exuberant display of color, beauty and love, in the ceremony where Fernand and Amanda became Monsieur and Madame Michaud. The morning dawned sunny, bright and full of promise, happy contentment ruled the day, and the evening witnessed a horse-drawn carriage bustling the newlyweds away to a train bound for Italy where they would honeymoon for the next two weeks.

The following day, after the guests had left for the airport, Tonie decided to make the trip to London that she had never made after the woodpecker had followed her to Bath and the police arrested Paul. Packing her bag and her prenatal vitamins, she set off to take the train to Calais and a ferry across the English channel to Dover. It would be longer than the Chunnel, but a much more spectacular trip, affording her the view of the magnificent white cliffs of Dover. A big plus was that the water should be calm at this time of year, unlike when she had made the dark and rough crossing and met Isaac.

Sitting atop the ferry in the sunshine with the wind softly blowing her hair, Tonie's thoughts flitted to the London she remembered. She had lived there longer than any other one place—nearly a hundred years including the time she spent in Bath. First there had been Isaac and Flora, then working as an instructor at the midwife school, the Harvey girls, living through the Great War and the terror of the bombings, then meeting Thomas and sailing for America. Her two husbands had been British. Maybe she would meet her next one there and forget all about Paul.

Nettie is tired of powdering her hair every day, of smudging her eyes with charcoal to age them, and of putting her hair up in a tight, matronly bun. She longs to cut it into a short, perky bob like all the young girls are wearing these days. Oh, to be carefree and light, doing things that a girl her age, well, a girl of her apparent age, should be doing—like having beaus and picnics in the park—not working at the midwife school where, after twenty some years, they expect her to be looking like a grandma.

So she rebels on that rare, sunny, late winter day, twirling her rich chestnut hair into a fluffy bun at the nape of her neck, fluffing out the sides and securing it with ribbon—creating a "faux-bob"—the look worn by women without the courage, or husbandly permission, to cut their hair. Nettie has the courage, oh yes, she has the courage, but not the opportunity. But a faux-bob will do, and no dark circles for her eyes today or heavy skirt down to the floor.

And, in keeping with her subliminal yearning for a new life, she defiantly drives into central London in her snazzy Austin Seven without her "old lady" disguise, to slowly begin withdrawing money from her bank account to add to her satchel in preparation for moving on. She doesn't have a plan yet, but she is taking a first step.

As she walks up to the door of the bank, a handsome young gentleman—not much more than a boy, really—is just leaving, and he gallantly holds the door for her, tipping his hat. Enjoying being noticed again, she smiles back at the young man. After making her withdrawal and leaving the bank, she is surprised to see her admirer waiting right outside the door in the same spot.

"Good morning, Miss," he addresses her. "I would like to present myself. I am Thomas Quinn, and this is my father's bank. I am in training as a future banker, and as such, I would like to ask you some questions regarding your opinion of the security of our bank. Do you have confidence that your money is safe here?"

"Well, yes I do," she answers back. "I trust that my money is well taken care of here in your father's hands."

"I am delighted to hear that. And, if I am not being too forward, would you trust me enough to walk with me sometime in Hyde Park, perhaps around the lake?"

While she does think it is rather bold of this young man to make such a suggestion without them being properly introduced, she is happy to accept. "That would be very nice, since I do know who your father is."

"Perhaps Sunday at three o'clock? At the lake?"

"Yes, I will be there." She feels her face blush and knows he is watching her as she returns to her car.

The internal restlessness that has been plaguing Nettie finds its answer in that propitious Sunday afternoon rendezvous. She and Thomas never stop talking, wrapping the circumference of the lake twice without noticing anything but each other. An adventurous young man, Thomas is bristling with energy to break out of the future his father is squeezing him into. He had wanted to fight in the Great War, but was thwarted by his age—only turning sixteen shortly before the armistice was signed. He then wanted to learn to fly the airplanes that had helped Britain win the war, but his protective father emphatically forbade him to enter such a dangerous profession. Now his idea is to sail to America and become a cowboy. Having heard stories of unending prairies of land—free for the working of it— Thomas envisions a cattle ranch and pitting his wits against the wilds. He cannot bear to think of sitting at a desk signing papers all his life, growing old and empty from meaningless work. He wants the wind in his hair and his seat in the saddle of a galloping horse.

Nettie falls in love with this boy who possesses all the enthusiasm for living that the years have robbed from her. Walking through the park, his hands fly out as he tells Nettie about the great expanse of the prairies just waiting for them in America. Nettie doubles over in laughter as he rides an imaginary horse, swatting the air behind him as he races across the acres of his imaginary ranch. Life feels good for the first time since she can't remember when. He reminds her so much of André. But as quickly as the boy she loved in her youth scampers into her mind, he scoots on out again. The past can't pull her in because the future is pulling her so strongly along in its stream—promising, bubbling, irresistible. Thomas's vision fits in neatly with Nettie's itching for a change of scenery. She bursts with excitement to go with this young man of courage who is willing to chase his dream across the world.

To this end, she begins wrapping up her old life. In the mornings she is old Nettie in a heavy skirt and gray hair—quitting her job, cleaning out her house, filling her satchel with money—and in the afternoons she is young Nettie in a teasingly short dress and flirty faux-bob, moving into a ladies' boarding home, shopping for new clothes, and meeting Thomas each day after work.

Throughout the spring and summer they secretly see each other. One sunny Sunday, sitting on a park bench in the secluded Queen's Wood, Thomas suddenly drops to one knee.

"Nettie, will you marry me?" He produces an elegant diamond ring that his grandmother has given him for when he marries someday.

Oh yes, she will.

But his parents have other plans for their son's life, plans that include marrying a rich girl from a prominent family and working in the bank. Nettie is an orphan and therefore not a suitable match for their boy and his bright future.

Not one to be easily discouraged, it doesn't take long for Thomas to think his way around this new obstacle.

"We will run away to Gretna Green in Scotland and get married by the blacksmith," he tells his beloved a couple days later. "You only have to be sixteen to marry there without your parent's consent. Then we will come back and tell my father that we are married and sailing to America."

"Are you sure you want to do that? Your father will be so angry," Nettie worries.

"I want to marry you, only you. We'll get married and go to America, and we'll start a new life where love is what matters and not how much money your family has."

So off to Gretna Green the sweethearts triumphantly flee, returning home with rings on their fingers and sparkles in their eyes, revealing their newlywed status to Thomas's family. For all his previous gruffness and bluster, Mr. Quinn is a romantic at heart and truly wants the happiness of his son. He breaks down and weeps, embracing his new daughter-in-law and wishing the couple Godspeed on their journey to a new land. He gives them money and letters of introduction to people he knows there. Nettie delights in the prospect that she is leaving all her sorrow and past behind her, and that she will find peace on the other side of the world. A brand new start in a brand new country, with the man she loves.

Tranquility soothed Tonie's frazzled nerves as she remembered that idyllic time of love and adventure. Gretna Green was famous for its runaway marriages—the first town across the Scottish border—where young lovers fled the confines of controlling parents in England and married their heart's beloved. Getting married in Gretna Green by the blacksmith was considered the height of romance. How she missed Thomas and his steady optimism.

The blasting of the ship's horn brought Tonie's attention to the present. The ferry made preparations to dock at the bustling town of Dover—with its commanding medieval castle keeping watch over its shores—and the time traveler reeled anew with the clashing worlds in her head. It was so long ago, yet so close at the same time. She had come to England with Isaac and left with Thomas. Now she came alone, with antiquated knowledge, hoping to find some spirit of her former self to help fill the hole inside her named Paul.

Chapter Twenty-Five

T ONIE ROAMED AROUND HYDE PARK, SOAKING IN the smell of the trees and the sounds of chirping birds and chattering squirrels. Each familiar sight, so well known yet so foreign, roused hitherto forgotten memories of her intoxicating walks with Thomas, heady with the rush of love. It was the same geographical spot on earth, under the same sky, and she let herself be swathed in kinship with it. The lovers that she saw strolling hand in hand evoked images of the young man who had become her husband and led her off to distant shores.

Many places were eerily exactly as she remembered. The Tower of London and the Tower Bridge stood rooted like solid, eternal sentinels, refusing to bend with the times, reminding the citizens of London of their place in history. The mighty Thames seemed a little smaller. Had it lost a little of its audacity, like she had? Had the years taken their toll? Perhaps it was really the same, only appearing less because Tonie had been younger then, the world brighter and more hopeful. The house in which the former Mrs. Stafford had shared with Isaac was gone, probably bombed out during the Nazi blitz of the Second World War. Skyscrapers now ruled the skyline, dwarfing St. Paul's Cathedral which had been the tallest building the last time she had been here. It was another pillar of society that had withstood the trials of time and the ravages of war, and now welcomed back its errant daughter.

Tonie slowly strolled across the modern, gleaming Millennium Bridge which led to St. Paul's. The pedestrian bridge provided an oasis in the middle of the burgeoning city, a temporary respite from the endless cacophony of cars and trucks. She tarried for a minute in the middle to breathe in the aura of this town that, while changing and growing, still beat to the same rhythm of busyness. Traffic lights kept order on the streets now, their unbiased, perfectly timed lights replacing the need of bobbies' hands to direct motor vehicles. Shoppers trod long concrete sidewalks, no longer forced to jostle for space on streets invaded by noisy, stinky buggies powered by gas engines instead of horses. London's facade may have slowly transformed through the ages, but its inner machinations still echoed the same yearnings of industry and progress.

As she neared the end of the bridge, she caught, out of the corner of her eye, a pair of eyes burning into her. Glancing over, she beheld the long searched-for woodpecker—full gray beard, tattered clothes, intense blue eyes piercing into her soul. Still angry at his part in the arrest of Paul, and the sense of violation that he was following her once again, Tonie marched right up to him.

"Why are you following me this time? There's no one to lead you to anymore!" She belligerently challenged this ageless man. She stared into his face, studying each feature closely, noting the smooth skin and blazing eyes, incongruous with the long, gray beard and straggly hair. His face whispered forty while his beard shouted eighty. Examining it closely, the makeup artist detected the tell-tale signs of her own trick—ashes. The beggar's beard was run through with ashes.

The enigmatic man leaned into her, his face alive, intense, peering into her eyes as if nothing else in the universe existed. Finally, his voice boomed out.

I know thee well, though you don't know me, your face informs your curse.

I denied our Lord, who loves us dear, I'm condemned to roam the earth.

My days, yes mine, will finish soon, when once more our Lord shall come.

But yours stretch through eternity and never will be done,

Unless you listen close unto my solemn vow:

Get thee to the church, my friend, to the Lord your knee must bow.

Around your neck your rebellious words have woven you a noose.

Take this advice from one who knows—Your servant, Ahasuerus.

Tonie backed up, stunned by the words and fervor of this madman, wanting to flee but held by the lock of his wild eyes. She stepped back four or five times, then broke free of his gaze and melded into a group of tourists headed for St. Paul's. Walking as swiftly as she could without running, expecting his claws to dig into her back at any second, she finally attained the entrance of the cathedral and stopped to glance around for her stalker. Not seeing him, she entered the church and sat in a side chapel, surveying the crowds of the devout passing reverently by. Figuring that he must know she had entered, she strategized to wait him out then leave by the western doors.

What a nut, she proclaimed, and scolded herself for tangling with him. But what did he want? He had followed her in Paris, and to Bath, and here he was again, now in London. She hadn't actually seen him in Bath, she conceded, but divined his presence there by the result of Paul's arrest. Had he traveled across the channel with her on the ferry? She hadn't seen him but that didn't mean anything, although he wasn't shy about showing himself on bridges. How could he know where she would be? Did he follow, then run up ahead to pop out at her?

Tonie focused on his words, trying to recall what he said. He spoke in verse and the language was archaic. It sounded like a dire warning. He was cursed, and she was cursed. Then some religious mumbo-jumbo. Your servant, Hazzuerus. That was weird.

Tonie leapt to her feet. He wasn't a spy at all. He hadn't been the one who followed her to Bath.

"He has the same curse as me!" she shouted out loud to the dismay of the praying parishioners. She must find him. Why didn't she catch that before, she angrily berated herself. The ashes in the beard, the young face.

For some reason he recognized her condition, but she hadn't recognized his. Running out of the cathedral she returned to the bridge, scanning every face to find him, but he was gone.

No! No! How could she have missed this? She had searched for years for someone just like her, someone who knew the pain of not dying at your appointed time, someone who might have an answer—like he apparently did since he said he was almost done. Her first impression of him in Paris had been that he bore the same affliction, but she had dismissed that idea when Paul was arrested and it had become firmly entrenched in her mind that he was a spy. Had he sought her out, or had it been a coincidence? How could he know her curse, and she didn't know his? How blind she was, she kicked herself.

She would stay here and watch for him until nightfall, she vowed, and then spend her remaining time in London searching for the man with the fiery eyes. Her efforts in Paris trying to find him had not paid off, but what else was left to her? This was her only thread of hope since the berries. Was he reaching his 950 years like Adam, and that was why he was at an end? Did she have another seven hundred years to go? Scarily, she heard the word "eternity" in there. She tried to remember more of his words but her mind was too jumbled at the moment.

Another week in London yielded no result. Tonie perched on every bridge in the city, hoping the woodpecker would swoop down and sing out another warning. This time she would listen, she swore. But the elusive bird had flown the coop, never to land in her tree again. With a mixture of hope and fear, the recipient of the dire portent boarded the ferry for home, determined to reconstruct what her oracle had pronounced.

Amanda and Fernand were coming back from their honeymoon this afternoon, and Tonie wanted to surprise them with a homemade dinner. Amanda had moved most of her belongings to Fernand's apartment before the wedding, but still had a few personal items to collect. Tonie would have an extra room now, and was pondering the decision whether to find a smaller apartment to save money or keep this one. Having no relatives who would come visit, she didn't really need the extra bedroom, but the apartment had been home to her for over a year. It was snug and comfortable, in a terrific location, so she was leaning toward keeping it, despite its connections to Paul.

"San Gimignano is an interesting old town, complete with a medieval wall and a town hall," Fernand enthusiastically described their trip to Italy over dinner that evening.

"Yes, it was charming and quaint, and so old fashioned," added the bride, glowing from her romantic honeymoon. "To me, the highlight of the trip was hiking the Cinque Terre. We stayed in Monterosso, then hiked on to the rest of the villages. The views of the sea were breathtaking, and we hiked though vineyards and citrus orchards. I imagined I was back in the time of the old Romans, the wind in my hair, surveying the horizon for boats coming up the coast from Rome. Then at the end, we caught a train back to our hotel."

Fernand laughed. "I was so sore that I couldn't walk for three days after that! Mon Dieu!"

"We needed all that exercise after eating pasta and gelato all week! I'm sure that I can no longer fit into my wedding gown!" The newlyweds gazed into each other's eyes at the remembrance of their lovely trip together.

"It sounds so romantic and wonderful," sighed Tonie. She had decided she would keep the news of her second meeting of the beggar to herself tonight, not wanting to bring up anything negative, and she didn't want to think of it either. She let herself be peacefully swept away at the delightful description of the honeymoon.

"C'était formidable," Fernand agreed. "I've been to Rome and Florence before, but I've never done the more leisurely things like we did. I would do it all again next week. Are you up to it, ma chérie?" the jaunty bridegroom teased his wife.

"Here," Amanda offered, digging through her large travel purse. "I've got some postcards from Rome." Out came her wallet, passport, ticket receipts, half a Milka chocolate bar. She piled them on the table until she found what she wanted.

Tonie admired the colorful images of St. Peter's Basilica, Trevi Fountain, the Colosseum, and listened to the story behind each one. Next came the camera with their personal photos. Tonie loved having the couple back and having dinner like old times. She guessed it hadn't been that long, but with the crazy month leading up to the wedding, then the two trauma-filled weeks that followed, she reveled in the ordinariness of this evening at home.

"I guess we should get going and let this poor girl get to bed." Fernand pronounced, rising from his chair.

Amanda went to gather some belongings in her old bedroom and then came back to reload her purse of everything she had pulled out in search of the post cards. The items had been cleared off the table and onto the counter, and she put them back in her purse, even the chocolate bar, then paused at the door with her husband.

"It seems strange not to stay here and go to bed. This will be our first night together in our new home, as a married couple." The bride turned to Tonie and asked, "Have you decided whether you want to keep this apartment or get another? You could probably save a couple hundred euros a month if you got a one bedroom or a studio. I would be thrilled to go apartment shopping with you, and I would help you pack up and move, too." More than familiar with the emotional toll of moving, Amanda wanted to ease the transition as much as she could for her friend.

"No, I haven't decided yet. Well, maybe I have. I can't envision moving, so I think I'll stay here," Tonie decided on the spot. "I like the apartment and the location, and I have enough money to swing it. And the extra room can't hurt with a baby on the way. There, I made a decision without agonizing, and I am happy!"

Monsieur and Madame Michaud said their goodbyes, and left to start the beginning of their life together.

Tonie took a shower and lay in bed. Seeing Amanda and Fernand get up and leave together brought home the reality that Paul was gone and she lived alone in a big apartment. "Well, that's that—on my own again," she concluded. "After each friendship comes to an end, after each husband dies, after my current husband dumps me, here I am alone. After your baby dies. Stop it," she warned herself. "I have a new baby coming…yes, that I'll have to bury someday. Alone."

The next day Tonie and Amanda met to go shopping for maternity attire. Nothing was fitting anymore and Tonie was tired on trying to squeeze herself into the largest clothes she owned, which resulted in making her look dumpy and frumpy instead of pregnant.

Walking along the north end of rue Mouffetard, the ladies enjoyed the narrow, trafficless old cobblestone street. The ancient roadway bustled as one of the oldest streets in Paris, rich with the ambiance of the earliest days of the city when it had been merely a Roman village named Lutèce. Lured into a shop of the cutest baby clothes that Tonie had ever seen, she set eyes on a little shorts and shirt set for a baby boy that had sailboats outlined in hand stitching, and her heart melted. She couldn't wait for her new baby. Obviously catering to the rich, the cottons were the softest cottons, each outfit original and charming. Finally settling for a finely knit yellow blanket, she made up her mind that she would return and get something special when she learned whether she was having a boy or a girl.

Along the same street, the ladies found a reasonably priced maternity shop where Tonie bought a cute, comfortable skirt with a low elastic panel, and a couple of longer blouses. She wore them out of the store because she was tired of stretching a rubber band from the button of her jeans across a four inch wide gap to the button hole.

With their feet starting to ache, the shoppers stopped at Café Clotilde for a lunch salad on the way home.

"Have you ever heard from Paul again?" Amanda asked, wondering if he would dare to try to contact Tonie against after his egregious behavior.

"Nope. I guess he was done. As soon as I had a problem he was through with me. Never mind that I stood by him during his flight from justice," the abandoned wife sniffed. "But I have never felt better. We did not click together. We were either breaking up or making up. Everything was fine until we came to Paris, so I don't know what changed."

"That is odd. Maybe it was the rebalancing of the power status. I wonder if at home he was the grand, respected professor, and here you stepped into your own and began to see yourself as his equal. Do you think, perhaps, he felt a little threatened?" Amanda tried to make sense of the flakiness of Paul.

Tonie jumped on this explanation, not willing to accept that her atheism had cost her her man. "That must have been it. It was always all about him. Oh, I never realized how passive I was about it. And here, here I was doing my research at the Sorbonne with Fernand, and I was respected. People think I'm smart. For the first time I had my own niche, and maybe I didn't idolize him in the same way."

It was true that Tonie had grown in confidence while doing her research. She felt more in charge of her life than she ever had, with the hope of an answer seemingly under her control. Another aspect to her growing confidence was the sense of self she derived from having found her childhood home and relics of her original roots in Paris. She had ceased being a wandering lost soul on earth, an orphan, and found the belonging she hungered for through the closeness she now felt with her parents and brothers and sisters. And, even though they were all long dead, she carried their love in her heart and it gave her strength.

"It's been over two months, I would have expected that he would have written at least," Amanda observed. "He is still married to you."

"Yes, and I've been thankful every day that I listened to myself and didn't tell him about the baby. I miss him sometimes, but I'm getting over it."

"That's to be expected. It takes a long time to become unattached, even if it wasn't the most phenomenal relationship. And, like you said, it was working until you came here."

"I know I need to file the divorce papers. I've been putting it off because I don't want to deal with it, but I suppose I should get it done. Plus, then he will have to come and sign, and that's awkward." Tonie sighed at the dilemma.

"Are you planning on finishing your research by next spring, with a new baby?"

Tonie smiled. "I don't know. Babies grow up so fast that I don't really want to leave my little sweetheart to go work on boring papers."

"Don't forget that you have a doting grandma and grandpa living a few blocks down the street who want their fair share of time!" Amanda smiled in anticipation.

"My baby already wants to play with you!"

New mama and grandma to-be walked home arm in arm, their roles reversed, in warm anticipation of the happy event looming on the horizon.

Chapter Twenty-Six

T HE SUMMER CANICULE DESCENDED ON THE CITY, the heat wave sending citizens by the thousands fleeing to the banks of the Seine for relief, creating "Paris Plage," the Paris beach, and it was only yet the middle of July. Tonie left her apartment early Sunday morning to do her weekly shopping at the Marché Bio on the boulevard Raspail.

Walking through the open-air market in the comparative coolness of the morning, she filled her net bag with carrots, zucchini, oranges and broccoli. Proud that she met her vegetable quota, she stopped at a booth with organic wines and picked up a bottle of red—her midwife assured her that one small glass a day with dinner was perfectly safe—and then she shopped for the most important items—French bread and pastries. Pain au chocolat was her very favorite, and she bought a couple. The net bag was burgeoning by this time, but as she smelled the rotisserie chicken she decided she could carry one more thing and bought a half chicken. She longingly passed tables of tangy, fruity tartlets; tender, golden crepes; fried potato galettes served on paper plates; fresh cream quiches; and sizzling sausages so smokey they summoned up ancestral memories of caveman days. But she declined, only because she didn't have another hand to hold one more thing.

Arms full, the shopper sauntered toward the exit of the market, pausing to watch two small children timidly petting goats in a small pen. A woman at the table was selling goat's milk and cheeses, and the mama-to-be's imagination flew to next summer when she would be buying milk for her own little one.

"They're pretty cute, aren't they?" a male voice commented from behind her.

Tonie turned to the speaker and beheld Paul, enjoying the antics of the perky goats with the children.

"Oh, hi Paul," a surprised Tonie greeted her long lost husband. She immediately shifted her shopping bag strategically in front of her thickening waistline. "I assumed you had probably gone back to the U.S., but... here you are," she stammered.

"I did, but now I'm back for Marc's trial. It's expected to last a week, and then I'll be going home, I guess." He smiled at her, hastily adding, "I wasn't following you. I came to the market for breakfast and ate my way through, and then just saw you this minute. I swear!"

"Oh, I wasn't worried," Tonie laughed, even though she was.

"How have you been?" the suspected stalker inquired, trying to appear innocent.

"I've been great. Amanda and Fernand got married and have returned from their honeymoon. Amanda and I found a new café that we love. It's halfway between our apartments so that's perfect. Café Clotilde. Do you know it?" she babbled, not knowing what else to say to this man she used to know intimately but who was now a stranger.

"Hmm," Paul tried to place it. "No, I don't think I've been there."

"Yeah, there are a lot of cafés in Paris," she nodded.

"I can see you have your hands full so I'll let you go." He paused. "Tonie, would it be okay if I call you up sometime this week before I go? Not for any other reason than to talk for old time's sake?"

During the conversation Tonie had oscillated between dreading he would ask this, and wanting him to so bad that it hurt. "Oh, um, sure." Their eyes locked for a second too long.

"All right." Paul brightened.

"See you." She veiled her eyes to reserve the right to change her mind.

Tonie hurried home with her heavy load, her mind spinning at the unexpected appearance of Paul. She didn't know what to make of it. All summer she had worked at forgetting him, trying to blame him for all their problems, but lately admitting that she may have played a small part in it too—a very small part, of course. He couldn't think she was too crazy, she deduced, because he approached her willingly. It would have been easy for him to turn around unnoticed. What did he want? Simply to talk? Did he want to try again? Maybe she was jumping the gun assuming he wanted more than a friendly conversation. He said to talk. Was his real motive just to get another peek at the circus freak-show to witness how over the edge she really was?

Tonie put away her groceries, conflicting emotions battering her heart. She was meeting with Amanda and Fernand at the Luxembourg gardens for a picnic lunch, and while she packed the chicken into a basket, along with some yogurt and macarons, she continued to rehash her meeting with Paul. Grabbing a water bottle, she headed out the door for the ten minute walk to the gardens.

Down the old, winding rue de Vaugirard she skipped, the street abandoned on this hot Sunday afternoon. Perked up by seeing Paul and feeling like she had options, she wished they could go back to their easy way of relating before they came to Paris.

The crowded gardens offered relief from the sun under its shady trees and cool plush grass. Tonie easily found the Michauds already ensconced on a blanket under their favorite tree, Amanda busily setting out a container of cherries and grapes.

"Bonjour!" Tonie greeted as she approached her friends.

"Bonjour!" returned Fernand and Amanda cheerfully. They made the round of kissing, then Amanda continued her lunch preparations, arranging a round of brie and buttered slices of fresh French bread on a plate.

"You are getting quite a, a baby bump, are you not?" Fernand observed. "That is what you say in the U.S., non?"

Tonie grinned. "Yes, it is what we say. Do you really think it's noticeable?"

"Oh la la, you can't miss it," he assured her.

The pregnant lady plopped down on the blanket and pulled out her food, adding it to the spread. She cut a wedge of brie and laid it on a slice of bread. Chicken could wait—she needed her French bread and brie fix, followed by grapes. Life didn't get any better than this.

"Speaking of which," she remarked after a mouthful, "I saw my baby-daddy this morning." She looked at Fernand. "That's another technical American term."

"What? Paul is in Paris?" Amanda asked.

"Yes. He's here for Marc's trial because he's testifying, and said he'd be here for about a week. He asked if he could call me."

"Non. Non," Fernand forbade emphatically. "I don't think you should see this man. He only wants to make love to you, and then he will leave again."

"You told me that when men fall in love it is forever, and they can't forget a woman," Tonie reminded him playfully.

"That is French men," Fernand corrected her. "French men love with all their heart, but American men want only one thing, and then they forget you."

"Well, at least I can't get pregnant," Tonie indicated her belly.

Amanda and Fernand both quit chewing and stared at her.

"I'm kidding! He said he wanted to call me, as on the phone, not see me or sleep with me. Trust me, I will not sleep with him."

"I think this man is bad news," her protective father-figure continued. "He will say sweet words to win you back, and you have such a tender heart that you will trust him, then, voila, he has left again without saying goodbye."

"I suppose," Amanda interjected, "it wouldn't hurt to talk to him. At some point you do need to discuss a divorce."

"That can be done through lawyers," Fernand pointed out.

"The only reason I've thought I should talk to him is to decrease the drama surrounding our break-up," Tonie stated unconvincingly.

Amanda examined Tonie closely. "Maybe it is time to address your differences now that cooler heads prevail, if you think there is any chance that you want to go forward in your relationship. But, you need to be careful, Tonie, and not take things too quickly."

"I know that's true. I just feel so torn. Part of me wants everything to be back to normal, but then I think of our problems, and nothing has changed there, so then I think it is hopeless."

"I'm not trying to take his part, believe me," Amanda continued, "but when emotions are involved it's easy to read things the wrong way, or even to say things you don't mean, and then misunderstandings arise. And, especially when issues of religion and power-balances come up, it can be extremely hard to figure out—with feelings being hurt on both sides."

"I did say some things that were hurtful," Tonie sheepishly admitted in a small voice. "He kept telling me how I needed God, and I felt disrespected, so I told him it was over."

"Oh mon Dieu!" Fernand exclaimed. "Les femmes! I'm sure his heart is breaking!"

Amanda laid her hand on Tonie's arm. "It sounds like you both have things to work out. In my opinion, you should talk to him when he calls."

Fernand sighed exasperatedly. "You need a father, young lady, to advise you and to give a stern warning to this man. I will be that father to you. Do you love him?"

"I don't know, that's the problem, and I don't know if he loves me." Tonie wavered in her uncertainty of Paul's feelings.

"What do you mean, you don't know? Of course you know! Are you happy he talked to you and wants to see you?"

"Well, yes."

"There you are. And, he would not have hung around your apartment, watching for you, if he did not love you. So you need to go back to him, and quit overanalyzing."

"He said he only happened to see me by accident," Tonie sought to clear up the misconception.

"He 'happened' to see you ten meters from your apartment? If he wanted to avoid you he would have taken a hotel in Montmartre, non?"

Fernand's "daughter" had to concede that it was true.

"If he didn't love you, then you would have never known he was back in Paris except for hearing on the six o'clock news that he testified at Marc's trial, and you would be sad, very sad, non?"

CHAPTER TWENTY-SIX

Tonie concurred. "Yes, when I think of that, I realize that I would be sad."

Fernand nodded triumphantly. "You see how easy? Always listen to your Papa."

With Fernand's insight that she and Paul still loved each other, a buried hope wormed its way into her consciousness. She wished with all her might that he would call sooner than later. She would keep their baby a secret, though, until she discerned his true sentiments, because she knew Paul was old-fashioned enough to think they should stay married solely because she was pregnant. There would be no end to misery in a marriage like that.

After a couple hours of soft, warm breezes, the afternoon grew hotter, to the point that the mother-to-be was beginning to get light-headed, so they decided it was time to head home to the wonder of air conditioning.

"My échographie is next week, do you want to come along?" Tonie invited Amanda, as they reached their parting in the road.

"I wouldn't miss it! Do you have any preference for a boy or a girl?"

Tonie pondered. Henri was a boy, and she worried that she might confuse them in her head if she had a boy, but she really did not think that was the case anymore. Would it be disloyal to him to love another boy baby? Emily had been her shadow as a little girl. Mother and daughter rolled out pie crust together, a little round of dough for Emily and a larger one for Mama. Baking bread was a joint venture, big loaf and little loaf, side by side raising in the sun. Nettie never picked strawberries without her helper, and when it came time to make jam, Emily measured the sugar. Yes, she knew she would be a good girl mother because of Emily. It was the possibility of being a boy mother that worried her.

"No, I really don't have a preference. I'm glad I don't have to decide because I couldn't," Tonie replied, not wanting to admit her worries.

"Fernand and I want to buy a baby bed for you. We could go shopping for that after your échographie, and then you will know what you want for colors and designs. Fernand said he would love to put it together for you."

"Oh, thank you! That makes it seem so real! I will decorate the second bedroom with little animals and soft colors. Somehow, I imagined the baby in a dresser drawer on the floor of my bedroom. What was I thinking? Thank you, Amanda! This will be so fun!"

Amanda looked at her with disbelief. "A dresser drawer? Tonie, you are too much!"

Tonie giggled inside herself. Amanda's mother had spent her first few months of life in a drawer, obviously not a story that had been passed on. Poverty is embarrassing when going through it, but a badge of courage after surviving it.

"Yes," Fernand added. "I am happy to help with anything. If you need me to pound a nail or change a lightbulb, you let me know. You shouldn't be standing on a stool anymore."

"I am five months along now, and I am getting a little off balance," the young mama laughed. "How am I going to hide this belly from Paul if he wants to see me?"

Fernand shook his head. "I don't agree that you should be hiding his baby from him. He has a right to know."

"But I don't want him to feel obligated to stay with me just because of the baby," Tonie wailed.

"Then tell him 'no' if he asks. That solves it."

"But, it's humiliating to know it's only being suggested out of duty."

"We already settled that you two love each other and want in your hearts to get back together, so trust in that and stop this nonsense," Fernand warned.

"Yes, Papa," Tonie laughingly complied.

Back in the coolness of her apartment, Tonie remembered the beggar and wondered why she was hesitant to confide her second encounter with him to Amanda and Fernand. They had been privy to her first brush with him, but this time it seemed more personal. It would bring up questions of why he would give her a warning, why he would talk about roaming the earth, why he would talk about bowing to God.

During the intervening months since seeing him in London, she had reconstructed his words until she felt she pretty much knew the content of them. From his discourse she took both comfort and dismay. Comfort that she was not the only person who lived past the normal age of humans and that there would surely be an end to the curse. And dismay that he spoke passionately about her need to bow to God, and that her curse would not be lifted if she did not. If he was indeed talking about living to the age of Adam, and that his time was almost done, she did not see why hers wouldn't also end when she was nine hundred or so.

But disturbingly, she also remembered that he said he would live to the second coming of Christ. Was that soon? The beggar said "soon." Struggling to fit that baffling phrase into the equation, she reasoned that he was attempting to make sense of what was happening to him the same way as she was, but since he didn't have knowledge of the berries and ancient diets, he shaped his understanding to fit his own logic.

Clinging to the double hope of not being the only person to endure this particular anomaly, and the comfort of being sure that there would be an eventual end to it, Tonie found the everyday living of life to be more bearable. Time stretched on, but not to infinity. While her mind could grasp the concept of long, it could not grasp "forever."

Chapter Twenty-Seven

I T DIDN'T TAKE LONG FOR PAUL TO CALL. TONIE'S
phone rang Monday night promptly at seven o'clock,
and, assuming it was him, she delightedly ran to
answer it. Paul chatted about the trial for several
minutes, then asked if she would meet him for drinks at
Habab's on the corner. Having anticipated that he would
want to see her, and not just talk on the phone, she
accepted and agreed to meet in an hour.

Racing around the apartment, her plan was to get
there before him and already be seated in order to hide
her changing shape. She wore her maternity skirt with a
chambray camp shirt which hung rather loosely,
therefore obscuring her lack of a waistline. In the event
she needed to stand up in front of him she carried her
largest purse, wider than her largest part. Inspecting her
figure in front of the bathroom mirror, she assured
herself that while she may appear a little fluffy around
the middle, Paul would never suspect that she was
pregnant.

Fresh lipstick, and off she ran, beating him there and comfortably installed at a corner table when he arrived. Ordering orange juice, she explained that she was working on some research and needed to put a couple more hours into it before going to bed.

"So, how is everything back in the states?" Tonie asked, to break the ice and enter into the safe waters of chitchat.

"Good," Paul nodded, picking up the oar of triviality. "My mother and father are very happy to have me back home, convinced that France is lurking with evil people." He laughed. "And my brother is getting divorced. It turns out that he's had a couple girlfriends on the side, and his wife found out." He rolled his eyes. "How are Amanda and Fernand doing?"

"They are very happy," Tonie reported. "They went to Italy on their honeymoon and had a fabulous time." Hesitating a minute, she mustered up her courage to quit back-paddling and dive straight into the rapids. "Paul, I want to apologize for my behavior the last time I saw you. I was so afraid of your reaction to my impossible claim that I don't think it would have mattered what you said. I was so sure that you thought I was crazy that that's all I heard, and I behaved badly."

"No, not at all," he passionately rebutted her statement. "I should have been more sensitive. I was sure that if you would turn to God then everything would be fine. That was my solution, and I didn't listen to you. I wanted to solve it for you and I couldn't."

"Really, it was my fault, and I want you to know that I recognize my tendency toward overreacting and assure you that I do try not to, not very successfully obviously, but I do try."

Paul shrugged and smiled. "You look happy. How is your research coming?"

Tonie brightened at the discussion of her favorite topic. "I am studying the diets of neolithic peoples this summer, and next month I am going to the dig in Jaffa for a couple weeks. They have been finding evidence of early bronze age habitation and I will be looking at shards of pottery that suggest different dietary patterns than what has been found at later dates. I'll be classifying fossilized plant remains and imprints that are waiting in the mounds of items piling up to be analyzed. Will you be teaching classes this fall?"

"No. I'm taking a year of sabbatical, and then I'll decide whether I want to go back or not. I am pretty disillusioned that no one stood up for my findings at the Lyon dig. It has all been swept under the rug. All my research, all my evidence, has been ignored. Even though I was exonerated of the charges, and Bonvalet and Marc presumably will go to jail, it doesn't make up for the wrongs done to me and the unscholarly treatment of solid evidence. But, enough of that. I have other plans that I hope to bring to fruition."

"The academic world will be losing a great mind if you go."

"I think the academic world wants someone a little easier to manage than me," he laughed. "But, we'll see. That's where I'm standing right now."

Making small talk about the weather, the American president, and the attributes of cats versus dogs, the estranged couple never ventured into deeper waters. After Tonie's thwarted foray into previous problems that had sunk them the last time they attempted a relationship, she realized that Paul only wanted to wrap everything up in a bow and end their association on a pleasant note. While agreeing with him that, indeed, the path was paved for any future collegiate encounters, her heart was disappointed. Fernand was right that she still loved him, but wrong that Paul loved her.

Paul offered to walk her home, and she rose from her chair, big purse in front, and they strolled through the soft, warm Parisian night. A formal good night at her apartment door, Paul thanked her for meeting with him, and the two former lovers parted without any ado and no plans for tomorrow. The end of an era. Well, that was that, Tonie concluded, once inside. She guessed she made a big fuss about nothing. But really, it was good to have tied up that loose end. Paul was right, and smart, to have made the effort to end as friends. Any weirdness was gone should their paths cross in the future. All that remained to be done was the paperwork.

Getting ready for bed, she studied her growing tummy in the mirror. C'est toi et moi, mon petit choux, she told her baby in the making. Contrary to her circumstances, a sense of security enveloped her, staving off the chill of loneliness. Life was set for the foreseeable future—a child and two loving grandparents, and a career that gave her purpose. Maybe tomorrow she would be crushed by Paul's disinterest, but tonight the crocodiles were sleeping as she floated down the serene waters on the river of hope.

The next day, Tonie met for lunch with Amanda who was eager for news of her evening.

"So, how did it go?" her best friend asked, confident of a positive answer.

"Well, Paul was polite and friendly, pretty much formal, but I guess he really did just want to talk and make sure things would be comfortable should we ever bump into each other again. So, we talked and parted our ways."

"Really? I am surprised. I honestly thought, what with him hanging around your stomping grounds and suggesting getting together, I thought he wanted more."

"No, but I'm okay with it. I mean, I would have preferred that we could work things out, but we do still have all the same problems. I have to hand it to him that he realizes this." A tear escaped out of Tonie's eye. "Oh, I hate that I am such a crier! I really am okay with this. If I weren't pregnant I probably would have forgotten him long ago." She dabbed at her eyes with a tissue and tried to smile.

"Of course you would have," Amanda reassured her. "A baby on the way puts you on hold, instead of moving forward. But, everything is going to be wonderful. It's wonderful right now. I think you were over him until he showed up again, so this is a tiny glitch that is meaningless. The next time you meet him you will have some sweet husband doting on you, and you will be thankful that the stars aligned the way they did to get Paul out of your life!"

The sad girl gave a little laugh and perked up. "Yes, just like you and Fernand at Jack's wedding bumping into your ex-husband. It was gratifying seeing that old cheat-bucket turn green!"

"When I got divorced I never dreamed I would find a fine man like Fernand and be so happy. Never in a million years! And here I am, and soon you will be too," dear Amanda encouraged her friend.

"Yes! I do believe that. My midwife appointment is tomorrow at one o'clock for my échographie. Does it still work for you to come?"

"I wouldn't miss it!"

"I'm having some uneasiness whether I should learn the gender of the baby. What do you think?"

"I want to know like crazy, but you need to do what is right for you. Why have you changed your mind?"

Tonie did not want to admit her worries, but whether she could love another boy as much as she loved Henri nagged at her mind. "I just don't know which I prefer. Will I make a better boy mother or a better girl mother? If I find out I'm having a boy and realize that I will be a terrible boy mother, then I have to worry about it the rest of my pregnancy. Maybe it would be better not to know."

"That's silly. You're going to get what you get, and you're going to think it's the most perfect thing in the whole world the minute you lay eyes on your baby. You are going to be a wonderful mother either way. You are so loving and kind. My worry is that you are never going to let me hold little him or her because you won't want to give him up for even a minute," Amanda teased.

Tonie smiled. "You make it sound so easy and natural. It's true, I really do want to find out."

The ladies finished their lunch—Amanda leaving for the hospital and Tonie heading to the Sorbonne to work on some papers. It was better to have her relationship with Paul defined, she decided once again. Before, there was always the vague hope that it would all work out, but this way she knew it was a complete impossibility, and she determined to quit hoping for it.

Cutting through the Luxembourg Gardens on her way, Tonie paused to watch the children launching toy sailboats across the pond with long sticks. Excited young navigators jumped with joy as capricious breezes billowed out the sails of their boats, briskly spiriting the seaworthy crafts to parts unknown. The children then raced to the foreign shores of the other side of the pond to retrieve and, once again, launch their boats to high adventure. Sunshine gleamed on their hair as they were completely submerged in the fantasy of their play. Tonie laughed as a duck climbed on board a boat that was caught in the doldrums of mid-pond by the fountain. The delighted owner of the boat tugged at his mother's skirt to make sure she witnessed the honor bestowed on his boat.

Jacques would have loved these boats, big sister Nettie reminisced. When Jacques was five years old, and Nettie fourteen, they had traveled with their papa to the Luxembourg Palace. Papa had business nearby, and the two children played for hours by the fountains to pass the time while waiting for him. It was all Nettie could do to keep her brother from throwing every rock and stick he could find into the pond, and to keep him from climbing into it, too. For months after that, Jacques begged to go back to the gardens, the memory of that outing looming as the grandest time to be had in the world.

Watching the boys now, thrilled with their hijinks on the high seas, Tonie imagined Jacques among them, calling out for her to watch each twist and turn and near capsizing that his daring ship encountered. At this moment, all Tonie's fears of having a boy baby vanished like the morning fog when the sun finally bursts through. Certainty that she would be a good mother to a boy bathed her in its glow—she knew boys, she had been a big sister to three boys. Losing Henri was not her fault. Henri would have loved to sail boats here, his hair shining in the sun, his smile infectious in his joy of living.

Tonie pulled herself away from the lulling vision in front of her, and set back out on her path to the school. The noise of the children slowly faded as she left the gardens, but the comfort of the scene accompanied her on her way. Soon it would be her skirt being tugged for attention. Soon she would be the mama being called to watch. Whatever she learned tomorrow regarding the gender of her baby, she would rejoice in it, for she knew that Amanda had spoken true—she would be a good mother.

Tonie lay on the cot in the dark examining room while the technician squirted cold goo on her stomach and spread it around with a wand. The expectant mother hoped the échographie progressed without delay because she had been required to drink a bucket full of water, and nature was calling already. Amanda sat in a chair next to the bed, anticipation sending shivers through her.

The two ladies stared in fascination at the screen while the technician pointed out Baby's beating heart, the stomach, the head, little kicking arms and legs. She navigated through the topography which would have otherwise been indecipherable to the untrained eye. Then she paused.

"I've got the money shot," she turned to them smiling. "Do you want to know the sex?"

"Yes!" Tonie and Amanda shouted out in unison.

"You're having a boy!"

A boy! Tears of surprise and happiness sprung from the eyes of the mother of the little boy. Nothing could be more perfect. Amanda stood up and kissed her. She was so happy that she cried too.

"And everything looks great for your little guy. His size matches your due date, November second. You can look forward to a normal remainder of your pregnancy." She wiped the goo off of Tonie's stomach and helped her sit up. She pushed a button on the machine and photos of the baby came rolling out.

"Here you go," she said, handing them to Tonie. "Baby's first picture!"

Photos in hand, two thrilled women walked arm in arm out into the bright sunshine.

"I know where I want to go to," Amanda liltingly sang out. "Remember that little shop on rue Mouffetard?"

"Yes! Me too!"

Eager shoppers descended into the first metro they found, ready for money to fly out of their purses.

Chapter Twenty-Eight

F ERNAND SCREWED IN THE LAST SLAT ON THE CRIB and returned the screwdriver and wrench to the toolbox. Giving the bed a shake to assure himself of its strength, he stood back to survey his work. "If I were a baby, I would want to sleep there," childless Fernand announced proudly, turning to see Tonie's approval.

Amanda waltzed in with an armload of crib sheets decorated with puppies and stars and began making the bed. Then she attached a mobile with musical bears. Finally, with everything in place—crib, sheets, blankets, pillows—the grandma-in-waiting pulled out a fuzzy white bear and laid it in Baby's spot, delighted at the scene.

Charmed, Tonie nodded her appreciation, admiring with awe the unfolding production of the crib with its dressings. "Three more months," she indicated her ever growing belly. "I seem to be getting larger exponentially."

The bed crew laughed.

"Have you decided on a name yet," asked the grandpa-to-be, "now that you know he's a he?"

"Not yet. I think I may have to wait to see what the little guy looks like. I wouldn't want to name him George if he looks like a Sam. I will name him when I see him."

"That's very wise. He might look like a Fernand, and if you had already named him Sam, then I would miss out!"

"Exactly," Tonie agreed.

Turning out the lights of the baby room, the happy group retired to the living room.

"Tonie, did I leave my passport here by chance? I haven't been able to find it. Not that I need it right now, but I was organizing the other day and realized it was missing," Amanda inquired, glancing around the countertop.

"Yes, you left it here after your honeymoon, and I put it in the safe." Tonie started to go get it for her when Fernand handed her the warranty form for the crib.

"You might want to keep this," he fatherly advised her. "Just in case something is not right."

"Oh, thank you." She took the papers from him and squeezed them into a drawer with all the other miscellaneous, jammed-in paperwork threatening to spill out.

Amanda continued on to the safe to retrieve her passport. Being that there were two United States passports, she opened up the first one she picked up to see whose it was.

"Tonie, what is this?"

Tonie, wary from Amanda's tone of voice, walked over and looked at what her granddaughter was pointing to.

"This is your passport, and it says here that you were born in Dry Creek, Oregon, on the same day and year as my Antoinette," Amanda stated, her voice weak and tinny. She stared at the document trying to make sense of it. "You couldn't have been. It's a small hospital, and no other babies were born that day. And definitely not another Antoinette Stevens."

Fernand strode to his wife's side and studied the passport over her shoulder. "What is this? I thought you were from Maryland?" His voice was calm and non-accusing. He peered at the hapless Tonie, waiting for an explanation.

The poser stood silent, not knowing what to say.

"Did you steal my daughter's identity?" Amanda asked, unbelievingly.

"No."

"Then what does this mean? I don't understand."

"I'm not your daughter, but, I guess, I did steal her identity."

"Why? Why would you do this?" Tears rolled down Amanda's cheeks, her reality shakily crumbling beneath her.

"I'm, I'm. I know this will sound strange, but it's the truth." The impostor glanced from one face to the other. "I am your grandmother—Nettie."

Fernand and Amanda stared at her, saying nothing, as if she had turned into a lizard in front of their eyes.

"I can't die," Tonie continued. "I was born here in Paris in 1773, and for some reason I quit aging at about the age of twenty, and I never die. I came to America with my husband Thomas in 1927, and later we had Emily, and then when she grew up she had you. I pretended to die when your mother died because at some point I had to go. It was getting strange, and harder for me to disguise myself as an old woman. Ask me anything. I will know it because I was there. I was there when Jack was born. And Antoinette. I was there when she drowned. Oh Amanda, my heart broke for you. Ask me anything."

"Why are you pretending to be my baby?"

"I had her birth certificate, and I had to establish a new identity. In the past I could move on and say I was anyone, but now a person has to have a birth certificate, and Antoinette would have been twenty-one when I needed to fake-die, and that worked for me. The day you walked into my biology lab I was so excited, and scared, and I wasn't able to resist wanting to be with you."

"But why didn't you tell me? Everything we've based our friendship on has been a lie. You're my best friend, why didn't you tell me?" Amanda's hands shook holding the dreadful passport.

"I was too scared you wouldn't believe me and wouldn't want to be around me anymore. I told Paul, and that's why he left me—he thinks I'm crazy. Do you believe what I'm telling you? Amanda, I don't want you to leave me. I'm living in hell, and I can't do this anymore, but there is no end." Panic started to rise in her. She lost Paul, and now she was losing Amanda. She

293

was in hell. This was hell. For all of eternity she was going to lose everyone she loved.

Amanda forced herself to be calm. Not wanting to lose control, she focused on soothing Tonie. "Tell me about your family, the one you were born into," she asked gently, sure that Tonie was in the throes of a nervous breakdown. She ushered the distraught girl to the couch, and they both sat down together. Fernand hovered protectively around his wife.

Amanda's warmth sparked a flash of hope in Tonie, a tiny, warm shoot, buoying her up on her endless sea of despair.

"I was the oldest child of seven, and my mother was a midwife, and I trained to be a midwife, also. We lived in Faubourg St. Antoine, east of the Bastille," the storyteller explained to her listeners, "and, I actually found the house I grew up in when I first came here last year. My father was a furniture maker. I had a little brother who was born when I was sixteen, who was like my own baby, but he died when he was only eight months old, and I loved him so much. Putrid throat came through our village, and he got sick with it."

Tears now welled up in her eyes. "He was the sweetest baby—smiley, and his eyes always lit up when he saw me. He trusted me, and I took care of him because Mama had so many other children to take care of. We called him our miracle from God because Mama said he was our special gift when she thought she was through having children. When he came down with putrid throat I assumed without questioning that my love was strong enough to heal him, but it turned out not to be."

"And then," Tonie continued flatly, "I realized there were no miracles from God. After that, even later when I married, I never wanted another baby. I was married one time before Thomas, and I secretly prevented getting pregnant, but with Thomas, I don't know, he was so set on children that I wanted to please him, and I figured, well, just one and I won't get attached, but if he looks like Henri then my heart will break. And that baby was your mother. I named her after my sister, Amélie, and I slowly grew to love her, who could not?" Tonie stopped and wiped her tears. "Thomas was over the moon with her!"

Amanda sat motionless, spellbound by her grandmother's candid memoir. "So what happened when my mother died, and you disappeared the same day?"

Tonie became Nettie again, telling her story, replete with details that no one else could possibly know. She told of her transformation into Tonie Stevens, then went back to her time in England with Isaac, and the Harvey girls, and finally meeting Thomas Quinn and sailing to America. The trio stayed up past midnight, examining every nuance of the long life of Antoinette Charpentier, daughter of Jean-Claude and Laetitia Charpentier. One person, one life, with years of memories. The cohesive telling of her life story created a feeling of continuity in her. A wholeness that she had not experienced in many years wrapped its comforting arms around her, soothing her and bringing a deep contentment in her soul.

After midnight, emerging from the immersion into the past, the Michauds decided the hour was late and they should all get to bed and discuss the situation further in the morning. Tonie fell asleep exhausted, but content. The sharing of her life lifted a giant weight off of her. She sensed that Amanda would love her regardless whether she believed her or not, but she somehow trusted that she did.

That night the befuddled couple stayed up several more hours after they arrived home discussing Tonie's revelation.

"What do you think about her story?" Fernand asked his wife as she put on a pot of water for tea. "I think she has snapped. She seemed out of her mind. Do you think it is because of Paul rejecting her once again?"

"It completely rang true to me, and I believed all of it," Amanda replied passionately. "At first I thought she was having a breakdown. She didn't do well that last time, when she ended up in the hospital, but this was completely different. She never wavered in her story and was never confused. It meshed with everything I know about her, and with everything in my own life."

"You believe she is your dead grandmother?" her husband asked incredulously.

"I think I do. She must have gotten off track somehow after her brother died. By her own words she was okay until then, and then she turned away from God, and I have a hunch that she sinned in some big way. By rejecting God she opened herself up to demonic possession. It makes complete sense."

"It also makes sense that she's perhaps mentally unbalanced."

"Who wouldn't be mentally unbalanced after spending hundreds of years in hell? Most people dream of living forever, but the reality must be exactly what she described—hell. God tells us that this world is not heaven."

"People don't live this long, and hell is a pit of fire. No one has ever lived this long, good or evil, and it seems to me that if God wanted to punish her He would give her a disease, or strike her with lightning, and send her to hell," Fernand contended.

"It sounds like she is in hell. It's kind of scary to imagine hell as tailored to fit the sin. Oh, Fernand! She knew so many details of my life growing up, stuff that nobody could know if they hadn't been there. I know it's true, and I have to help her find an answer. I'm sure it's spiritual, but she's so resistant to any suggestion of turning to God for help."

"Paul didn't believe her and he left her over it. I have to agree that it's a lot to swallow, although I do see your reasoning. But, I just can't accept it."

"What about her botanical studies? She's spent the last few years studying ancient diets. That ties right into her search for a reason she is living so long. And the berries? She's sure there is a physical reason, but I see a spiritual one."

"Did you consider that perhaps she is a con artist who studied your family thoroughly in order to fool you? Maybe she wants to get money from you. Is she a girl that Jack used to date, and she can't get over him?" Fernand got carried away painting a vivid picture of Tonie the madwoman. "Maybe she was once at your house with him and stole the birth certificate, and then when they broke up she decided to take over your daughter's identity to stalk him and stay close to the family. That makes more sense than that she was born in 1773."

"That doesn't make any sense at all. Until I took that biology class I had never seen her before. She couldn't possibly have known I would take that class. And she has knowledge of things that Jack doesn't know and that I didn't know," Amanda countered.

"Then how do you know they are true?" Fernand grunted.

"Because they have a thread of continuity. She describes the feeling and the mood of the situations. She doesn't have just stray facts, she has the emotional content of what was going on. A stranger would not have any of that. Plus, I know her. And I believe her, and I am going to help her get back to God. I know in my heart that this is where the issue lies. And," Amanda declared emphatically, "even if I thought she was as crazy as a dingbat, I would help her because I love her."

"I guess it explains Jack's pictures of your grandmother," the dissenter softened.

"Oh! I forgot about those! Yes! She was the spitting image of my grandmother in the photos."

"Let's go to bed, Madame Michaud. It's almost morning."

An hour later Amanda sat up in bed and proclaimed, "I just remembered something I read in a book by C.S. Lewis! He said he believes that people who go to hell can get out any time they choose, but nobody ever chooses to. I think that is exactly what is happening here. Tonie is in hell, and she could get out if she chose, but she can't choose to because she refuses to turn to God."

Fernand stopped snoring for a minute then turned over and went back to sleep.

Chapter Twenty-Nine

T ONIE SLOWLY AWAKENED THE NEXT MORNING with unidentified tentacles of anxiousness worming their way through her consciousness, until her thoughts took form and she remembered being caught red-handed the night before of having assumed Amanda's daughter's identity. Fear and courage struggled within her, yanking her back and forth between them, each ferociously vying for control of her mind. Courage took the lead as she thought of Amanda's selfless love, then fear raised its ugly head to remind her that neither Paul nor Lydia had believed her. Courage surged into dominance by claiming that Amanda knew her and loved her, and had even had a vision that she would be free.

Beleaguered, Tonie dragged herself out of bed, and decided it was a good time to fill her friend in on her meeting with the woodpecker in London. He was more evidence that she was not the only person this had happened to, and it would bolster her claim of a great age. Leaving a message for Amanda to meet her for coffee at Café Clotilde, Tonie left the safety of her apartment to face whatever the day would throw at her.

Amanda was already at the café when Tonie arrived. At the first sight of her, Amanda ran to her.

"Tonie, we are going to find an answer to this. I want you to know that, no matter what, I am by your side, and we will figure this out."

"Oh Amanda, you don't know what it means to me to be able to talk about this. I've been locked up with my secret for so long that I can't remember that I was ever normal. Even if we don't figure anything out, the relief is palpable from the enormous oppression lifted from me!"

The ladies sipped their coffee while Tonie related her story of running into the woodpecker again in London.

"I think the same thing happened to him as to me— he must have eaten the berries," Tonie conjectured. "My first impression of him, when he asked me for money on Pont Neuf, was that he knew of my curse. But after Paul was arrested, I concluded he must be a spy, so I dismissed that idea. With my second encounter with him, I realized that my first assessment of him was right, that he really is someone like me who can't die and is trying to warn me. I've tried to reconstruct his verses, and he said something like this, but it all rhymed—he has been condemned to wander the earth, but his time is almost finished, but I am cursed for eternity unless I bow to God. And he said his name at the end, which is something like 'Hazzuerus.' He said, 'Your servant, Hazzuerus.'"

"If his time is almost finished, does that mean he is about to die?" Amanda questioned.

"That's the way I took it, and I am afraid that if he dies, I'll have no hope of finding him again and I won't be able to find out the solution. He said his days of wandering are finished when the Lord comes again, which he said would be soon, so I'm not sure he really understands why he has been doomed to wander, but he does seem to think he will escape his curse before too long."

"Darling, this all points to a spiritual issue. If we are to believe the beggar, he is saying that he has wandered the earth for some unspecified amount of time, but when the Lord comes again—the second coming—then he will be free. Then he goes on to say that your curse will be over when you submit to God, and if you don't, then you will wander the earth for eternity. You don't need to find him again, he has already given you the answer. The berries have nothing to do with either his situation, or yours." Amanda looked tenderly into Tonie's confused eyes.

"That would mean that I'm in hell for real." Her mind spun frantically for any solution other than that.

"I think you are in hell, but you can get out any time you choose."

"I am choosing to all the time. I have been searching for a way out ever since I learned my curse. I really believe the beggar was just trying to make sense of his situation, but he doesn't know anything about the berries. I never did either until I took that biology class. I am telling you about him because, if I can find him, maybe between the two of us we would find the answer." Tonie desperately tried to hang on to her rapidly dissolving theory.

"Do you really not believe in God, or are you mad at Him? Is denying His existence a way to punish Him for letting little Henri die? If God appeared right here beside you, this very minute, what would you say to Him?"

Tonie spluttered as if a hand had leapt out and slapped her in the face. "I would be too angry to talk to Him," she declared, pinching her lips tightly, filled with fury at the thought of a God who would let her suffer for so long.

"God loves you so much more than you can imagine, and His heart breaks for you for losing your baby brother. He loves Henri as much as you do, even more."

"But why would He let a baby die?" Tonie accused.

"I have agonized over this as much as you have. I used to wonder if Antoinette was spared something hideous that God could see coming and I couldn't. There are some things so awful that I would rather that she died when she did than to go through them. And, I've wondered if I was being punished for my failings. But, this is what I really believe after all these years: I know that my faith has grown incredibly, I love God more, and I trust Him more, He is my everything. Does Satan want that? No, God wants that, so I have to believe that the most painful suffering in my life was God ordained, and therefore, ultimately, a good thing. Antoinette has been in God's arms all these years. She is loved and cared for and happy, so who am I to question God's goodness? He has stuck by me through all this, and His goodness overwhelms me. There is a bigger plan than just this earthly life, Tonie. So much bigger, that we would willingly suffer for it if we had even an inkling of it. Just like Jesus did."

Tonie sat frozen, Amanda's words clashing with the ideas that had driven her for so long. Her confidence faltering, she doggedly tried to keep to her theory.

"I really think the beggar is nearing the natural end of his life as someone who ate an ancient food that gave him the lifespan of Adam. He may not comprehend why he is living so long, but I do. From the beggar I discern more than ever that I am going to live until I'm nine hundred or so years old. That means I have another seven hundred to go, but that's not forever, and that's not a curse. It's a misfortune. I mistakenly ate 'the berries of life' and now I'm paying the price. He told me his interpretation of what he views as a curse, just as I considered my longevity a curse, but now I don't. I would like to find him again and exchange stories—what unusual foods he ate, how he passes his time, stuff like that."

"All of that may be true, but, won't you study the Bible with me, for a year, and find out what you really believe?" Amanda coaxed. "Maybe the berries did cause this, but you could spend the next seven hundred years with the comfort of God if you find out that not believing He exists is your way of punishing Him for the death of Henri. Henri is with God whether you believe it or not. Do you not think Henri is in heaven?"

"Of course Henri is in heaven," Tonie spat out. "He would surely go to heaven because he was perfect."

Then she leaned in close to Amanda and whispered, "It's too late for me. I cursed God." The words came out of her mouth without her permission, without her even knowing the thought was there.

Amanda's eyes opened wide. She hastily tried to hide her shock. She stared into the depths of Tonie's tormented, pleading eyes. "It doesn't matter, that is what Jesus did on the cross for us. He died for our dumb mistakes. Claim that forgiveness, Tonie, and you will live in heaven with your brother. The beggar said it—you have to bow your knee to God."

"Are you sure? I'm pretty sure I am damned forever."

"No, you are not!" Amanda proclaimed. "Oh! Tonie, remember my vision? I didn't know what it meant then, but now I do! Oh, Tonie. You are going to be free! You are going to soar like an eagle!"

A rent in the fabric of her being tore through Tonie. One minute she was chasing the blurry shadow of an empty promise, and the next her whole world came into focus and the truth of the beggar's words became crystal clear. Truth so close and real that it burned through her, forcing her to cover her face.

Amanda jumped up and took her by the shoulders. "Let's go to the church and talk to the priest. He will know what to do. Is that okay with you?"

Nodding, Tonie leaned on Amanda for strength. The two partners in the tumultuous boat called life ambled down the street together, propelling themselves in the direction of Notre Dame de la Consolation.

Amanda led her into the church and sat her in a pew while she summoned the priest. For an hour the delivered girl moaned and wailed, all the lost years of despair ripped from their long-held residency. She cried out the pain of interminable bondage to an insatiable, evil master, unable to completely grasp her freedom. Then the tears that came were from the sheer realization of the reality of God's love. Amanda brought kleenex and sat with her that long hour.

Father Jacob listened closely to Tonie's story, paying special attention to her anger at God following Henri's death. Questioning her after she finished, he heard the groaning of a lost soul, never finding peace because she searched everywhere except where the true answer lay. The bishop arrived from Notre Dame, and the two priests led God's penitent daughter, and Amanda and Fernand, to the altar, sprinkling the entire gathering with holy water.

"Antoinette Isabeau Charpentier. When you blasphemed God you drove the Holy Spirit from you, leaving a vacuum that enabled Satan to build his stronghold within you. Do you renounce Satan?"

"I do."

"And all his works?"

"I do."

"And all his empty promises?"

"I do."

Tonie knelt down on both knees and bowed her head. Amanda and Fernand knelt behind her with their hands on her back. The priest made the sign of the cross on himself, then on the rest. The bishop then again sprinkled all present with holy water.

"From all evil, deliver us, O Lord. Save your servant who trusts in you, my God. Let the enemy have no power over her and the son of iniquity be powerless to harm her. Lord, send her aid from Your holy place and watch over her from Zion."

"Amen."

"I command you, unclean spirit, along with your minions now attacking this servant of God, to depart from this creature of God, in the name of the Father, and of the Son, and of the Holy Spirit."

"Amen."

Father Jacob made the sign of the cross on Tonie's brow, lips and heart. He again sprinkled her with holy water.

"May the blessing of Almighty God—Father, Son, and Holy Spirit—come upon you and remain forever with you. Amen."

"Amen."

Tonie stood up, light and airy. She was herself as she had never been before, absolute peace flowing through her.

"Am I forgiven?" she asked.

"Oh, my child, you are forgiven! God is dancing in heaven that you have returned to the fold, and the angels are rejoicing! Yes, you are forgiven!"

"Am I normal? Have I rejoined the human race? Will I join my family in heaven someday when I die?"

"Yes, that too, trust me," Father Jacob assured the girl with the shining countenance.

Tonie swooped her arms out and up over her head, turning to Amanda and smiling. "I am soaring!"

Entranced by her story, the priests bubbled around her after the service, drinking in the description of her many years on earth. Tonie then thought to tell them of her meeting with the beggar the two times, explaining that at first she mistook him for a spy. When she told them of his verse, and that he referred to himself as, "Your servant, Hazzuerus," the men of God exchanged glances.

"Hazzuerus? Was it Ahasuerus?" Father Jacob asked, astounded.

"Oh yes, that's it," she agreed.

"What did he look like?"

Tonie described his long gray beard which clashed with the age of his face, his piercing blue eyes, his rhyming verse that she reconstructed as accurately as she could.

"You have met the Wandering Jew!" the bishop exclaimed. He told them the story of Ahasuerus, who denied rest to the suffering Jesus as he bore his cross to Golgotha.

Tonie stood too stunned to speak, marveling over all the seeming coincidences that God orchestrated to bring her back to the fold.

Joyfully walking home with Amanda and Fernand, the new woman in God pondered, "So, how old do you think I am? I was seventeen when Henri died. Did I age after that?"

"It is my understanding from the priests that you quit aging at the moment you denounced God, and your curse began. Therefore, your body is seventeen years old," Fernand the scientist propounded.

"That makes me a teenage mother, then. An 'about-to-be unwed' teenage mother."

Amanda laughed. "There are a lot worse things to be!"

Chapter Thirty

MEANDERING THROUGH THE PÈRE LACHAISE Cemetery on the crisp October day, yellow and orange leaves crackling under her feet, Tonie no longer envied these inhabitants their eternal beds of repose—knowing that someday she would follow, in the natural order of the world. With her return to the living, that earthly bond now swept her along in its current, seamlessly with the flow of humanity since the beginning of time. She stepped into its binding cord, sealing the break where she had left her spot empty, unable to be filled by anyone else. The beggar, too, she knew, would someday reclaim his spot which was waiting for him.

With three weeks left until her due date, Tonie's concerned midwife had warned her this morning that her blood pressure was rising on the high side and wanted to check it again tomorrow. Her first reaction had been complacency—years of assured rebounds from all mishaps rendered her unfazed by bodily concerns—but a little tiredness reminded her of her human status and she agreed to be checked. Things did seem to be moving along in her pregnancy. The last few days she had some tightening low in her back, which the midwife had pronounced normal and nothing to worry about. Tonie was confident that, in her many, many years as a midwife, she would be able to detect labor when real labor occurred.

In the middle of her musings, she noticed a headstone that read, "Beloved Wife and Mother." She bent down to examine the inscription, and realized the young woman had died at age twenty-two, leaving behind a husband and a child. Now that Tonie had regained her mortality, she also regained an attachment to life, and a love and longing for this little person growing inside her. Mortality was a double edged sword. While bestowing the love of life on one side, it guaranteed death on the other. Years of wishing life away when she had an endless supply had now given way to the fear of losing it too early. I guess there's no making the humans happy, Tonie sighed to herself. But, she wouldn't trade back to her undying state for anything.

Walking beyond the avenues of ornate shrines as big as houses, she came to a section of graves that were plain, their headstones simple markers sinking into the dirt, forgotten like the grave that harbored her once-promising berries that she had worked so hard to find. She bent down and pulled the overgrowth away on one of the oldest graves, wondering what story of human passion and endeavor was waiting to be revealed here.

Rubbing years of dirt from the stone face, she was finally able to read a name. Jean-Claude Charpentier— 1746-1804—Beloved Husband of Laetitia. That was Papa's name. Confused, Antoinette Charpentier studied the dates. That would be right, but Papa had not been buried here. She bent over the headstone next to it. Laetitia Charpentier—1751-1803—Beloved Wife of Jean-Claude. Mama. The cemetery wasn't here at that time. Her mind reeled back to Papa's funeral in the small fenced-in cemetery of the church down the road from their house. The sun had blasted uncaringly in the sky that day, not having the decency to cover its face in respect for the enormity of the loss taking place. She and Amélie had clutched each other's hands tightly.

When did Mama and Papa get moved here? She had looked for the graves at the family church when she first came back to Paris, but the entire graveyard was gone. They must have been moved here during the citywide cemetery cleanups in the1800s.

Tears welled up in Tonie's eyes. Clarity engulfed her and a sense of completion surrounded her. First her home and now her parents. She belonged, and she knew would never leave Paris again. Everything she had done between leaving her homeland and coming back receded into a blur, and now was her only reality.

"I'm sorry, Mama, that I added to your load of care instead of lightening it for you. I'm sorry, Papa, that I didn't rise to the occasion and be the backbone of the family while you grieved your son." Huddled over these graves, Tonie glimpsed who she used to be—through the eyes of her parents, through the eyes of God, as an outsider looking in—and for the first time she saw herself for who she had really been all those years ago—a young, confused, grieving girl, trying to deal with one of life's hardest blows amid the turmoil of a family in crisis. And she forgave herself.

Moving on, she searched around the other tombstones in hopes of finding more family members, but she didn't find any. Tonie knew that many cemeteries had been dug up with the revamping of the city, their residents thrown into unmarked mass graves where people now paid to laugh and gape, and she could only assume that that was what had happened to most of her relatives. God knew where to find them when the trumpet sounded, and that was all that really mattered. When her little boy was big enough to understand, she vowed, she would bring him here and show him his lineage, where his grandparents lay, the story of uncles and aunts in heaven, and of her long road home.

The expectant mother stood up heavily, having a hard time finding her balance. She looked around for a bench to sit on but didn't see one. A twinge squeezed across her lower back, warning her to return home. Stumbling a few steps, dizziness forced her to sit on the ground. She glanced at her watch. Amanda would be teaching English lessons, and Fernand would still be teaching his class. Sitting in the cool fall sunshine thinking about what to do, she jokingly wondered if a baby had ever been born in a cemetery. She had overdone today, she admitted, and needed only to rest a few minutes to regain her strength. What with her midwife appointment this morning, the jogging, lurching metro ride over here, and then walking around for the past hour, it had been too much for her in her advanced state of pregnancy. She debated calling Fernand's secretary in the office, but decided she didn't want to come across as some Nervous Nellie crying about every ache and pain.

Another twinge crossed her back, stronger than before. Maybe she should try calling Amanda, just in case she had finished early. Tonie dialed her number and waited. No answer. She left a message to call her back.

After a minute, an elderly couple passing by with a bouquet of flowers saw her on the ground and came rushing over.

"Madame! Puis-je vous aider?"

"Oui, I need to rest on a bench."

The couple helped her to a bench around the corner, and she sat down. The old gentleman wanted to call for an ambulance, but Tonie insisted she was all right. His wife refused to leave, sitting down beside her and rapidly firing questions regarding her condition. Just then her phone rang, and it was Amanda calling back.

"Amanda, I'm at Père Lachaise, and I don't feel very well. Could you come help me walk to the metro? I can't make it home by myself. I can barely walk."

"What? I can get the car and come get you. Do you need me to do that? I could be there in twenty minutes." Alarmed, Amanda bolted out the door of the school building. "I'm at the school but I'm running home now to get the car. Just sit there and don't try to walk."

"Okay, I'm waiting."

"Are you having any contractions?" Worry flashed through her friend's mind.

"Just a couple twinges, oh, ouch, there was another one. I'm sure it's just false labor, but it's a little bothersome. There are some people here to help me, and they want to call an ambulance. Maybe you better hurry, Amanda."

"What? An ambulance? Oh my goodness! I'm coming right now!" Amanda ran down the street full gallop like a crazy woman. "It will be okay, Tonie! Everything is fine!" she shouted into the phone, trying to convince herself.

Twenty minutes later, Amanda came running into the cemetery and found Tonie still sitting on the bench exactly where she said.

"Are you okay? Are you having more contractions?"

"Yes, I need to go home. I think I might really be in labor, but I know first babies take a long time, so I'll be fine." Tonie considered this a first birth since it had been eighty years since the last one.

"I left the car right at the entrance. Can you walk that far if you lean on me?"

The old woman who had stayed by Tonie the whole time shook her head and addressed Amanda. "She needs to go to the hospital. I have five children and seven grandchildren. I know when a baby is coming. My husband should call the ambulance."

"I want to go home," Tonie replied adamantly, standing up and leaning on Amanda. A gush of water trickled down her legs.

"Olivier, call an ambulance for Madame," the old woman stated matter-of-factly to her husband.

"Oh my goodness! Amanda! The baby is coming now!" Panic crossed Tonie's face.

Amanda pulled off her coat and laid it behind a leafy hydrangea bush, out of view of the path. Old Madame and Monsieur followed suit, pulling off their coats too, laying them end to end with the other. Amanda lowered Tonie onto the soft bed, asking Monsieur for his shirt, which he happily supplied.

Five minutes later a lusty wail filled the air.

"It's a boy," Amanda shouted out to the old couple who were keeping guard over the privacy of the new mother. "A very beautiful boy!" Tears of relief and happiness filled her eyes.

The faithful guardians clapped and yelled out, "Bravo! Bravo!" to the bush.

A few minutes later, paramedics came tumbling down the path carrying a stretcher, searching for a laboring woman. Old Monsieur motioned them over to the hydrangea bush, where they found the beaming mother with her petit monsieur wrapped up snuggly in the man's shirt.

Amanda held Tonie's arm as they descended the steps of the hospital with two-day old Jean-Fernand nestled tenderly in her arms while Fernand brought the car around. Grandpa had installed the infant seat into the back, and he now carefully took the sleeping newborn from his mama and adeptly fastened him in. He had been practicing this important task with the white teddy bear for the past two days and was now confident with the real thing.

At Tonie's apartment, Amanda opened the doors and ushered the new mother in. Tonie stopped and stared at the sight that greeted her in the middle of the living room.

"Oh, Amanda! What is this? A dresser-drawer bassinet?" Standing in front of her was a Louis XVI dresser drawer mounted on a pedestal with four legs sweeping outward and ending with claw feet. The little bed was lined with a mattress and white silk sheets with lace trim. The yellow knit blanket that Tonie had bought on the rue Mouffetard hung draped over the side.

"You said you wanted to put your baby in a dresser drawer, so, voila, there it is!"

"Where in the world did you get this? It is absolutely beautiful. I have never seen such a thing!" The enchanted mother walked around it admiringly, touching the gold drawer pulls and marveling over the rich patina of the wood.

"It wasn't easy," Amanda burst out delightedly, her secret finally finding freedom after weeks of solitary confinement. "I searched the city over looking for just the right dresser so I could get a drawer. I only needed one drawer but I anticipated having to buy a whole dresser, then I found this antique shop out in Montmartre, and the owner had this drawer back in a corner, and it was exactly what I envisioned. So then, I had to find a woodworker to make the legs in the same style. I wanted to tell you so badly! I thought it would be perfect to put by your bed until Jean-Fernand is a little older. Since babies wake up so much in the night, you can pluck him up without having to get out of bed!"

"Oh, Amanda! I love it! Now I can tell you a story. I didn't want to admit this before, but when your mother was born, I used a dresser drawer for her first bed. We had an old dresser from Sears and Roebuck that we had bought second-hand, and I emptied my clothes out of it because we didn't have much money, and she slept in it for about three months. I've gone full circle!"

"I guess it's a family tradition then," Amanda laughed, delighted in Tonie's appreciation for the bed. Taking the newest addition to the family in her arms, she gently laid him down, covering him with the yellow blanket. "Jack and Colleen want to come for his baptism, so I said I would talk to you about dates so they can buy their tickets."

"I would think when he's about a month old, wouldn't you?"

"That sounds splendid. I'll let them know." Amanda hesitated, then added, "Also, I told them who you are. I hope you don't mind, but I thought they need to know, because, not only are you Jack's great-grandmother, you are a remarkable testament of faith."

"Me? No, I am living proof of how low a person can go. I will never brag on what a wretch I was, or that it was my faith that saved me. I had no faith, it was you who led me, kicking and screaming, back to God, and it was God in His infinite mercy who forgave me. Every minute of those years was panic and despair, and I would still be there if not for you. You are a testament to faith, not me, and I will thank you forever for never giving up on me."

The two kindred spirits hugged, tears of happiness spilling down their cheeks.

Chapter Thirty-One

C HURCH BELLS PEALED MERRILY AS THE TRIUMPHANT party slowly processed out of the sanctuary and flowed into the narthex, lined with stately marble columns, and statues of the apostles staring with their blank, sightless eyes. Jean-Fernand Stevens, wearing the same baptismal gown worn by his great-nephew Jack, was baptized amid two doting grandparents, a very proud aunt and uncle, and his helplessly smitten mother. It seemed to Tonie that an abundance of clergy had attended the service this morning, all bustling about and eager to hear her story—not only about Ahasuerus, but also about her newest adventure of giving birth in the cemetery.

"Yes," she agreed with a young priest as they stood chatting afterward. "It is an unusual location on a birth certificate for 'place of birth.' I had hoped after my conversion that I would be able to look forward to a more normal life, but it seems God has a funny sense of humor."

"Oh, yes, indeed." He started laughing and had a hard time pulling himself together. Finally he swallowed and mirthfully added, "You will have quite the story to tell little Jean-Fernand when he gets older."

Tonie smiled and nodded, not really sure she found as much humor in the circumstances of her baby's entry into the world as did this young man, but conceded that she might still be a little too close to the situation. Tired of all the attention her life was generating at the moment, she set off across the room to Amanda, who was gootchy-gooing the tiny star of the show in her arms.

"I think this little guy is getting hungry," Grandma Nona observed, handing him over to his mama.

Tonie found a quiet corner in the church to nurse him. What a happy day. She reveled in the joy of this special event in the life of her child, enjoying the peace of it all the more for having walked through the fires of hell.

Colleen peeked around the corner and found her. "Can I talk to you?" she whispered.

"Of course." Tonie smiled at her...her what? Her sister-in-law? That sounded nice. Maybe her sister. She loved having a solid position in her new family.

"I wanted to find a private time to talk, which isn't easy," she continued to whisper. "I am amazed at you, Tonie. I wanted to tell you that. My heart breaks for you for what you went through, and rejoices for your miracle at the same time. Finding out about your past has changed my faith, and Jack's, and has brought God's mercy alive for us."

"Thank you, Colleen. I worried about Jack's reaction because it's really strange for him, and I had felt that he didn't trust me, which I can't blame him being that I had his great-grandmother's face and his sister's name."

"He is thrilled. And I wouldn't say that he didn't trust you. He's a very thoughtful man and I know that you struck him as odd, but now it all makes sense. You know how you read about God's miracles, and it seems normal when they happen in the Bible, but then, when you come face to face with one, it really twists your reality."

"That is so true," Tonie wholeheartedly agreed.

"I also wanted to tell you that Jack and I are expecting a baby in June," Colleen confided. "We haven't told anyone yet because we didn't want to take away from Jean-Fernand's special day."

"Colleen, I am so happy for you! I think it adds to his special day! Let's go back to the others, and you can make the announcement so the priests can give you a special blessing. Amanda is going to be over the moon!"

"May I carry him?" Auntie Colleen put out her arms. "I need to start practicing!" The two sisters walked back to the narthex to rejoin the merriment in progress.

Tonie sat on the floor of Amanda's apartment, trying to keep Jean-Fernand from crawling off the blanket, but he determinedly climbed over her legs and made a beeline toward Amanda. His Nona plucked him up." I should put you in my suitcase and take you with me. I am going to miss you so much!"

"How is Colleen feeling?" Tonie asked, taking back the little escape artist so Amanda could get her clothes packed.

"Everything is perking along well. She has two weeks until her due date and is working on a water color that she hopes to get finished before the baby comes. Did I tell you they decided on a name?"

"Really? What is it?"

"Amélie Margaret. After Jack's grandmother, with the French spelling," Amanda smiled and winked, "and Colleen's grandmother's name is Margaret. Isn't that sweet?"

"What a lovely name! I can't wait for these little cousins to meet. Hopefully they can come for Christmas."

"Yes, that would be wonderful! If I go there once a year, and they come here once a year, at least I will see them every six months. That's not too bad," Grandma Nona philosophized. She finished folding up clothes and squeezed them into the suitcase. "Okay, that should do it. I hope it will close!"

Paul shook hands with the rector of the parish, then he and Louie stepped out of the rundown Church of the Good Samaritan into the sun-dappled streets of Paris. They were in the midst of organizing a soup kitchen in the church for the poor and homeless of the city. It had been a year in the planning, and now the legwork had begun to find a location. Their mission was to provide food for the hungry as well as to restore their dignity and help them to become productive, functioning members of society. Always in the back of Paul's mind was the memory of his time in Bath where he had become invisible. As an outcast and "non-contributing burden" on society, each and every small kindness had been balm to his weary soul.

The vision burning in their hearts was to build a self-sufficient community where each person had their task—preparing and serving meals, washing dishes, repair work on the premises, cleaning after Sunday services—in exchange for their daily food. As the men and women came to know their worth to each other and to God and developed a job skill, they would leave the mission to go on to work and serve others. Starting small, Paul and Louie saw no end to the possibilities for reaching out.

With plans to meet up later in the day, Paul said goodbye to Louie and ran down the steps two by two into the buzzing metro station to catch a train to the sixth arrondissement. Seven days of criss-crossing the city, searching every park, eating his way through the Marché Bio more than a couple times, and lurking on the street outside Tonie's apartment—perhaps her former apartment for all he knew—had yielded no results of finding Tonie. Not that he was still in love with her, he continually assured himself, but only because he wondered how she was, and if she were still in Paris.

After meeting with Tonie the summer before in the pub, and strongly suspecting she was trying to hide a pregnancy, his hope of resurrecting their marriage crumbled like a cookie in the hands of a toddler.

However, she never requested a divorce, and he didn't either. Wouldn't she want to marry the father of her baby? Did her atheism really allow her to live in adultery with another man? Paul had a hard time believing that about her. For all her bluster against God, she lived a moral and circumspect life. Did she make a one-night mistake? Was her lover an atheist, he wondered? For her sake he hoped not. He sighed and wished he had handled things differently.

Sauntering through the Luxembourg gardens, eagle-eyed as ever, he glanced over at a woman under a tree with a baby carriage. Dark-haired like Tonie, he inspected her a little closer, and then the woman's laughter caught on the breeze and floated over to him. He knew that laugh. She was on the phone, her face happy and shining, then he heard her say, "Bye, I love you." Paul froze in his tracks. Should he or shouldn't he? She was an old friend, he rationalized—actually a current wife. But, regardless of their legal connection, he was now "accidentally" bumping into her for the second time. Why didn't he send her divorce papers like any man with half a brain would do? Ignoring the voices in his head, his feet carried him over to her.

"Tonie?" Paul greeted her with great surprise.

"Paul? What are you doing in Paris?" Startled, her mind immediately began spinning how to explain her baby.

"I'm here for a visit. Paris has a way of getting under your skin, so I'm back for my fix. I'm also meeting with Louie about working on a project together. But mostly, I'm having fun. You're looking great. Life must be treating you well."

"Yes, I just got off the phone with Amanda. She's in the U.S. and called to say that Jack's wife had her baby this morning. So, that is really good news."

"Tell them congratulations for me," her husband jubilantly responded, happy to hear that it wasn't to another man that she had been professing her love.

"Thank you, I'll pass that on."

"Have you decided to live in Paris, or are you still working on your schooling?"

"I took this last year off, but regardless of whether I continue or not, I have decided to stay here permanently."

Tonie studied Paul's face, wondering if he still considered her mentally unbalanced for asserting she was so old. She hated that she had confided her true story to him and that he had not believed her. While not wanting to lie to him, she did want to take back her secret for which he had judged her so harshly.

"I wanted to tell you that I've come to my senses and I know who I am now. And, I've found peace in my life." All of this so very true.

"And a new man?" Paul hinted.

Tonie laughed. "No, I haven't found that."

"So, who's this little guy here?"

"This is my son, Jean-Fernand."

"Well, that was fast. I guess time flies. I noticed you were expecting the last time we met, but my mind still somehow imagined a newborn."

"No, he's eight months now. He's losing his baby-ness and turning into a little boy," Tonie prattled on, confused by Paul's remarks. Why had he not said anything at the time if he had thought she was pregnant? Wouldn't he want to claim his child?

"Eight months? Let's see." Paul's cheeks flushed as he squinted into the sky to do the math. "Eight months, plus nine months…make seventeen months. We were together seventeen months ago." He stared hard at this stranger sprouting horns right before his eyes, wondering what lie she could possibly come up with to save herself.

"I didn't want to tell you about my pregnancy for fear that you would feel an obligation to stay with me out of duty, even though you didn't love me. I know you are old fashioned that way."

"This is my son?"

"Of course he is. What did you think?"

"I don't know what to think. When I came back to Paris for the trial, I looked for you, hoping to somehow get back together and work out our differences, and then, when I met you at the pub, I saw you were pregnant and assumed you had…moved on."

"I thought you wanted to tie up loose ends so we wouldn't have to worry about bumping into each other and it being awkward. I wanted to tell you about our baby, but I didn't see the point when we had such insurmountable problems."

Just then the object of the discussion woke up with wide saucer eyes, staring at his mama talking to a stranger. Tonie bent over and plucked him up, nestling him onto her hip. "Jean-Fernand, this is your daddy."

The newly awakened baby peered at his father suspiciously. He didn't look a thing like Fernand, the only other man in his life.

Paul put out his hands invitingly and, after a moment of indecision, Jean-Fernand leaned into them. The new father gazed into his son's face, a face he had never seen before but which was infinitely familiar at the same time.

"Were you ever going to tell me about him? You owed me that." Frustration tugged Paul back and forth between the joy of having a son and the huge betrayal at the hands of this woman.

Tonie's determination to lie evaporated into thin air, the immensity of her deception jumping out at her as she witnessed its impact on Paul.

"Hiding Jean-Fernand was a decision made in my lostness, and I never reexamined it again until just now. I've found my way back to God, and I've been delivered from the wrong path I was on for so long, but that is not to say that I have yet discovered all the offenses I've committed. Hiding your son is one of them, but I didn't realize it until this minute. I am relearning how to live, and I...I apologize, from my heart, for not telling you."

Paul knew he should forgive her, that the law of God demanded forgiveness, but it was not right now in his heart to do so. He had suffered at her hands too many times, and this lie was beyond his comprehension. He shook his head at the thought of a lifetime of never knowing Jean-Fernand had he not come searching for Tonie on this very day.

"I'm not sure what to believe from you anymore. I stood by you when you needed me, and yet you were lying to me the whole time. I need some time to think on this." Paul looked down at his son then reluctantly handed him back to his mother. He stormed off toward the gate, anger flashing hot through his veins, trying with all his might to not say any of the mean things darting through his brain right now. But his mind demanded some kind of resolution; he couldn't stand for this inane circus to keep making a mockery of his life. Stopping, he turned back to this vixen of a woman whom he felt he had never known.

"I guess there's no time like the present to come to a decision of our...our *marriage*," he shouted across the gap. "I think now, especially since there is a child involved, that we need to file divorce papers and figure out a custody arrangement."

Several passers-by stared at him through sideways glances, but Paul stomped back to Tonie oblivious of his audience.

"For whatever reason, I've always kept this vague fantasy that somehow we would get back together and live happily ever after. But it is now painfully obvious that will never happen."

"What do you mean, you've had a fantasy of getting back together?" Tonie fired back. "You thought I was crazy and never let me forget it. And I was crazy. Crazy for thinking you would believe me, crazy from living all those years in a nightmare, a nightmare of hell with no hope of escape. You didn't stand by me, you stood above me looking down on me for my lack of faith. You judged me for it instead of reaching out in love, and I couldn't live with that. It was too heavy of a condemnation."

"I tried every way possible to help you. You can't deny that I tried, and even if my efforts weren't able to help reestablish your equilibrium, they were heartfelt. And somewhere else you were able to accomplish what I wanted for you all along, but don't tell me I didn't try."

"Well, I really am hundreds of years old. That's the truth. I have no more lies."

Paul's bluster drained from him. "You said that you have found God and know who you are now. I don't understand."

"Remember the beggar that I thought was a spy looking for you? It turns out that he was another grave sinner, like me, condemned to wander the earth until he acknowledged God. He approached me again and revealed my curse to me. I am that old, but through my repentance I have rejoined the human race and I will age normally from now on."

The ground dissolved under Paul's feet. He floundered in disorientation, like a log being rolled along in the surf, round and round, helpless, until finally he was spit back up on the shore. Like the final piece of a puzzle dropping into place, Tonie's assertion rang so true that he had the sensation of having always known it.

"And I didn't believe you."

"No, but I don't blame you. It does sound pretty crazy. Do you believe me now?"

Paul slowly nodded. "I should have believed it all along, and I think I did at first, but then I decided to get logical and deny it. That is where I tend to go wrong... when I decide to get logical."

"Don't feel bad—it took me 240 years to quit shaking my fist at God. How blind is that?"

A closeness to this woman enveloped Paul. He was bound to her and could no more walk away from her than he could cut the very feet off his legs. "Do you really believe we have insurmountable problems?"

Tonie searched Paul's face. "Not now that I realize God's love for me. I could never accept anyone's love while I rejected God."

"Human love is imperfect, Tonie. I love you, and I promise to stand by you and be for you for the rest of my life, and into the next."

Husband and wife strolled through the gardens like shy new lovers just getting to know each other, taking turns holding their little boy who delighted in throwing himself back and forth between his two parents.

That evening, the phone rang while Tonie was brushing her teeth getting ready for bed. Day was in full bloom in Oregon, and she guessed this would be Amanda calling to give the full report on baby Amélie's second day of life.

Quickly spitting her mouthful of toothpaste into the sink, she answered the phone, eager with news of her own.

"Hello?"

"Tonie, I had a dream!" Amanda burst out. "In it, you and Paul were coming out of the cathedral, and you were in your wedding dress, the one you got in Rouen, and Paul was wearing a tuxedo! It was so real that I had to tell you!"

About the Author

J. A. Olson has always been an avid storyteller and now enjoys channeling her passion for a lively tale into the written word. Her interest in French history inspired her to write *Nettie at the Well*. Originally from Fairbanks, Alaska, she currently resides in Vancouver, Washington. She is also the author of *The Ghost of Anna*.

CPSIA information can be obtained
at www.ICGtesting.com
Printed in the USA
BVHW07s0946220718
522263BV00002B/9/P

9 780985 527525